IN DREAMS WE ROT

BETTY ROCKSTEADY

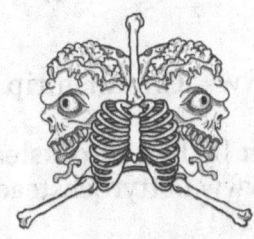

Ghoulish Books
San Antonio, Texas

In Dreams We Rot
Copyright © 2024 Betty Rocksteady
First Edition 2019

Second Edition

All Rights Reserved

ISBN: 978-1-943720-79-8

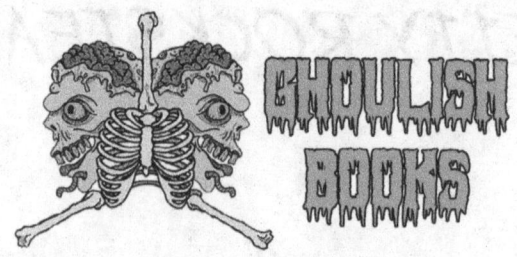

www.Ghoulish.rip

Cover by Betty Rocksteady
https://www.bettyrocksteady.com/

Also by Betty Rocksteady

Arachnophile
Like Jagged Teeth
The Writhing Skies
Soft Places

Copyright Acknowledgements

Love is Not a Handful of Seeds | *Unpublished, 2016*

Tiny Bones Beneath Their Feet | *Dark Moon Digest #34, 2019*

Something is Coming | *Turn to Ash Volume 3, 2017*

These Beautiful Bones | *DOA III, 2017*

The Botany of Desire | *Unnerving Issue 3, 2017*

The Desert of Wounded Frequencies | *Lost Signals, 2016*

Root Rot | *Unpublished, 2018*

Postpartum | *Eternal Frankenstein, 2016*

This Narrow Escape | *K-Zine Issue 14, 2016*

The Language of the Mud | *Utter Fabrication, 2017*

Lonely Hearts Club | *Ravenwood Quarterly Issue 1, 2016*

Our Feral Skies | *Dark Moon Digest #29, 2017*

The Taste of Sand on Your Lips | *555 Vol. 2, 2016*

Dusk Urchin | *Looming Low, 2017*

Larva, Pupa, Moth | *Dark Moon Digest #26, 2017*

Elephants That Aren't | *Lost Films, 2018*

First, A Blinding Light | *Lost Contact, 2021*

Lullabies from the Formicary | *Turn to Ash Volume 2, 2017*

Crimson Tide | *DarkFuse Dark Borne Muses Series, 2016*

The Backwards Path to the Limbus | *The Outward Inn, 2019*

She Sleeps with Crows | *Winner of Grey Matter Press'* I Can Taste the Blood *Contest, 2016*

CONTENTS

BETTY ROCKSTEADY IN 3D

TRYING TO FIGURE out how I met Betty Rocksteady, exactly, has been a constant source of frustration. When I concentrate and look back, I cannot recall a day in our past when we haven't had some semblance of a conversation. But I know it must have started somewhere. If I browse her bibliography—specifically, the table of contents in the very collection you currently hold in your hands—it appears the first time we worked together would have been on her short story "The Desert of Wounded Frequencies" in our anthology *Lost Signals* (July, 2016). With this in mind, I conducted some gmail investigation and pulled up when she originally submitted the story to us: October 30, 2015.

However, while looking this up, I happened to discover this wasn't the first time she submitted fiction our way. In fact, apparently I'd previously rejected two other stories from her, which I am literally learning right now, as I write this introduction. The first story she ever submitted to us was something called "The Clown Society" back on November 5, 2014. Betty, if you're reading this introduction—and I hope you are, considering this is your collection—please answer one question for me: What the *fuck* is "The Clown Society"?

Okay, apologies. You have to understand, ghouls, Betty and I talk every day, and not once has she ever mentioned any type of *clown society*—and, honestly, I find it a little rude. But this introduction isn't about that story. It's about her collection, yes, but also the overall work of hers we've been lucky to publish. It is also about our friendship. I don't believe the friendship started with the *Lost Signals* story, though. If I had to pinpoint it, we started really bonding after I sent her the most unprofessional acceptance of all time for her novella *Like Jagged Teeth* (initially titled *Broken Stairs*) on November 27, 2016:

> "Hey! *Broken Stairs* is great. Cool and spooky and right up our alley. We want to publish it next year. I meant to send this acceptance a couple weeks ago, but then . . . forgot? Anyway, I've already edited half of it. I guess I thought I already accepted it? I don't know! But yes. ACCEPTED."

Listen, I cannot stress enough that publishers should never, ever behave this way. It is so insane and unhinged that it's difficult not to laugh when I think about it, and I think Betty feels the same way, which is how we went from "publisher and author" to "actual friends." If I'd accepted anybody else's book in such a manner, I think I would die from embarrassment.

Around this same time, Betty also recommended a movie to me she thought I would like titled *The Hole*. I want you to do me a favor, and go over to IMDB and search for a movie with that name. What you'll find is a plethora of holes. Now, Betty claims she gave me the release year and even the main actress from the version she meant, but I have no memory of this, so I'm unsure if I'm actively being gaslit here, or what. In any case, I did not watch the version of *The Hole* she meant. To be honest, I still don't know which one I was supposed to watch. The only *The Hole* I've ever seen is *The Hole in 3D*, a 2009 children's horror movie directed by Joe Dante. Why would she recommend this movie to me, specifically, I still haven't figured out. Ask her and she might tell you that wasn't the version of *The Hole* she was talking about—but honestly, how are we to know for sure, right? Maybe she's so embarrassed I wasn't blown away by this movie recommendation that she decided to pretend like I'd watched the wrong one. We will never know the truth.

Either way, this mixup, for whatever reason, concreted our friendship, and I am not sure we've gone a day since without chatting about something, whether that be Aesop Rock, crafting story atmosphere, drawing grotesque cartoon penises, or how often we crave death. I am honored for her to be my friend, and I am honored to have published a significant percentage of her fiction.

Book-wise, as of November 2023, we have released her novellas *Like Jagged Teeth, The Writhing Skies,* and *Soft Places*. We have also published a ton of her short stories, many of which you'll find in this collection.

It has been thrilling to witness Betty's writing evolution. Aside from "The Clown Society"—which I cannot comment on, as I only recently learned of its existence—the fiction of hers I've read has always been *interesting* and worth reading, certainly, but I think it was sometime during the writing of *The Writhing Skies* that she started really leaning into her true passions: weird shit, yes, but also *old* weird shit, specifically the old weird shit typically found in black and white cartoons.

There's a short story in this collection titled "Elephants That Aren't"—which was originally published in the *Lost Films* anthology—that I believe is the most obvious turning point of when her writing style hit new ground. I remember when she was writing it, the way she'd talk about the whole process of figuring it out. This was a new kind of excitement. The kind of excitement people have when they feel like they've finally found Their Thing, and after reading the story I would say it's hard to disagree there. "Elephants That Aren't" is the type of story only Betty Rocksteady could possibly write.

MAX BOOTH III

The stories you are going to find in this collection are weird. They emphasize atmosphere over plot. When you read Betty Rocksteady, you are inviting yourself into a dream. Nothing will make sense—yet, at the same time, *everything* will make sense. The reason why I've spent so much time in this introduction talking about how we became friends, instead of the actual stories, is it's not easy preparing someone for the type of fiction she writes. These stories are best experienced going in cold. I'm not promising they'll warm you up, though. If anything, you might finish this book feeling colder than you've ever felt in your life.

So let's do it. Don't dip your toe in. Don't test the waters. I want you to close your eyes, and I want you to leap head-first. And, when you're as deep as you can go, I want you to open your mouth. I want you to scream.

—Max Booth III
Publisher, Ghoulish Books
November 9, 2023

LOVE IS NOT A
HANDFUL OF SEEDS

THE POLICE CALLED off the search after a week, but Nicole kept circling the same paths in the woods, choking back tears and pretending it was all going to be all right. For three endless months she searched. When the last trickle of hope was ready to die in her chest, she found something: a scrap of blue cloth the color of his eyes, tangled on a tree branch. She rubbed it between her fingers, convinced herself it carried his scent.

She walked deeper into the woods. The paths were well-worn; her feet knew the way. The trees revealed their secrets slowly. She stumbled upon a group of foxes, chewing wet mouthfuls of something. They scattered when she came.

There he was.

He looked the same as the day he had vanished, except pale and still. Only his eyelids fluttered. She fell to her knees and took his hand in hers, but it crumbled, became a jumble of twigs on the forest floor. She tried to wrap her arms around his shoulders, but his tattered clothes fell apart, scattered pinecones and dandelion puffs and seeds.

His eyes shone glassy and wet. She kissed his lips and they crumbled like brittle leaves. A beetle glinting with iridescence skittered through his hair and his golden locks turned to grass. Her love fell apart, scattered by the breeze.

When the police came, they shook their heads. They

couldn't meet her eyes. She sat in the mud, sifting through forest debris, pushing it together, trying to reassemble love. They pulled her to her feet. Before they walked her home, she stuffed her hands in her pockets. She hated to leave any of him behind, but they gave her no choice.

She planted him in the stillness of night. The damp earth accepted her offering, and his branches cast shadows across her face.

TINY BONES BENEATH THEIR FEET

IF YOU HELD a gun to his head, maybe Harold would have admitted he felt it coming. It was something in the way the cats moved, the way their eyes flickered. Yes, he felt it, somewhere deep in his bones, and when the knocking started, the muscles in his shoulders tightened.

Already?

His favorite cat was expecting it too. Cora had been perched in his lap for hours now, twitching her tail, unable to get comfortable. She was one of the few cats he had named, after an old girlfriend. At the first knock, her eyes blinked open, and with her nimble feet, she was yowling at the door in seconds.

Any other day, they would have ignored the knocking. Over the years, visitors had become more and more occasional. Family, friends, concerned neighbors eventually disappeared, whether by anger or death or eventual disinterest.

Harold wasn't as limber as he used to be. Cora paced impatiently back into the room, and finally he got up and stretched the ache out of his back, displacing several cats from the couch as he stood. They scattered, whiskers twitching, tails bushy, eyes wide.

He opened the door a few inches. A woman faced away from him, as if she were contemplating walking the trail back to her car, and he cursed himself for not being just a

3

little more patient. But what difference would it make? He could put it off perhaps another week or two, but eventually she would be back.

"Ah, you *are* home!" The woman's hair had grown out since she had dyed it last, revealing a few inches of fuzzy grey roots. Her eyes were small but intelligent, and they flickered quickly over him, his stained bathrobe, the cats at his feet. "I'm Susan. I'm here to help you, if I can."

"And what is it you think I need help with?"

She talked fast, as though reading off a script. "Well, it's about the cats. I'm from a TNR group—trap, neuter, release. We help out stray and feral cats by spaying them and returning them to the wild, with a caretaker—that would be you—to feed them and let us know when vet care is necessary. We've been helping out a lot of cat colonies in the city, and we've had a few reports from your neighbors that there are a lot of cats in your area. I've come out to offer our help. We would have called, but—"

"I don't have a phone."

"Ah. Well, that would explain it. I wonder if I could come inside? I'd love to get some information on the size of the group you care for, and figure out what help we can offer."

"I'm not sure that I need your help. Things here . . . things are good. Fine. I've got it under control." Cora peered curiously from between his legs. In the front yard, a group of tabbies watched with interest.

"There's no shame in getting help. We've helped over 50 cat communities in the last two years alone, all through community donations. It doesn't cost you a cent. In fact, it will save you money." She shuffled through her paperwork and produced a flyer. He glanced down at it briefly. "How many cats do you have out here?" She tried to peer over his shoulder into the house behind him, as if that would reveal the answers he was reluctant to give. "I'd love to come in and have a talk with you."

He hated her already. He wanted to close the door in

4

her face, go back to his sofa, his dreams, but Cora chirruped and Harold sighed, opened the door wider.

"I guess you better come inside."

Susan hissed in a breath. He knew how he looked. An old man, living in the middle of nowhere, curly grey chest hair poking out over his collar and a spreading middle that loomed dangerously over his sweatpants. And in the house, behind him . . . well, he did his best, but he was a bachelor. And the cats . . .

They weren't all inside. Of course not. They couldn't be contained, they came and went as they pleased. As it was, dozens of eyes blinked open as he led the way inside, heads popped up and peered around corners. A few curious chirps escaped, but they stayed back, out of the way, all except Cora, who kept close to Susan's heels.

He led her to the kitchen. Even if she was a cat lover, he knew better than to offer her a seat on the fur-covered sofa. There were two tabbies napping in the sun on the table, but they scattered with a nudge. A little coffee remained in the pot from this morning. He considered offering her a cup, but by the way she hesitated next to the chair, arms loaded down with paperwork, he had a feeling she wouldn't accept anything he offered. "My, I haven't seen such a large colony in a while . . . maybe ever." Cora leapt up on the table, nudged her head against Susan and received an absent stroke. "How many cats would you say you have here?" She turned back a few pages in her pile, pen in hand.

"Oh, I have no idea." She might not want to sit down, but he certainly did. His back wasn't as strong as it used to be, and he didn't spend any longer standing up than he absolutely had to.

"Just an estimate is fine. 50 or so? You know, we can help you with feeding them as well. What are you currently feeding? Wet or dry?"

"They feed themselves."

"Ah, yes, a lot of people still think of cats as mousers,

5

birders, but they really do better with a consistent and complete source of nutrition. How many did you say? 50?"

"Oh, more than that."

"A hundred?"

"I really don't know. More."

She chewed her lip. "Ah. I see. So they mostly live inside with you? Any vet care previously?"

"They're out back too. No vet care. They don't need it."

"Well, I know in the old days we didn't take cats to the vet much, but things are different now. There's a lot of simple care that can help them live better lives. Not to mention spaying and neutering—the most important. I guess you don't have any idea how many breeding females you have? Many kittens at the moment? We can often adopt out kittens, even if they're feral, with a little work—"

"No."

"I understand you're attached to them all, but it's often better—"

"No, I mean no kittens. There's never any kittens. Lots of cats. No kittens. All full grown. They don't get sick. I've never seen them die. I don't even know what they need me for. Maybe just to watch." Susan blinked, then looked back down at her papers. Maybe he was being difficult. This wasn't the best way to make her understand. "Why don't you come out back, and I'll show you? You'll get a better idea of the . . . " he gestured with his hands, hunting for the right word, "the scope of it."

"That sounds great. Do you mind if I take some pictures?" She reached for her purse, but Cora had draped herself over it and she hesitated.

Harold met Cora's eyes. "You'd better not."

"We're not judging you, of course. It'll just help us with decision-making, how many traps to bring, stuff like that."

"I'd really rather you didn't." Although, did it matter? He knew how this day would end. The only way to move was forward. He opened the door and gestured Susan outside. He pocketed a clean cloth from the counter.

6

The yard itself was fairly small, but his land extended deep into the woods. He hadn't had the energy to care for the lawn much this year, and the grass had grown long and clogged with weeds. Dozens of cats lounged in the late afternoon sun, grooming themselves, purring and pouncing and darting between the overgrown grass. "Wow," Susan breathed.

He had long since given up estimating how many there were, but they had to be in the hundreds, and that was just the ones visible at the moment. New ones seemed to pop up every day. The longer you looked, the more you saw, peeking between trees or huddled together as if in a private discussion, hidden in the shadows of his ancient barn. Cora darted out between his legs, and the crowd of cats parted to let her through.

There was a sudden wet plop, and Susan gasped again. A shaggy tuxedo cat had dropped a headless mouse at her feet, blood still oozing from the stump. The cat looked up at her expectantly, his muzzle stained red and dripping.

"Nothing to be upset by," he reassured her. "They do what they have to."

"It's not that. Not just that. I've never seen a colony this big. Usually they max out around 30 . . . I've seen up to 50, but never anything like this."

"Ah. Well, it's the woods where they're most active. Hunting and such. You know."

Most of the cats in the yard had stopped what they were doing when Susan spoke. They didn't see many humans, or at least as far as he knew they didn't. Hell, he didn't know what they got up to when they were out of sight.

"You can't possibly have many more than this? Feral cats only live a few years, and if you're not seeing kittens . . . " She scanned the yard as she spoke, and all the cats looked back at her. So many eyes. She stumbled over her words, then took a breath. Her voice shook. "I've never seen a colony get this large. Not near this large."

Cora waited impatiently by the entrance to the woods, pacing back and forth. She was right. The sun would be setting soon, and they had much to do before nightfall. "Well, I'm sure you'd like to see the woods then, get an idea of the whole thing?" He started down the stairs, and cats crowded around his feet, muttering.

He was midway there before he noticed Susan wasn't in step with him. When he turned back, her face was pale. He sighed. It wasn't that he was in any particular rush for what came next, but he had never been good at dealing with other people—why else would he have ended up out here? He didn't know what to say to reassure her.

Susan grimaced. "I really should get a few more of the girls out here. It's a lot to take in all at once. I think I have enough information to get started. I don't want to take up any more of your time, I'll just leave some paperwork on your table and see myself out . . . " When she turned back to the door, a half dozen cats pressed out—white and grey and tabby. Judging from the look on her face, she didn't yet see what he saw. It annoyed him. A woman familiar with cats shouldn't look so frightened just because there were a few more than usual. But when the cats padded forward, she backed down the stairs, and then he was there at her elbow, and he took her arm. Her skin was clammy. He thought of the last time he had touched a woman—it had been Cora, of course, the first Cora, and that was decades ago, long before all this.

"Come on, this won't take long." She let herself be led, or let herself be carried away, but the result was the same. She came with him. To the woods.

He was hyperaware of what lay beneath their feet, but Susan didn't seem to notice. That was fair, of course. There was a lot to take in, and the bones were so small. If you didn't look closely, you might mistake the trail as some sort of rock purposefully pressed into the earth. The trail wound labyrinthine between the trees, doubling back occasionally as it spiraled ever inward. He led her deeper into the woods.

After a few minutes of walking, Susan pulled her arm away from his. "It seems like we're backtracking. I really need to go. I can tell there are lots of cats here, I don't know if I'm getting any more information from this . . . and I have somewhere to be soon, I really have to go. I'm meeting someone." He didn't believe her. There was no one waiting for her. And even if there were, well, in the long run things would go as they should. They always did. But still, he let her pull away.

The woods rustled around them, the occasional mewls of the cats echoing between trees, a faraway hum that might be the purr of a very large cat. The path had crisscrossed in multiple places. Her face sank. She would never find her way back. Not without help. A small black cat approached, then another, and another, spitting and mewling, clustering around her, pressing against her legs.

"It's not much further." This time he took her hand. Again, she came with him, a faraway look in her eyes.

"The path . . . are those bones?"

"Yes. Mostly mice and birds."

"Why would you . . . ?"

"Oh, I didn't."

Her eyelid twitched. "What do you mean? You don't expect me to believe . . . "

"I don't expect anything. I don't know exactly how they do it, but they do. They hunt and feast and leave the remains, and I follow their path. And now you do too."

In her fear, the wrinkles in her face smoothed slightly, and he could see the little girl she had once been. "I want to go home."

"We're here, though." They had followed the path all the way, crumbled the last mouse bones beneath their feet. The tangle of trees opened into a small clearing, and in the centre of it, surrounded by cats, there was a shallow grave dug into the dirt and mud. The cats stopped their sunning and licking to stare as Harold and Susan neared.

"I want to go home." The purr was louder now, seemed

9

to fill the clearing. Cora popped out from somewhere and wound through Susan's feet, sending her off balance. Harold caught her and turned her to face the grave.

She looked. She had to.

The grave was rough-hewn but neat, dug out a long time ago with teeth and claws, kept tidy over the years by Harold's hands, and perhaps by the hands of others. In the bottom, an opening, just wide enough for a large cat to slip through. The tunnel cleaved deep into the earth, and just before your eyes gave out to the distance, you could see what lay on the other side. A perfect circle of the night sky, shadows of trees stretching up into it, and the sliver of a crescent moon. He didn't like to look too long anymore. He didn't have the resilience he once did, not with these old bones. Perhaps Susan did, although he had been much younger than she was when he had first come here.

He looked at Susan, at the tears she didn't notice dripping down her cheeks. He allowed her a moment, then gently turned her face away.

A cat approached, businesslike, not stopping for their benefit, a bird still twitching in its mouth. It jumped into the grave and slipped through the hole, obstructing their view.

"What are they doing?"

"I'm not sure. I try not to wonder anymore . . . I think it has to do with the bones. It must be the bones."

Susan brushed the tears from her cheek, but they just kept coming. She didn't look like the sort of woman who cried much, too much of a tough nut. The tears softened her face, made her seem more beautiful. "We have to call someone, this is . . . cats don't do this. Someone needs to see this."

"Who do you want to call?"

She gestured uselessly. "I don't know—a scientist?" She shook her head, and for a moment he felt sorry for her.

"Yes, of course."

"Or . . . at least the others from my group. People need

to see this." Cora wound between her feet insistently, mewling. She hopped, trying for Susan's hand, her back arched, begging for a stroke.

"What does all this mean? How . . . why haven't you called anyone? The news, something?"

Cora stretched, digging gentle claws into Susan's pant leg. Finally Susan reached down to stroke her, and there was a flash of teeth as Cora sank her jaw deep into the webbing between Susan's thumb and index finger. Susan screamed, and Harold's own finger webbing ached in sympathy. Cora released her, a scatter of blood on her muzzle, and brushed against Susan's leg before dancing away.

Blood dripped from Susan's hand; her eyes were wide and frightened. "Oh my God . . . "

"It's okay, we'll get you cleaned up." He handed her the cloth he had pocketed earlier, and she pressed it to the wound. A dark smear of red seeped through the material.

"It doesn't feel right, her teeth . . . "

"Ah, Cora's fine. It'll be fine. Come on now, we'll get it cleaned and bandaged."

She slumped against him. "Cat bites are dangerous, they get infected."

"This one won't. Don't you worry. Don't worry about anything." He led her back through the woods, a straight path this time, not following the bones. There was no need to, not on the way back. In only a few moments, they were back in the yard again, the cats happy now, sunning and playing and curling up to each other.

He led her into the house.

"I don't feel good, I need my phone. I need to call someone . . . "

He led her past the kitchen, straight into the bathroom. It was narrow, cramped, and a little dirtier than he would have liked for a guest, but soon she wouldn't be a guest at all. He put the lid down on the toilet, and she sat there with her head between her knees while he rummaged through the medicine cabinet.

"Hold your arm up, it'll slow down the bleeding." He got out the cleaning supplies, and took her hand gently. She winced as he yanked the cloth off. The wound was deep and purple, but the bleeding had slowed down to a trickle. She pulled away when he dabbed it with peroxide, but he grabbed it back to smear Polysporin on and bandage it up. It was all window dressing anyway. It would be fine in the morning. It would be deep under the skin then.

"I need to call my niece. I don't think I can drive. I feel . . . weird. I want to go home." Her legs shook when she stood up, and he steadied her.

"Yes, of course. Why don't you lie down for now? I'll bring your purse to you and you can make your calls." He half-carried her to his bedroom. He was too old for this. The cats that were currently sleeping on the bed shuffled aside as Susan sat, then settled back in around her. A faint smile touched Susan's face as they pressed against her, and she lay back among their purring bodies. As she drifted, Cora hopped up next to her.

There was still a faint pinkish stain on Cora's fur. He reached out a hand, and she leaned against it. He stroked her, looked into her eyes, as wide and luminous as the night sky. "Goodbye, my friend," he whispered, and she blinked at him slowly. Then Cora curled around Susan's feet, and Harold walked away.

Tomorrow Susan would wake, surrounded by purring warmth, rested, healed, and ready to do The Work.

Outside, the sun was setting, filling the yard with a golden-pink glow. His favorite time of day, but it had been a *long* day, and he didn't feel like stopping to enjoy it. He was tired. He hadn't realized just how tired, but now it fell over him like a heavy blanket, weighing him down, and all he wanted was to get it over with.

In the glow of the sunset, cats bathed and feasted and lived their strange lives. Their eyes flickered to him as he passed, acknowledging his presence. At the lip of the forest, he removed his clothes. He folded them neatly and placed them on the ground. A small black cat curled up on them.

For the last time, he walked the trail, tiny bones nipping at his bare feet. When he reached the grave, he kneeled, and then he collapsed, tumbled inside, the empty opening pulsing at his back. The purring intensified, and cats peered down at him, then hopped in beside him, and he was blessed, he was so blessed.

Their purring bodies surrounded him, and he felt the thrum of the universe in their voice, and they began to lick, their rough little tongues quick and fast, coming at him from every angle, first caressing, then tearing open his old, delicate flesh, and he barely felt it at all, he barely felt anything as they licked every last scrap of flesh from his bones, he just closed his eyes and kept them closed until the day his bones cracked and broke and tumbled into that other world.

SOMETHING IS COMING

THE WOMAN IN the grocery store looked around to make sure no one was watching. When she was satisfied, she lifted up her skirt, displaying a shapely behind. She adjusted her pantyhose and let the skirt fall back down. She exited the aisle and the video clip ended.

That was enough. Leah should go to bed. She had to get up in the morning, and she was starting to feel gross. She shouldn't be watching these. She shouldn't be spending so much fucking time on this website.

No one was getting hurt. They would never know. The only one she was hurting was herself, staying up way too late, smearing her laptop keys with salt, and wasting way more time online than she should. But once you got started, it was hard to stop.

HACKED WEBCAM! GUY FUCKS A DIFFERENT CHICK PRACTICALLY EVERY NIGHT

Not tonight. Tonight he was just watching television, hand down his pants, rubbing listlessly, looking down at his phone every couple of minutes. Not that different from her. Tonight he was just wasting time. She liked that. Sure, sometimes the stuff she watched was more titillating than this, but . . . it wasn't about that. Not really.

Dozens of people could be watching him, and he had no idea. This was the real him. The most natural. The side of himself that even he wasn't aware of.

He turned the TV off and left the room, and Leah was left watching the spot on the couch he had once inhabited.

14

Crumbs dusted the area where he had been. She waited a few minutes, but it didn't look like he was coming back. A good time for her to log off herself. But instead she closed the window and clicked the next link.

Just one more.

CAPTURED FOOTAGE, COUPLE FIGHTING IN ELEVATOR

It was so much better than manufactured drama. She couldn't hear what they were saying, but she could see the honesty in their faces. The snotty way the girlfriend rolled her eyes. They thought this was private, between them, but someone had uploaded this to the internet, and instead their private moments were shared with . . . well, how many other people frequented these forums? Dozens? Hundreds? They left the elevator, still arguing, but Leah saw the switch on their faces as they prepared for the outside world. The masks that smoothed out their features, the shifts in tone, nearly imperceptible.

Leah sighed, wiped her hands on her pajama pants, clicked on the next link. It was almost midnight and she had work the next morning. One more.

Before it loaded, a cheerful tone rang out from her purse. A *familiar* tone. Leah's heart leapt, even before she fully realized what it meant.

Kaitlyn?

She hadn't heard from Kaitlyn in months. Not since the wedding. She shoved the laptop off her lap and onto the coffee table, fumbled the phone out of her purse.

Hey, sorry I haven't been in touch things are weird, I need to get outta this place Matts a dick can I crash at urs? Sorry I know its late.

The smile that beamed across Leah's face was wrong, but she couldn't help it. She *knew* Matt was a dick. She *knew* Kaitlyn shouldn't have married him, and goddamn, she missed her friend.

Of course you can do u need cab money or? She barely had time to rethink her words—should she have asked more questions? Should she have expressed pity? But Kaitlyn was typing already.

Actually I'm starving can u meet me at the pub by yours? They serve food late right?

Yah! 20 min?

OMW

Oh shit. Her apartment was a mess. She was a mess. She had enough time to get changed, but probably not enough time to clean up. Shit, shit, shit, Kaitlyn would think she was a slob. She tossed the phone in her purse and reached for the laptop.

A man was looking at her.

No, not at her. Looking at the camera, the room behind him awash in a sickly green glow. This video shouldn't be on the forums. He knew he was being filmed; he was staring right at the camera.

His eyes were wide. Too wide. Sunken and muddy and deep, and as she made eye contact across the screens, his smile widened. He didn't blink. Heavy eyebrows framed his deep-set eyes and he just kept grinning.

Leah shuddered and closed out of the video. She didn't have time to make a comment or notify the site owners, so she just closed out of the forums entirely and deleted her history. Just in case. They usually kept things pretty well-monitored, so all the videos really were candid, but every now and then some creep would come through. Someone who got off on being watched. Well, that was hardly any creepier than what she was doing, was it?

Forget it.

Kaitlyn was coming over, and she was leaving her shitty husband, and Leah tried to stifle the joy that bubbled through her.

She really was an awful friend.

～～～

She probably didn't look great, but she wasn't *that* bad, and it hardly justified the way people stared at her as she walked to the pub. It was freezing out and she hated walking at night and they weren't looking at her, not really, she was just being paranoid.

Kaitlyn was already there when she arrived, alone at a table in a corner, one of the bar's many televisions streaming sports over her head. Something sharp fluttered in Leah's chest—it had been months. She tugged her t-shirt further down her hips. She had put on a couple pounds, and Kaitlyn was bound to notice.

Even from the three-fourths view she had, Kaitlyn looked great. Her cheekbones could cut glass, and her blonde color had grown out, but the roots just made it look more punk rock. Leah tucked a faded red strand behind her own ear. Should she get a drink before she sat down, or . . . ?

Kaitlyn turned, and a grin lit up her entire face, and then she was hugging Leah and she smelled familiar and fantastic and Leah couldn't help but laugh.

"Hey, I missed you." Leah sat down.

"I know, it's ridiculous, I've been really busy, and I know that's not an excuse, but . . . ugh. I just feel like shit all the time. I'm glad you're here. Thank you." There were wrinkles near Kaitlyn's mouth that weren't there before, and something about them made her seem so much more down to earth.

"No, don't worry about it. Did you order yet?" Ugh, what a stupid thing to say, but Kaitlyn shook her head and grabbed the menu. Leah had been eating chips all night, but what the hell. They couldn't quite stop bubbling over with conversation, but finally they ordered, and it was over their appetizer that Kaitlyn finally gave her a hint of what had happened.

"He was just getting too jealous." Kaitlyn loaded a sickening amount of salsa onto her chip. "I can't even have guy friends anymore. There was this one guy I was talking to online, Daniel, and he was just so sure there was something going on there, but we were just talking about the band, and I don't know. Matt got all pissy and I just didn't want to deal with it anymore and it turned into a huge fight and here I am."

There was more to it, and Leah was sure it would come out over time. It always did. But she couldn't help but pry, just a little bit. "There was nothing going on with the other guy?"

"Not from my side of things . . ." but she saw the look in Kaitlyn's eye. Someone else might not have caught it, but Leah knew her too well. Didn't matter. She had her friend back, for a few days, at the very least.

"Well, you don't have to put up with his shit anymore. You can do whatever you want."

"Exactly! And I don't want to be settled down." Kaitlyn laughed. "I don't know what I was thinking. That's not me—you said it before the wedding, and you know me better than anyone."

She didn't know the half of it. Kaitlyn slurped on her beer and realized it was empty, and so was Leah's and she looked up to flag down the waitress and that was when the television above Kaitlyn caught her eye. The newscasters stared out of the screen, their eyes fixed on Leah, a beat too long. Their mouths gaped open slightly, the papers caught mid-shuffle in their hands. There was enough time for Leah's mouth to go dry, and she swallowed with difficulty, and then it was over and they were talking again and the scores were up and the moment passed, and the beers came, and Kaitlyn was smiling and everything was fine.

"Do you have any wine? We should stay up all night and watch a horror movie, like we used to." Kaitlyn's cheeks were flushed pink and Leah already felt a little bit drunk, but what the hell? It was way past a reasonable bedtime already. Leah could always call off in the morning. She had hit a few too many sick days the last few months, but another one would hardly affect anything, not at this point.

"I think I might have a bottle. What do you want to watch?"

Leah poured glasses of wine while Kaitlyn browsed the DVD shelves. It didn't matter what she picked, she always talked through the whole thing anyway. Leah shoved dishes into the sink in an effort to make things look a bit tidier in the kitchen, and Kaitlyn read titles aloud from the living room and Leah couldn't help but smile.

"Is there anything here we haven't watched 15 times already?"

"Probably not. Check Netflix."

"I think I'll get changed first, wash my face. That way if we fall asleep, I don't turn into a hideous monster in the morning." Kaitlyn slid into the bathroom. Leah heard her humming to herself as she walked by and noticed the door open a few inches, like an invitation.

Leah placed the wine glasses on the coffee table and hesitated.

She shouldn't.

It was like being a teenager all over again. Alone in Kaitlyn's room, surrounded by stuffed animals, the bathroom door cracked open while Kaitlyn brushed her hair, washed her face.

Did she still brush her hair naked?

She remembered Kaitlyn's smooth olive stomach, the buds of breasts hanging loose over the gentle slope, long strokes through her soft hair until it was shining. Leah's stomach churned, not unpleasantly.

She shouldn't.

But she did. She crept past the hallway again, back into the kitchen. The door opened onto the mirror above the vanity, and she caught a glimpse of flesh as she walked past. Her heart thudded in her ears and her face felt hot.

"Do you want anything to eat?" Her voice cracked.

She hovered in the doorway to the kitchen. "I have some chips . . ."

Kaitlyn's voice was like a song. "Nah, I'm fine. I'll be out in a few minutes."

"Take your time." Leah walked slowly through the hallway this time, trying not to let the floor creak under her feet. Quiet steps. She neared the doorway, kept out of sight, peered in, heart in her throat, and the mirror looked back at her. Kaitlyn's eyes were huge and round, and she made eye contact with Leah, and Leah's heart sank from her throat to her gut.

"I'm sorry." She looked down at her feet. "I didn't mean to."

"Huh?" The door cracked open further. Kaitlyn stood in front of her, toothbrush hanging out of her mouth, pale legs peeking out from beneath an oversized band t-shirt. Her mirror image peered over her shoulder, eyes black and mouth gaping slightly. Leah gasped, and Kaitlyn looked back and the mirror matched and everything was fine. "What's wrong?"

"The mirror . . . you . . . ?" The mirror echoed Kaitlyn's furrowed brow. Leah felt mildly nauseated, but she pushed it aside. She was imagining things. She needed sleep. "Never mind."

Kaitlyn pushed past her. "Well, did you find anything to watch?"

Leah looked back at the mirror once more. Only her own face looked back, her skin washed out but normal. She followed Kaitlyn back into the living room.

Kaitlyn crept closer in the darkness. Leah couldn't concentrate on the movie. She didn't want to, anyway. It was too low-budget or something. The actors kept glancing at the camera, their gazes resting there a moment too long.

Instead she watched Kaitlyn, kept her profile in the

corners of her eyes. She blinked slowly. She was sleepy, but refusing to give in. Every now and then she let out a long sigh, and when she did, she inched closer to Leah. Their shoulders brushed now. Kaitlyn's arm was so soft against hers. Her eyelashes brushed her cheeks as she blinked, slow, and Leah felt the urge to kiss her.

The faces on the screen kept glancing back, looking to their director for advice.

Kaitlyn turned her head slightly, licked her lips, and her soft hair brushed Leah's face.

"Are you tired?" Leah asked, breaking the silence suddenly.

The characters thrashed around the woods, confusing twists and turns, as the creepy music rose to a crescendo.

"Not really." Kaitlyn's voice was low. Her eyes were shadowed in the darkness. She leaned into Leah. "Thanks for letting me stay here. I keep making mistakes, and you keep being there to help me pick myself up again."

"It's no problem . . . you're my friend." Kaitlyn's face was so close to hers. Leah swallowed. Her throat felt thick, and her heart strained in her chest. Kaitlyn was just so pretty. So soft.

Kaitlyn leaned in an inch, and Leah knew it was a mistake, but she leaned in the rest of the way, and the world fell away and there was just Kaitlyn, Kaitlyn, Kaitlyn, and who knew how long it would last this time, it didn't matter, her lips were so soft and she smelled so good and Leah dove in.

It always came at the worst times. After the funeral. Before the wedding. Now. But who was Leah to resist? Who had she ever been? Kaitlyn's breath came in little gasps and Leah kissed her cheeks, her neck, her shoulder, and time fell away and Kaitlyn's shirt came off and Leah's followed and Kaitlyn's eyes smiled up at her, and Leah took her soft hand in hers and she was about to suggest they move to the bedroom when Kaitlyn screamed.

The actors were watching them, dark shadows beneath

their eyes, and those eyes were familiar, weren't they? Yes, they were a little familiar, and a dull pounding started in the back of Leah's head. "What the fuck?" Her voice sounded muffled.

Kaitlyn giggled. "Sorry, it just startled me . . . what's wrong with the movie? Is it . . . frozen or something?" The smile looked pasted on her face.

"I don't know." Leah didn't want to look at it anymore. She grabbed the remote, changed the channel. Cartoon faces stared back at her, eyes bulging and red. Kaitlyn sucked in a breath, and Leah changed the channel again, and the eyes kept looking and she changed the channel and then she clicked the television off.

She could feel Kaitlyn looking at her. She was afraid to turn. Afraid of what she would see in Kaitlyn's eyes. But Kaitlyn touched her knee, and when Leah looked at her, she looked away. "I don't like this."

"Weird, huh . . . " Leah had never noticed the crow's feet by Kaitlyn's eyes before.

The television lit back up on its own, making the girls jump. The actors were back, clustered in the woods, hands over their faces, peeking out between their fingers. Someone was whispering.

Something is coming something is coming something is coming

"Are you doing this?" Kaitlyn's voice was shrill. "You're freaking me out!"

"How could I be doing this?" Leah snapped.

My eyes are open

Something bleeped from Kaitlyn's pocket, and she pulled out her phone, so quickly it was like she was expecting it. Her smile looked real for a moment, and she typed something quickly. "Thanks for letting me stay, but I think I'm going to get going. Daniel finally got back to me."

"Daniel?" The people on the television looked blurry. Leah could barely pull her eyes away from them.

22

Kaitlyn glanced up at her. "I was telling you about him earlier. I think I'll just crash on his couch instead. It's closer to work." The feelings that coalesced in Leah's stomach were distant, dull—sadness, yes, confusion, hadn't they *just* been kissing, did Kaitlyn really not care at all? And—

Something is coming

Kaitlyn sounded irritated. "Can't you turn that off? It's giving me a headache." No, not irritated. Something else. Leah picked up the remote and turned the TV off, but it was already off, and she turned it back on and he was staring at her again, the man from the computer earlier, and Kaitlyn shrieked and Leah turned it off again and this time it stayed off, but she could still see him, like he was imprinted on the screen, or beneath her eyelids.

Kaitlyn hadn't brought much with her: a purse, a knapsack. She gathered them together quickly.

Leah couldn't just let her leave. This was happening too fast. "Why don't you just stay the night . . . it's late." She glanced at the TV over her shoulder. There was something they weren't talking about. Something didn't feel right.

Something is coming

"To tell you the truth, I'm a little creeped out. I'd like to get out of here. I don't feel right." The room was tight around them.

"I thought . . . I want you to stay." Leah's voice was small. It was hard to think around the pounding in her head.

Kaitlyn turned from the window, and something fell away from her in that moment. She looked like a regular girl, the way she would look when you were used to her face, when you were sick of her, when her smile didn't light up the whole room anymore. Her skin was sallow. She looked tired, and the wrinkles around her mouth were more prominent now. "I don't want to stay."

"Okay." Leah was too tired to argue. She wanted this to be over.

Kaitlyn looked out the window again. "There's people out there." Her voice was shaky.

23

"What?"

"Leah . . . what's happening?" She sounded miles away.

Leah crowded into the window beside her. Kaitlyn's skin felt clammy against her own.

The darkness was thick. The houses across the street were distant and indistinct, muted by the streetlights that flickered and died. It took her a moment to pick out the people, blurs in the darkness, shrouded in it.

They didn't move. The more she looked, the more there were, but she could only focus on one at a time, and they *didn't move*, they were frozen in mid-stride, and the only thing that was clear was their eyes, and they were staring right at her, and Kaitlyn made a strangled sound and backed away from the window.

"I wanna go. What's taking him so long?" She pounded at the keys on her phone furiously and then she dropped it. Leah let the curtain fall. She looked down. Kaitlyn had received a picture message, and *it was him*, and his face was a smear across the phone and his jaw was slack and his eyes were so, so wide.

"I'm calling the police." Leah's own voice sounded far away, but she tapped 911 and didn't even think of what she would say—what could she possibly say, and the voice that came out of the phone was wrong, it was awful. *"Something is coming."*

She hung up. Kaitlyn was looking at her and Leah squirmed in her gaze.

"What happened? Why didn't you say anything? What's happening?" She looked back out the window, then pulled the blinds shut. She looked sick. "Give me that." She took the phone from Leah, and Leah let her. She didn't know what to say. Kaitlyn dialed and Leah watched, breathless, and Kaitlyn's face fell, and then she turned the phone off.

"I'll try the computer."

Leah sank down on the couch again. The shadows in the corners of the room loomed and changed, making her nauseous. Kaitlyn came back, looking pale. She sat next to

Leah and took her hand. Leah put her arm around Kaitlyn, drew her in close, but it didn't feel the same. Kaitlyn's scalp smelled sour.

"I don't like this."

"It'll be fine in the morning." Leah couldn't think of what else to say.

"I don't feel good. I want to lie down."

Leah's bed was unmade and she tossed the blankets quickly into a tidier shape. Kaitlyn followed behind her, didn't seem to care. She turned to the corner and pulled the blankets around her shoulders, over her head.

The television turned on in the other room and Leah did nothing. Too many voices whispered, but she didn't want to leave the room and walk back out there alone.

She left the light on and curled up beside Kaitlyn. "Are you asleep?"

"I'm scared."

She pulled Kaitlyn close.

She didn't remember closing her eyes.

She dreamed of him, floating, blotting everything else out, his smile too wide with too many teeth, and he wouldn't stop looking at her *he wouldn't stop watching her* and she woke up and the room was dark. The only thing she could see was Kaitlyn's eyes, wide open, bright white in the darkness.

Leah screamed, and Kaitlyn didn't blink.

"Kate?" Her own voice wasn't familiar anymore.

Kaitlyn's cheeks looked hollow, and her eyes . . .

They weren't her eyes.

The green light of the computer screen lit the room.

Kaitlyn kept staring at her.

No.

Kaitlyn was looking at something behind Leah. She was looking over her shoulder.

Leah's heart thudded. She was too afraid to turn around.

THESE BEAUTIFUL BONES

THE CRACK ZIG-ZAGGED across the basement, ripping it nearly in two. That was definitely where the draft was coming from. Rather than fixing the fucking thing, the landlord had covered it with boxes stuffed with junk, cutting corners wherever he could. Suzanne was sick of this dingy place already, but it was the only thing she could afford. Well, the only thing her mother could afford, and that cash was running out quick.

How did the landlord even get insurance on this place? The dirty floor smelled awful. Musty, but in a very human way. If she was being honest, it smelled like an unwashed cunt. The opening ran deep into the earth. It was probably full of bugs and rats. The piles of boxes concealed it at a glance, but there was no hiding it once you got down here. There was no hiding anything down here. Tacked-up posters peeled away to reveal walls covered in graffiti or drawings or something.

Suzanne sighed, shoved boxes back in place. They must be creating at least a little bit of insulation. The stack of cardboard wobbled, spilled out a mess of torn clothing and dirty magazines. Suzanne grabbed a handful of clothing and dropped it again. Bits of lace and pliant leather, combined with the nudie magazines . . . gross. She stood up and brushed her hands on her jeans, frowned at the mess. This was disgusting. She tried to shove the pile aside with her foot and just made things worse; more boxes tumbled and spilled—a stack of photos that she didn't even want to look at, stained paintbrushes, a dagger.

She paused.

It was dangerous-looking, even in this pile of junk. Something moved in her stomach, and she reached for it, but drew her hand back when she noticed the handle—it was intricately carved, and right where she would wrap her hand around it, it was shaped like a gigantic, exaggerated penis. Her cheeks went hot. She kicked it back into the pile with the rest of the stuff. What the hell was wrong with him, renting the place out like this?

She yanked out her phone. Anger churned in her stomach, but what good would calling him do? He must know about the crack and all this shit already. He was the one who hid it. Who else could she call to complain? Her mom was already worried enough, and Eric . . .

The phone rang in her hand and she nearly dropped it into that disgusting hole. God, how would she ever get it out? She couldn't imagine reaching her hand down into that gap, moist and earthy and unknown.

The phone rang again.

It was Eric.

She didn't want to answer it, but it rang again and again and finally she did. She had to. Who the fuck was she to resist? She peeled a bit of a Coke poster off the wall, revealed a sliver of whatever was painted beneath. She didn't say anything.

"Suzy?"

The sound of his voice was familiar and awful. It wound into her ears, clutched at her heart.

"Suzy, don't hang up. I'm so glad you answered. I've been so worried about you."

She trudged up the crooked basement stairs. "Oh, poor you. So worried." She found her purse, rummaged out a pack of smokes.

"What have you been doing? Where are you? When are you coming home?"

"I'm fine. It doesn't matter where I am. And when I'm coming home is up to you." She sat on the back steps, stared into the forest. The leaves were starting to fall, the branches bare and cold without them.

"I'll come get you anytime. You have to come back. I know you will. We belong together, you and me. You've been gone long enough already."

"Did you fire her?" She lit a cigarette and tried not to cough.

"Suzy, are you smoking again?"

"Who cares?" She blew smoky O's, an old trick she was happy to see she could still do. Through the haze, she realized there was a little hut or . . . something she hadn't noticed before, out in the woods. A shed. It must be a shed.

"I care. You know that."

"Did you fire her?" Her voice was sharp. "Did you?"

She could hear him breathing on the line. He was trying to think of a way to make it sound better. "I can't do that, honey. She needs the job. Besides, what would my boss say? She's a good worker. How would I explain it?"

"How will you explain it to me?"

He didn't answer. He always had an answer for everything, but he didn't have an answer for that one.

She should hang up, end on a powerful note, but she couldn't help herself. "Are you still fucking her?"

He hesitated again. She could picture the look on his face. Eyebrows folded into concern, a smile tugging on his lips, urging her to forgive him. Before he could say anything else, she cut him off. "Forget it. Call me when she's gone." She hung up. Again.

She rubbed her eyes. She was so fucking sick of crying. He didn't deserve her tears. He didn't deserve anything from her. So why did she keep answering his calls, and why did she keep checking her phone when they didn't come?

Fuck it. She stubbed her smoke out. Her phone rang again and she tossed it on the step. She should check out that shed. Maybe she could find some wood or something to board up the hole in the basement. Maybe she could distract herself for at least a couple of minutes.

She hopped off the step and into the trees, where branches snatched at her hair and mud sloshed onto her slippers. The woods yawned open to reveal piles of rock and dirt. The overgrown grass abruptly gave way to bare earth. There was no shed, just a huge slab of stone, balanced atop a jagged staircase that reached nearly to her bust. What the fuck *was* this? It must have been used for something at one point in time, but now it was broken and disused, like everything else around here.

Something else to complain to the landlord about.

She climbed the stairs. The top was stained with rust. She ran her hand over the surface, smooth and warm. It must have been baking in the sun all afternoon. She sat down, dangled her legs over the edge, lit another smoke. From this angle, she could see a pile of disturbed earth, nestled beneath a tree. Some attempt at gardening?

The tree was hideous, dead, coated with black rot. Maybe they had been trying to dig it up by the roots and just gave up.

Her eyes lazily traced the curves and angles that jutted out every which way. A hammer lay atop the pile of earth, from the same set of tools as that dagger—its handle was shaped into a massive phallus. Someone had carved something into it once, but she couldn't make out the letters; they were all jumbled together. It reminded her of something. Something wordless. She felt it, deep in her gut.

The rock seemed to move, pressing up against the seat of her jeans. The warmth and firmness felt good. She shifted, and the seam of her pants rubbed against her crotch. The breeze was warm for fall, but her nipples stood to attention. She pressed against the rock, felt a wetness grow between her thighs.

The carving on the hammer was so detailed.

Jesus Christ, she was getting horny. Pathetic. It had been ages since she had gotten laid. Even the last few times she had fucked Eric, she could tell his mind just wasn't in it.

Maybe she should go to the bar downtown and pick someone up, bring them back to this shitty rented house and fuck them. But it would be just her luck to run into someone Eric knew. Then she would have to explain herself, and honestly, it was far more likely she would bring someone back here and end up crying because they weren't Eric. It was his familiar body she wanted in her bed.

What the fuck was she doing out here anyway?

The rock pulsed beneath her cunt. She tore her eyes away from the hammer, tossed her cigarette and went back to the house, feeling even worse than before.

"Have you heard from Eric?"

"Only every day."

She heard the *click click click* as Mom snapped her tongue against the roof of her mouth, sending shivers of annoyance up Suzanne's spine. "Why don't you just come home?"

Why didn't she? "I can't, Mom."

Eric could still turn things around. But she was so tired of being stubborn, of waiting for him to make the right choice. What was there for her back home? Move back into the room she had spent her childhood in, get a shitty fucking job, try to figure out who she was without Eric. She blinked tears away.

"I'd love to keep helping you, honey, but I can't afford to wire you anymore money. If you want a plane ticket home, that's one thing, but I can't just keep sending you money every week. You need to figure out what you're doing."

What the fuck *was* she doing? She couldn't go crying back to Eric just because she had nowhere else to go.

"I have to say, Suzy, as sorry as I am for you, I'm not surprised this happened."

30

"Is that so?" The words tasted bitter on her tongue.

"You know how you two got together in the first place. He's too old for you, anyway."

It was true. Everyone told her it would happen. A man who leaves his wife for a younger woman is the type of man who will leave the younger woman for his secretary. And now here she was, all alone, with ten lousy years of memories to keep her warm at night.

"He might fire her. He misses me." He wouldn't fire her. He would keep fucking her and whatever Suzanne did, she couldn't change that. "Never mind. Can we talk about something else? Anything else?"

"Sure, honey. What have you been up to lately? Are you looking for a job?"

"I'm fucking miserable, Mom. I have not been looking for a job."

"Are you getting out of the house, at least?"

"I've been walking," she lied.

"That's good. It's important to get some exercise. That's bound to get you feeling better. What are you up to tonight?"

"I don't know, I might tidy up or something. Read. Watch TV."

"Oh, your father's home. I better get going. Remember, call me anytime. There's always money for a ticket home."

Suzanne hung up the phone, listened to the silent house. She flopped back on the couch and flipped through channels. The colors and shapes blurred, made her eyes heavy. Another exciting evening.

The moon glared through the window bright and angry, and Suzanne woke up confused. Springs from the couch dug into her side, and the TV droned some bullshit infomercial. How long had she been asleep? She fumbled for her phone, couldn't find it. Her head felt light, strange, and a dream danced through her consciousness, just out of reach. Something red and wet and ripe. She could smell that scent from the basement.

Something about the basement.

Something about the walls.

Had she seen something behind the posters earlier? Or had that been part of the dream? Her mouth tasted sour. The solution to something dangled just out of her reach.

Moonlight dribbled down the walls, surreal waves that made her feel dizzy.

She stumbled into the kitchen for a glass of water. For something to clear her head. The basement door loomed open, and the smell was so strong. She was halfway down the stairs before she knew what she was doing. She yanked the chain for the light, and it swayed, revealing thick tears in the haphazardly hung posters. A faded strip peeled away as she watched.

Weird that they had covered this up. There was a mural on the wall, and it looked clean and fresh, much nicer than the shitty posters it had been covered with. Fresh, but old-fashioned. People, dozens of people, faces . . . and so much skin. They were all naked. Something religious?

No, not religious. She yanked more posters down and wondered if she was dreaming again.

The landlord was a pervert, or whoever lived here before her was a pervert. It was a giant orgy. Maybe he would be pissed she was ripping these posters down, but they were so fragile they practically flaked away in her hands. Hell, just since this afternoon they had started falling apart.

The smell got stronger. It was so familiar, the way it wormed into her brain. Damp and musty; a sex smell. It made her think of Eric. Her gut twisted painfully.

It must have taken forever to paint. Complex configurations of men and women, cocks and pussies and assholes and tongues, licking and sucking and fucking, wet and sweaty and frantic. Every position you could imagine was displayed. Who would go to the trouble to paint this?

She tried to swallow. Her throat felt tight and sore. She had torn the paper down in a frenzy, and now she regretted it.

One character repeated itself throughout the mural. He was beautiful. Tall and blond and smiling, his body as hard and glistening as his enormous dick. The rest of the figures were a little more stylized, their faces indistinct, but he was rendered in loving realism—especially his throbbing cock. Much bigger than Eric's.

Despite herself, Suzanne was getting wet. She had always wondered what it would be like to take a huge dick. The figures in the painting seemed to enjoy it. His grin nearly split his face in two as he shoved it into every available hole. The artist had captured a certain charisma in that smile, one that fluttered butterflies in Suzanne's belly.

She had never been one for pornography—Eric had wanted to watch it with her once. He had even suggested they make their own. She hadn't done it, but maybe if she had, maybe if she had been a little more experimental . . .

Maybe if he had made her feel a little more comfortable.

Maybe there was more to her than that vanilla side.

Her eyes scanned the painting. Men with men and women with women and women with men and everywhere she looked, that beautiful man with the huge penis, everything hard and firm and beautiful.

Her hand slipped inside her blouse.

Two women bent in front of a line of men, their sweet faces surrounded by massive erections. Wet, glimmering parts spread out. Legs scissored across each other. Huge hands on buttocks, leaving behind imprints. Crooked smiles. Heavy breasts and small breasts and dainty little tongues licking swollen clits. Faces buried between thick thighs. Faces blurred, indistinguishable in their pleasure.

Swollen cocks ready to burst, mouths twisted in pleasured screams, pubic hair lush and shining.

Suzanne slipped a hand between her legs. So much naked skin, so many hands and legs and nipples and pussies. Asses laid across altars, pointed in the air, inviting. Her vision swirled, coalesced on an altar and that beautiful man, penetrating women in turn, one after the other, sliding his cock in and out, in and out. Suzanne thumbed her clit, slowly at first, then faster.

His huge cock throbbed and gleamed and he was ready to come, and so was she.

No.

Something was wrong.

The scent let up, a breath of fresh air, and her head cleared and all that wet pleasure became something else. Suzanne whimpered, and her vision sharpened suddenly to pick out details she hadn't noticed before.

The smiles were more sinister than she'd thought. Some of the women held knives, gleaming with redness so wet she felt like she could reach out and touch it. Pussies spread open, ripped too far, gaping puzzles of flesh torn all the way to their assholes. Their faces were contracted with pain, not pleasure, but still they writhed against each other.

It was horrid, grotesque. They pulled out knives, made new holes to fuck, and tore each other apart. Men smiled around wet mouthfuls of flesh. Women impaled themselves on wicked branches from trees, and that beautiful man in the centre of it all, atop the altar—and fucking Christ, was that the stone and tree from the backyard?

This was some kind of joke. What kind of person would paint this? How had she not seen this? Sick guilt churned her stomach. Suzanne pulled her sticky hand out of her panties and heaved herself up the stairs, slammed the heavy basement door behind her. She didn't stop until she was outside, cigarette in hand, blinking back tears.

Even she deserved better than this.

A dozen donut holes and an extra-large café mocha. Not a great use of her last five bucks, but honestly, how far would that five bucks have taken her anyway? A mouthful of chocolate and she was pawing at her phone again, making sure she hadn't' somehow missed a call in the thirty seconds she'd managed to tear her eyes away.

She *should* call the landlord. She *wanted* to call Eric. Why couldn't she just go back in time and not read the emails? Suspecting but not knowing. Christ. Couldn't she just have ignored it a while longer, at least gotten a better plan in place? Suzanne dabbed at her eyes with a napkin, refused to meet the eyes of the older couple sitting next to her. Their sympathetic smiles made her want to puke.

Okay. Deep breath. Call the landlord. The place was a dump, and if she complained, if she threatened to take her complaints further . . . maybe she could stay in the dump for a while longer while she figured out what the hell she was going to do with her life.

She fucking hated confrontation. Her chest clenched while the phone rang. And rang. Fuck it. She hung up, groaned, ran a hand through greasy hair. The couple next to her got up and left, and she dabbed her eyes again.

Now what?

Call Mom and give up, get a ticket and try to imagine a new life for herself, or call Eric? Either way, she was accepting defeat. She tapped chewed fingernails against the table, brain tugging in one direction and then the other.

She had a few more days to think about it. Put off the inevitable a day longer. She tossed the rest of the donut holes into the trash.

She kept her phone in her hand as she walked home. Maybe he would call tonight. Maybe their last conversation was the push he needed.

The night was still warm, but the moment she stepped into the house, she was freezing. The air was cold and damp, and the basement door was wide open. 'Her stomach clenched. There was no way she had left it open. The landlord?

"Hello?" Her voice cracked, and she hated the sound of it. She peered down the stairs, into the darkness. The air was moist against her cheeks. She could almost taste it, salty and thick. "Hey, is someone down there?" There was no answer, of course. God, with her luck, there was probably some crazy person down there. Whoever lived here before, whoever painted that weird fucking mural.

Maybe she should call the police.

She held her breath, listened. She didn't hear anything. She couldn't call the police. She wouldn't be the hysterical woman all alone, getting paranoid every time something creaked.

There was no one down there. But she had to make sure. She groaned, grabbed a knife from the kitchen. Like that would do anything. Like she knew how to use it.

Maybe the psycho would kill her and do her a favor.

"Hey, I'm coming down there now. If anyone's down there . . . I have a knife."

The light played shadows across the walls, and the walls were covered with paint, and there was nothing obscuring it anymore. Just brilliant, lurid color, covering every inch of space. And that *smell*. Spicy, thick, musty, *sexy*. Her head wobbled. Her thoughts felt far away. The pictures swam out at her, and her eyes couldn't keep up.

God, she had never imagined being fucked in so many ways before. Thick cocks crammed into tight holes everywhere. Her own hole pulsed, grew wet. But it wasn't just cocks going into those holes. It was knives, it was spikes, and she had never been interested in any of this shit before, had never even thought . . .

She slid a finger in her mouth, wet her lips.

No matter where she looked, there was more to see, and He kept smiling at her. At her.

She reached out to the wall, stroked it, and the faces seemed to look at her. Some of this looked so familiar—that twisted tree out back, and those women, with their knives, thrusting, thrusting into a man, and he loved it *he loved it* and his cock spurted cum and the phallic hammer swung and blood rained over the altar.

Suzanne's phone buzzed. She shook and yanked her hand from her pants with disgust. What was she doing? Eric was on the phone and she couldn't answer it, not now, the colors were too bright and something was not right in her head.

She slammed the basement door behind her. It was sure as hell shut this time, and it was going to stay that way.

Blood and sex swam in her head. There was still a bottle of wine in the fridge. She curled up on the couch with it, and every time she closed her eyes she could see them writhing.

Hands groped their way up her thighs, oily wet, smooth against her skin. Someone moaned—was it her? Firm hands on her tits, squeezing her nipples, too hard, and it *was* her that moaned this time. Her cunt was wet and slick; someone was licking and chewing and it was *so good*.

She stirred awake, and so many sets of painted eyes were on her.

She was in the fucking basement. How did she get in the fucking basement? Her pussy pulsed, begging, and she scrambled to her feet, and there was a sound of something tearing, a great groaning, and that wet cunt smell overtook her. She stumbled back, heart pounding, thighs shaking. She had to run, but she couldn't tear her eyes away from the mural.

The figures had turned away from each other. They

were looking at Suzanne, smiling, all those teeth, all that red. Static blared from everywhere, from nowhere, from inside Suzanne's head. Her clit was wet and huge and throbbing. The wall warped, turned liquid, and there were so many eyes, looking at her, *wanting* her, there were hands all over her body, touching her, prodding her, needing her. Something huge was ripping through the floor and she was ready to bend over and take it, every inch of it, she was filled with red hot pulsing need and she was coming, she was coming, oh God, she was coming.

She was on the floor, ass in the air, thighs trembling. She couldn't catch her breath. The moon had gone dark, and in the shadows, the painting moved.

Her stomach churned; she felt like she was going to throw up. She lowered her head to her hands, closed her eyes, tried to remember how to breathe.

That was fucked up. *She* was fucked up. There was something wrong with her. She was an emotional fucking wreck and she was half asleep and she let this stupid fucking house get the better of her. It was just the work of some pervert. It was nothing. She wouldn't look at it.

'Her legs shook. She looked out the window, to the trees.

That mound outside. The mural. The dreams.

She had to know for sure.

She pulled on sneakers, but didn't bother to change. The landlord had left a shovel in the porch, and she grabbed it before she stepped outside. Wind tickled through her nightgown. The moon was bright enough to lead her.

She shouldn't be doing this, she *knew* that, but there was an insistent nagging in her brain that wouldn't let her stop until she felt the dirt beneath her fingernails.

The trees were still; the stone structure loomed between them. The dirt next to it was loose and light. Grass had never dared to grow back in.

She dug.

She was grateful for the breeze that broke her sweat as she shoveled. She was grateful for the trees that kept her out of sight of the neighbors.

She caught the scent of herself in the air, musty, unshowered, insane. Her back ached. There was nothing out here. She was cracking up. It was time to go back inside.

But her shovel struck something, and she crouched down to push dirt aside, revealing a sliver of something hard and yellowed. She clawed deeper, snagging a nail, and was rewarded with the gentle curve of clavicle. The wind raised gooseflesh on her arms, tickled her thighs.

She had to call the police.

Blood pounded through her ears. She needed to see the whole thing. She shouldn't. She should be terrified. She should be upset. She should be running back to the house *right now*. But she kept digging, gently, unearthing it bit by bit.

Muck had picked the flesh from the bones, leaving the skeleton filthy but whole. The top of the skull was shattered and splintered where it had been caved in by the hammer. She cradled it, feeling strangely tender toward this man she had never known. He had been discarded too. Fucked and left for dead, and wasn't that kind of the same as her? Fucked and used and thrown aside.

The eyes of the skull were dark and beautiful. She slid her hand down, caressing his cheek. The bone was rough and dirty beneath her fingers. Hard. It was so intimate to touch this part of a stranger, the deepest insides, the last piece that remained. Her nipples were so erect it was painful.

The man had been beautiful once. She knew it. Even in death you could see that. These beautiful bones laid out before her, strong and whole but for that wicked head wound. Shining beetles crawled through his ribcage.

She slid her hand down his arm, took his chalky hand

in her own. The bones creaked as she led the hand to her cheek, turned her face to kiss the cold death of his palm.

There was a pulsing in her groin.

Something wasn't right.

She dropped the hand, disgusted with herself, but it fell so gently, caressing her, brushing against her nipple on its way down, making her sigh.

She had never been with anyone but Eric before. Had never even thought of it, really.

She crouched in front of the bones. She was lost. Her hand slid down the bumps of his vertebrae and across the cage of his ribs, where his heart had once pounded in fear.

She took his hand again, licked the tips of the fingers. They tasted like dirt. She slid the hand down across her breast. Bumpy phalanges tore her thin nightie apart. The bones were cold and rough, their caress pinching, teasing, as they slid down her bare belly.

She sat astride the pelvic bone, grinding down, gasping as the curve of hip jutted into her wet panties. She slid back and forth, took fingers deep into her mouth, stared into empty eyes. Blood pulsed in her ears, along with the pulse of something else, deeper, but she was so fucking horny she couldn't concentrate, she could only buck and writhe and gasp.

It wasn't enough.

Hard fingertips scraped her breast, rough and jagged, releasing bright trails of blood. The pressure it released felt good. She leaned forward, pressed her forehead against the cool, rough skull. Her tongue glided across his teeth. They tasted dirty. She felt dirty.

She slid her hands over herself, smearing blood and dirt across her pale skin. She yanked her panties off. Her pussy was hot and wet, throbbing, and she straddled the hipbone again. This time it rubbed against sweet bare flesh. Bits of dirt flaked, sandy against her clit. It still wasn't enough. Her head swam. She could barely breathe. This wasn't her, but she needed more. She needed to be closer. She needed it inside her.

She pulled the bones from the mud, dragged them atop the huge stone altar. She could move freely now. The femur pulled away from the hip bone with a snap and she stroked it, let fibula and phalanges dangle into her lap. The head of the bone bulged obscenely. She sucked it into her mouth, greedy, swirling her tongue around. She groaned. It was so hard.

She slid it between her legs.

It was too big, and she bucked her hips in frustration. She wanted it, she wanted all of it. Everything in her body was screaming with want and need and desire and she thrust her hips down, hard, and her pussy ripped and it felt so fucking good.

Blood soaked her hands as she thrust the bone inside, again and again, forcing her cunt to accept it. Tender skin tore; warm wetness flooded her thighs. Her hand was covered in hot wet blood and she rubbed her clit and fucked herself harder and harder until her eyes rolled back in her head and everything shivered and quaked.

She came painfully. In those seconds of black stillness, she saw something, she saw *him*, his body exquisitely sculpted, beautiful, his face a blur of black sketchiness, the mask thrown aside, his cock massive and throbbing and perfect, ready to rip everything apart with its strength, ready to fuck great fissures into the earth, tear it apart from the inside out.

And then she was sitting amid the trees in her backyard, astride a skeleton, bleeding and cold and stuck, her insides screaming with pain. She tore the bone from her pussy. Hunks of flesh and hair came with it and gore soaked the stone.

Blood splattered the kitchen tile. She was woozy. She needed to call 911, but God, she just couldn't help herself.

"Hello?" Eric's voice was sleepy. Was the bed next to him empty, or occupied?

"It's me. Can . . . Can you come? I hurt myself." Her legs trembled.

"Suzy? What's wrong?"

"I can't talk about it. I just need you to come. Please?" Her forehead was soaked in sweat. Everything she touched was smeared in blood. She needed a doctor. She needed stitches. She needed mental help. First, she needed Eric.

"I'm so glad you called. It's time to come home. "

"No, Eric, I just need you to come here. Please." She choked off a sob. "Something weird is happening. I'm at a place on Baker's Lane. The last house on the left. Just come here, please."

She turned the phone off so he wouldn't call back. She didn't want to talk. She just wanted him to come.

Suzanne was dressed and soaking through a pad when the car pulled up. Even in this bizarre situation, she felt nervous. What could she even say to him after all this time? How could she explain this?

She opened the door and he smiled, blue eyes shining. How had she never noticed they were dead inside?

He took her into his arms and the smell of his cologne teased her nose. She should have showered. She must smell awful.

"Suzy, what the hell is going on here? You look like shit." His eyes softened. "I'm happy to see you, but you don't look well. God, I'm so happy to see you. Look at you. You need me. You haven't been taking care of yourself."

"I've been doing fine." She pulled away from him. It hurt to walk. "This is all going to sound insane. I need to show you something in the basement."

"I'd rather talk at home. I'd like to get you in the bath first. Jesus, what have you been doing out here?"

"Please, I think it would be better to show you first."

42

He shrugged. "Have it your way, but let's make it quick. This place is disgusting. "

"You don't know the half of it." She gestured towards the kitchen, led him to the basement door.

"Can we just get to what's going on here? Are you limping?" His brows furrowed with concern, a robot imitating human emotion.

"Really soon, yes, we'll talk. I just want you to see this so you can understand. Please?"

He followed her down the stairs, into the darkness. "What is that smell?"

"Just . . . " She gestured a limp arm at the wall. At the painting. "Look. Just look. I'll explain."

But she didn't. She couldn't tear herself away. All that wetness. The blood and the sex and the guts and the come. Eric frowned. "Did . . . did you paint this? What the fuck is this?"

"It was here when I got here. Does it look right to you?"

"I'm not gonna sit here all night looking at some old porno painting. What is going on with you? Have you been drinking?" He reached for her, but she swatted his hand away.

"It's not what you think . . . just . . . look at it a little longer. It's the only way for you to understand what's going on here."

"And then you'll come home?"

"Just look."

"What am I looking for?" He turned back to the wall. She reached down. The hammer was heavy. Need was growing in her chest, in her gut. She would know when the moment was right.

Red spurted from the wall and Eric turned to Suzanne, confusion in his eyes, and Suzanne swung and the sound the hammer made when it connected with his skull was music.

Flesh split from skull, bone crunched beneath hammer. Eric swayed, grimaced, his mouth an O of

43

surprise. She wasn't strong enough. She had to hit him again.

He fell from the couch, his eyes squinting beneath the waterfall of blood. The dent in his head was the size of a baseball. "K . . . Karen . . . " he muttered.

"Who the fuck is Karen?" She swung again, hit the opposite side. His eyeball turned to liquid, squelched against the floor. Something rasped deep in his throat and he collapsed.

He didn't even look human anymore. He looked like art. Thick fluid pumped from his shattered face. His remaining eye flickered. She thought he was still breathing. She swung again and a spray of brain matter misted her face. She licked her lips, tasted salt. She swung again and again and chips of bone and meat sprayed new blood on the walls as his skull finally shattered.

She yanked off her sweater and her jeans. There was no time for teasing. She wanted him *now*.

The knife was dull. She hadn't had much time to prepare. It was a lot of work to open him up. Grunting with effort, she slid through his flesh. Fat and muscle slipped away from her hands, and she opened him wide, like a present. He smelled like meat, like blood, like sex. She could hear laughing, somewhere far away. Was it her own? Her face hurt from smiling. She slipped her hands into the opening. He was so warm and wet inside. Rib bones scraped against her hands, sending a chill through her body.

His heart came out with a wet squelch.

It was hers, finally.

Blood spurted over her teeth. It was thick and bitter, but it tasted delicious. Juices leaked onto her face, her breasts, made her wet and warm and slippery. She slid her hands over her breasts and God, she had never been so fucking horny in all her life.

It had been wrong to fuck the skeleton. She knew that now. She belonged to Eric. She would make it up to him. And all the eyes in the painting could watch.

She cracked his rib bones with a snap, shoved their jagged ends into her own smooth skin. She wanted everything of him to enter her, everywhere. Her flesh was unwilling but yielded. She stabbed broken bones into her stomach and a beautiful arc of bone jutted out beneath her sternum, like a crown.

She wasn't patient enough to slice through tendon and meat to get to the bone. She needed it all *now*. She tried to carve his arm off, but the thick muscle and bone was too much for her knife. She groaned in frustration. She would have it anyway. He still wore their wedding ring, but her pussy was ripped too far open to feel it when she shoved his fist inside.

"God, that feels good." She moaned and leaned forward to kiss him. She slipped her tongue inside what was left of his mouth, tasted blood, swallowed shattered teeth.

There was so much of him; bones and muscles and tendon and meat. She wanted it all.

The knife was sharp enough for her own soft skin. The ruin of his head gaped at her as she slid a blade between her tits. Exquisite pain jolted through her body. She slid a finger inside the cut, teasing, coy, and carved a muscular ribbon from his thigh. It curled around her fingers, and she slipped it inside the wound, greedy fingers shoving, until his flesh was hers.

She could stuff every bit of him inside herself if she just made enough holes.

She cut and screamed and fucked and came. Painted figures screamed in ecstasy. The floor turned red beneath her, and blood dribbled into the hungry mouth that tore the basement in two.

THE BOTANY OF DESIRE

THE FLOWER HAD grown through the wall overnight.

The petals were highlighter yellow, brighter than any flower he had ever seen. Clint pulled the stem from the wall and it made a sucking sound as it detached. Beneath it was just plain paint, no crack or mud or anything that would have made it make sense.

He was running late already. He yanked on his frayed denim vest and headed out the door.

Holly was already at their table. He was late again, but she didn't look mad. Not at all. She leaped up to hug him and her hair tickled his nose.

"You look so cute with your little flower!"

He glanced down. He didn't remember taking it with him, but there it was, bobbing out of his pocket. "Hey, this must be for you!" He presented it to her with a flourish. She smiled and tucked it into a braid. Her hair was a wild mess of browns and reds, and the flower looked perfect there.

"Aww, thanks! I never figured you for the flower type."

"I'm full of secrets, I guess. You already have a coffee. Can I get you anything else?" She shook her head, but when he got his own coffee, he couldn't resist buying her favorite donut.

She was so cute, sitting there doodling little monsters in the margins of her notebook. She laughed when he brought the treat to her, and he loved that laugh, loved that her reaction to surprise was always joy. She wasn't jaded like his other girlfriends had been. Not that she was his girlfriend. Not exactly.

"So what have you been up to since last week?" She needed space. And normally he did too, but it was driving him crazy trying not to freak her out. He liked her too much. He didn't know how to relax anymore, too busy trying to plan the exact right moment to message her and the exact right thing to say.

"Eh, not much. Working, hanging out. Nothing serious." She sipped her coffee.

"Hanging out, huh? Anything . . . anything you think I should know about?"

She raised an eyebrow, and her smile faltered for a minute. Ugh. Why had he said that? "Well, do you feel like it's something you need to know about?"

"No, no. I guess not." His gut twisted. He was not built for casual dating. He knew it was a dick move to pretend he was okay with it when he wasn't, but he kept hoping . . .

"Let's change the subject." And her smile was back, just like that. "What movie do you want to see?" His gratitude made him feel like a dog, slobbering and happy for scraps.

She picked the movie, and they walked home slow. He was happy to listen to her talk. Happy to delay the inevitable. His house was closer to the theater than hers. He always walked her home, of course, but first he had to ask. Had to try.

Clint pointed at his apartment. The gesture was useless. She knew where it was. "Did you want to come up for a bit?" Nervousness fluttered through his chest. Sometimes she said yes. Sometimes.

"Can I just come up for a minute to pee? I shoulda stopped before we left the theater, but you know how I am with public bathrooms."

"Sure! Yeah! Of course!" Why did he sound so enthusiastic? She brushed his cheek with her lips.

He kept his apartment pretty neat, but walking through the hallways was always taking a bit of a chance. Some of his neighbors were on the seedier side, and it was embarrassing bringing her here, but what could he do? He unlocked the door, and she stood close to him, her breath warm on his neck. "Do you want a beer or something while you're here?" He was dying to spend more time with her, and if she left now he probably wouldn't see her till next week.

He would never get the hang of this.

"Whoa! More flowers?" She pushed ahead of him. Clint was more surprised than she was. There *were* more flowers, a half dozen of them, scattered around his *Trainspotting* poster. "They're not real, are they?" She touched one, drew her hand back. "They are real! How did you do that? It looks like they're growing right out of the wall." She looked so impressed, but he could barely enjoy it.

"I didn't do anything! They weren't here when I left to meet you." He ripped the poster down to examine the wall. The stems grew directly out of the plaster.

"What kind of flowers are these, anyway?"

They were different from the one he'd found this afternoon—blood red and royal purple, inky colors. The petals rippled like the ocean.

"I have no idea."

She must have heard the distance in his voice, because her smile faded. "You really didn't plant them, or . . . I dunno, superglue them or something?"

Clint took out his phone. "Should I call my landlord, do you think? Like . . . it can't be right that they're just growing like this."

She smacked the phone out of his hand, playfully. "No way! Really? You're going to call him and complain that beautiful flowers are growing out of your walls?" She laughed again, and it did sound silly. She leaned over and echoes of red and purple shone onto her face. "I've never seen anything like it before." The smile that curled on her lips was familiar and welcome. She kissed him. Her lips were sweet, and the scent of the flower in her hair was intoxicating.

"Do you work tomorrow? I don't work till the afternoon." Her voice was husky. He could barely speak, only shook his head. She led him to the bedroom. Petals scattered across the floor, but he hardly noticed them.

After, she was snoring lightly, limbs splayed out, sheets shoved to the side. He didn't want to close his eyes, didn't want to miss a moment. The moon shone in the window, making her glow. He could see her veins through her skin, delicate webs that looked green in the moonlight. Her hair spread, tangled around the pillow, and as she shifted, he saw that the stem of the yellow flower had twisted its way into the shell of her ear. He reached for it, and its scent wafted into the air and permeated the room. He drifted.

A vibrant splash of wildflowers bloomed in his hall, a scatter of bright green grass and clover between them. It wasn't normal, but it was hardly awful, was it? It wasn't as if the place was dirty or dangerous or anything like that.

And it had thrilled her so much.

He couldn't focus. Not on such a non-problem. He was still daydreaming about her soft skin, her masses of hair, her fruity sweet smell. His phone buzzed. He glanced at the number and a pleasant feeling of surprise pulsed through him. Holly had never called him before. He had always been the one to get hold of her, and hell, who called *anyone* anymore? They always texted. Besides, she should still be at work—oh shit, maybe something was wrong?

"Holly?"

"Clint!" Her voice was bright and cheerful. "I've been thinking about you all day!"

"Really?" His cheeks felt hot. "You just left a couple hours ago."

"I know! I had such a great time last night! Can I see you again? Tonight? I'm working till 9, but I can stop by after that. I'll bring a pizza or something."

Oh thank God, maybe all this nonsense of playing hard to get was over, and he could stop trying to swallow his feelings all the time.

"I'd love it if you came by."

"Then I will!"

He kept checking the plants, half-expecting them to disappear as suddenly as they came, half-hoping that more would grow. It was silly. It didn't matter. She hadn't slept with him just because some flowers had sprouted up in his apartment.

Did they need watering or something? He was so stupid; he should have Googled it right away. If they were here, the least he could do was take care of them. He was partway through forming a Google search when she showed up.

She hadn't brought pizza. She looked fantastic. Her cheeks were red with the cold, her smile was electric, and her hair was an insane cloud around her face with dozens of new flowers tucked into it.

"Hi!" She pulled him close. She smelled rich and green and it made him dizzy. "I'm here!"

"Hey, more flowers."

She winked at him. "Yeah, I grew 'em myself. Picking up a green thumb like you."

They spent the evening curled pleasantly together, watching television, her hand entwined in his. The scent of the flowers in her hair made him sleepy, and his eyes were half-closed when she moved suddenly and woke him up.

"Look, there's more."

He could hear them growing, a faint groaning beneath their feet. A stem snaked between cracks in the hardwood floor, its velvet-purple head thrust toward them. Something quaked within him and he started to stand up, but Holly held him back, hushed him. Whisper-quiet, the petals unfurled and released a pungent scent. Leaves crackled together like applause around the room.

"It's beautiful."

It *was* beautiful, but it was also very, very strange. "This is getting really weird." The purple flower seemed to glare at him. He wanted to reach for it, pluck it out, tear it to pieces. Instead, he looked at Holly, and her eyes were soft.

"What's so good about normal anyway?"

The bed shifted and he woke up gradually. Her side was still warm. A few dreamy moments passed, but she didn't come back. He heard his name whispered, or he thought he did, over and over. His mouth tasted sweet, like fresh grass.

He sat up in bed, and a canopy of vines crowded his vision. His heart thudded, and he realized how shallow his breathing was.

"Holly?"

There was no answer. A breeze dusted pollen into his face, and he breathed it in, choked on the powdery taste. He crawled out of bed, left the sheets rumpled, and stepped into his living room.

No, not his living room.

A jungle.

A dim yellow sun illuminated huge inky flowers and twisted trees that snaked up where there should be walls. Clint's stomach lurched, and the rich, living scent made it difficult to breathe.

The grass was vivid green beneath his bare feet, so green it didn't look real. It couldn't be real. It wasn't real. He had to be dreaming.

He could hear singing.

Something buzzed past his nose, something too large to be an insect. His face felt sticky.

He was done with this dream. He wanted to go back to his bedroom, let the morning come; but when he turned, his bedroom door was gone, and blue plants gaped back at him, the patterns in their leaves like faces.

"Clint?" Her voice was honey, a salve, a sliver of sanity. He turned, and leaves parted, led him deeper into the woods.

"I'm coming!" His voice was too loud in this place, and the plants rustled in response. He followed the path further. It was too much. He should be in his living room, he should be tripping over the couch, but there were only leaves and flowers and gasping breaths and bushes and—

And Holly.

She was naked on a bed of flowers. Her skin was luminescent, nearly green, her Janis Joplin hair spread out in tendrils, eyes sleepy-lidded. "What took you so long?" Her smile tilted crooked at him.

A wave of dizziness came and he sat down too quickly, fell over the bottom of his pajama pants. She cat-crawled over to him, took his head in her hands.

"This is fucked up." He didn't know what else to say. Her cool hands felt refreshing against his hot skin. Did he have a fever?

"Everything usually is." Her eyes glowed yellow—were they always that color? She kissed him, and she tasted like ripe red fruit, and he was falling.

She pushed him back onto velvet-soft leaves. She

opened for him, and everything was wet. Flowers bloomed around his face, changing color with the rhythm of her hips. He gasped and she rocked and stroked his face and kept him calm and the panic that rushed through his head was overtaken with rhythm and explosions of scent as flora burst into life around them.

He didn't last long. He couldn't. He was overwhelmed, overstimulated, and when he came his head shot back and between the branches, petals danced in the sky.

Later. There was no light. There was nothing. The dark covered everything, and he could imagine he was back in bed, safe, if it weren't for the sounds of the jungle around him.

Clint's heart beat too fast. Waking up hurt. Holly stroked his chest with light fingertips. He took her hand in his and felt the hair on his chest, but it wasn't hair anymore. It was sharp and smelled like grass.

He jerked up, straining to see.

"Lay down, love, it's all right." Her voice didn't sound like her voice. It sounded like rustling leaves, like the buzz of insects.

"We've gotta get out of here. This is really wrong. Something is really wrong."

"Shhh."

The darkness abated as the cloud cover shifted.

And then he saw her.

She was very still. Her skin was delicately veined with thin, leafy lines. It was hard to see in the shadowy light. He couldn't be sure she was there at all. She might be a bed of flowers, her hair just a pile of weeds, lips of petals, eyes of seeds.

"Holly?"

"Stay with me." Her lips didn't move.

He wanted to touch her, to prove it was real skin

beneath his hand. He wanted to scream her name, force her to get up from the ground, but something about that stillness was terrifying, and he didn't want to wake it up.

"I have to go . . . I have to get help." This wasn't a problem he was equipped for. Someone else could solve this. He just needed to get out of here. He just needed to get back to his apartment and find his phone and call someone who understood.

"Stay." It was not her voice at all. It was the wind between leaves. Clint ran.

Grass crackled beneath his feet and the screams of tiny budding flowers erupted. Something like a sunflower burst in front of him, and it had Holly's face, and her eyes were full of tears. "Clint, stay here, please. Please hold me." Leaves clutched at his wrists and he tore them apart, and their green juices stung his fingertips.

Her face was everywhere and all the leaves whispered his name.

Tiny blue flowers rippled beneath his feet, stared at him with her eyes.

He kept running.

The forest grew thicker around him. Thorns and branches tore at his skin. He wouldn't look down at the blood because *what if it wasn't red*. His progress slowed to inches. He broke branches and ripped away flowers, and finally, finally, the door to his apartment appeared, covered in vines that tore at his fingers as he pulled them apart.

"Clint, please! Please don't leave me here!" He turned, slowly, and between branches she swayed, pale as petals, skin like silk, vines and leaves tangled around her feet, arms branching upwards, too tall, her hair a mass of leaves and twigs, her face frozen.

He had to go back for her.

He had to get her to safety.

He had to run.

He turned to open the door. Buds sprang forth and flowered and revealed vicious teeth. He tore at them but they kept growing and it was impossible to get any closer. They bit his hands and he tried to kick down the door but his feet wouldn't move and he couldn't look down, because then he might see the branches that twined around his legs, rooting him deep into the earth.

THE DESERT OF WOUNDED FREQUENCIES

THE CAR WAS a piece of shit, but it would get him home and that was enough. Adam didn't have a lot of money left, but nothing was gonna stop him from getting back to Karen. He'd made a mistake, but there was no more running from it. She would never blame him. No matter what had happened.

The old man looked as bad as the car did, faded jeans and mustard stains. He kept quiet the whole time Adam looked at the car, started it up, checked under the hood. Adam probably could have taken off with it then and there. The creep wouldn't have done nothing, but Adam wasn't that kind of man. Not anymore.

"How much?" he finally demanded, and the old man's eyes snapped up at him, startled out of a half-doze.

He chewed his lip, stared with sunken eyes at the car. "I can let her go for 500 bucks?"

"I'm just using it as scrap. Piece of shit will probably break down before I get it halfway across town. I'm doing you a favor. 200."

He shook his head, slowly. "Can't let it go for that low. Need to make my rent this month." He nodded back at the shack where the car was parked. Didn't even own the shithole. At that age and still paying out his ass, lining someone else's pockets. Revulsion crept into Adam's stomach.

He could have paid the 500, but he saw the weakness in the man's eyes. It wouldn't take much to break him. Adam stood tall, squared his shoulders back. His eyes were steel. He reached slowly into his wallet, counted out four 50-dollar bills and handed them to the man. "Get the paperwork." There was no arguing with him.

With the paperwork signed, the old man handed him the keys and Adam threw his bag in the backseat. He could be home in two days if he kept on cruising. Karen would be happy to see him. They could deal with the rest of it later. The man kept watching as he put the keys in the ignition and at the last moment, tapped on the glass. Something was in his eyes that Adam couldn't interpret. He was sick of this weak old man, but he rolled down the window.

"I wouldn't bother with the radio if I was you. Broke. Just leave it."

Whatever.

The second day on the road, the silence began to bother him. It was slow going, but he was in the home stretch now. He spent the night at a motel and grabbed some snacks, nearly exhausting his supply of cash. Didn't matter. Karen would have kept working. She had to, for the baby. He'd find work and they'd settle back down into how things used to be. He just needed to make it home.

But now he was out of the rush of the cities, with even the occasional small town far behind him. The car had started to smell. There was no air conditioning in this old heap, and the desert roads were hot and ripe. Even with the windows wound all the way down, there wasn't so much as a goddamn breeze. He hadn't slept well last night; never did. Downed a couple beers in the shitty bar next to the motel. Maybe a couple too many, because now he found the heat and the monotony of the road tiresome. His eyes kept drooping closed.

The last store he stopped at had a batch of used tapes and CDs for sale, but this car was so old that all it had was the radio. The radio that didn't work. Fuck. Nothing ever went right, huh? At least if he could blast some tunes, maybe it would keep him awake. So close to home, but with the sun boiling down and the stuffy air, he was liable to pass out and go off the road and get impaled by a fucking cactus. It was the old man's fault. Shoulda got the thing fixed up before trying to make a couple bucks off it.

The road ahead of him was straight as an arrow, miles of sand tapering off into the horizon. Eyes so heavy they felt like they were fulla sand, but when he rolled up the window, the stuffiness made it impossible to breathe. Adam grunted and pounded his fist against the dash. A hiss of static shrieked, startling him awake.

"Jesus fuckin Christ." He yanked the volume down until the static turned to a dull hum. Didn't work, his ass. Fucker just wanted to make sure his trip was as miserable as possible. He adjusted the knobs, searching for a station. Futile. There was nothing out here in the middle of nowhere. Might have done him some good when he was back in the city, but he had trusted the old creep and fucked himself over once again.

"Asshole," he muttered, and silenced the radio. The static continued to mumble. Adam stabbed the knob again, but the crackling continued to fill the car. He spun the knob and the irritating sound whined louder. He turned it the other way with no effect.

"Fuck off." He yanked at knobs and spun through channels, swerving over the empty road. The sound didn't change.

"Of course. Of course he's gotta make this whole trip fucking miserable. A guy tries to do a good thing, go back to his fucking fat loaf of a wife and idiot child, but ya can't cut him a break. Always gotta have shit like this happen." Adam's face flushed hot and red. He pushed the little car faster. "Get me outta this fucking desert." His map lay useless on the seat next to him. Straight fucking line the whole way in this hunk of junk car, and now this fucking maddening static as his accompaniment. Could it get any worse?

He kept driving. There was nothing else to do. The visions he had had of his homecoming were tainted now. He had figured he would get home, Karen would be thrilled to see him, get a little poke in before she made dinner. Have a couple beers. Back at it again. But now, after this shit drive, he knew he would have a fucker of a headache. He might be better off stopping at the next motel and cabbing it the rest of the way home. There was no sense going home in a sour mood—he had some serious sucking up to do to get back in Karen's good graces again. Hell, it shouldn't take too much. She needed him. She better.

He had been doing fine for a few weeks, burning through his money, drinking, meeting girls. But then one of them had noticed the tan line on his wedding finger and asked what happened. He gave her the abbreviated version, but that got him to thinking. If he was doing this, what would Karen be up to? He pictured her and that horny neighbor talking about him, and it sent that red hot anger through him. The dude had just been waiting for his chance to get Karen in the sack. The real sensitive type. Always asking to hold the baby as if it weren't a whining crying sack of shit. That made him real mad, and he realized that meant it was time to go home and collect what was his.

Karen wouldn't have done anything yet. She was the faithful type. Real forgiving. She knew how a woman was supposed to behave. He would be safe, he was sure of it. He never shoulda run off in the first place.

While he was lost in thought, the static changed. There was something beneath it, getting louder. Something breathing.

"The fuck?"

After all this driving, he had to be getting close to the

city, or at least some signal somewhere was strong enough for this hunk of junk to pick up. Fucking weird, though. Sounded like some greasy mouth-breather just leaning over the mic and jerking off or something. Adam fiddled with the radio again, but it was the same on every channel.

"Fucking weird-ass stations out here." He glanced at the map. Reading all those fucking lines and numbers was a headache.

The breathing grew heavier and faster, the static more discordant. Annoying motherfucker. He still had the old man's number circled in the paper, he'd call him up when he got home. He deserved some of his cash back.

"OH GOD, OH GOD, WHAT DID YOU DO?" a woman's voice boomed through the car, and Adam screamed, swerving to the right, dangerously close to going off the road.

"What the fuck was that?"

The radio buzzed and he stared at the dead dumb thing, tense, waiting for it to yell again. His heart rattled in his chest, but the radio remained silent.

He levelled the car back out and drove on. His mouth tasted sour. He stabbed at the radio buttons. He had just picked up on some Christian station or something, one of those weird ones they have out here in the middle of nowhere. People going slowly insane, thinking they have a direct line to God or something. Dumb sonsofbitches. It hadn't really scared him, not that much. Fucker.

The radio buzzed on in a shrill whine. So fucking annoying. He didn't want to listen anymore, but what the hell else was he supposed to do? He was stuck out here. The desert was fucking endless. There was no way to distract himself from the sounds that crept in beneath the static. As much as he hated to admit it, he should have listened to the old man and not turned the fucker on. Not only was it annoying, but it was dangerous. Loud sounds outta nowhere would startle anyone. If he weren't so far away, he'd be tempted to turn back and confront him, demand his money back. But there was only going forward now. Back to Karen. Back to the baby.

On the bright side, maybe those choking sounds meant he was getting closer to civilization. Closer at least to wherever this station was, or wherever this weirdo was holed up in their basement transmitting. A voice murmured, but it was impossible to make out beneath the other sounds. A woman. Sounded like a woman. Singing. Hey, maybe that was a good sign. Maybe there was some normal programming after all. Or maybe she was screaming.

A thin sheen of sweat covered Adam's face, and he rolled the window down. The wind had intensified outside, but it didn't bring any fresh air. More like hot breath on the back of his neck, spattering sand into the sweat. He tried to roll the window back up, but it stuck. This car really should have been used for parts. Piece of shit. He heard a honk and glanced back, but there was nothing for miles. Just the empty road. He was rewarded with another hot gust of sand, irritating against his skin, biting like glass.

He turned back to wipe his face on his sleeve and there was someone in the car next to him. A woman. She stared at him. Her eyes were too dark. Endless. He lifted his head, heart thudding, and she was gone.

The mumbling on the radio turned to soft words. Adam's throat constricted. Something... He could only make out a few words, but it was a woman. Saying something in a singsong voice. Uselessly, he spun the knob. The voice rang out clear as bells. A lullaby, one he didn't recognize. The music accompanying her didn't sound like normal instruments at all. The plucking sounded more like the creaking of a bed than guitar strings. Something dripping. She chuckled.

"Shut up, you creepy bitch." His voice cracked as he spun the knobs. Jesus Christ, would he ever be out of this fucking desert? It shouldn't have taken more than an hour or so to get through this stretch of road, but it was creeping up upon suppertime now. His guts cramped, but he wasn't hungry. He should have been home by now, talking his way back into Karen's bed.

"Do you think she forgives you? Everyone knows." The voice was louder than it had been before, the static shocked into silence. Adam's heart sank deep into his stomach.

Fuck kinda radio show was this?

The static droned, wet sounds beneath it, breathing and something else. Something unpleasant. The skin on his arms prickled. The sweat and sand that stuck to his skin, begging for a shower. Fuck getting home tonight. As soon as he got out of this desert he was checking into a motel, getting a hot shower, and ditching this shitty car. He would call Karen and she could pick him up.

The static gave way to a gentle sobbing. Who the hell broadcast this shit? This bubbling anxiety was an unfamiliar sensation to Adam, and he tried to keep it under control. This wasn't who he was. He clenched his teeth. The sweat stains beneath his armpits weren't who he was.

He trained his eyes on the road. Focus. The sobs faded back into the static, and his eyes grew heavy again. In the distance, near the horizon, he spotted a shape. The first landmark for miles. Good. He must be getting closer to . . . something. All this desert could drive a man crazy. He drove faster, eager to see a change of scenery.

He got closer, and the shape gradually turned into something recognizable. His stomach went sour. It was a baby carriage, empty, abandoned among the endless sand. As if triggered by this, the gentle sobs of the woman gave way to a baby crying. Fuck. Fuck. Fuck. The most irritating sound known to man. The squalls and shrieks were maddening. Adam pounded his fists against the steering wheel. "For God's sake, how fucking far do I have to go? Fuck's sake."

The screams grew louder, shrieking, begging, needy, and suddenly they stopped. Abruptly. Just like...

Static.

His foot went heavy against the gas. The desert was too long. Something was wrong. He must have taken the wrong turn. He should be in town by now. He should be driving down city streets instead of this fucking desert. Jesus Christ, he didn't even give a shit about getting back to Karen now. He wanted a cool glass of water, and then a whisky. And another whisky. He felt like he had been driving for days.

The static grew steadily louder the faster the car went, until it was screeching in his ears, discordant offbeat sounds pounding and pounding until he wanted to scream. He slammed on the brakes and the car screeched to a stop and he got out. He just needed to stand up for a minute. Take a breath. Get his senses back. Faintly, he heard the familiar sounds of traffic, but the desert was empty. The sun was setting, turning the sky blood-red. This was impossible. Ridiculous.

He could still hear it.

The static surrounded him now. He took shaky, weak steps out into the road. The hiss rained down from the sky, along with all the other sounds beneath it—the honking of horns, the screech of brakes. The voices. The murmurs. The screams.

"Stop it. I'm going home! I'm going home! I don't fucking care what happened to the baby!"

She would forgive him. She always forgave him.

The baby screamed and screamed and he remembered how it felt when he shook it and shook it and its head jolted back and forth until it finally stopped screaming. It was better now. It was quiet. Still breathing, just a trickle of blood from its eyes. It would be fine. He had run but he was done running now. He was going home.

He took a breath.

The static couldn't hurt him.

He got back behind the wheel. The seatbelt jammed. Fuck it. He was going home. He pressed the gas pedal to the floor. The static was too loud, deafening, but he didn't care; he was moving. He was driving. Next to him, the dark woman turned and stared at him. He didn't want to look at her, but he looked and her eyes bled tears and she opened her mouth and a scream of static poured out and she was screaming and the baby was screaming and Adam was screaming and

The desert sky wavered. Warped. It peeled away. The city was there. Oh God, he was so close to home. Traffic was congested and there were cars and people everywhere and he was not in the desert anymore. He could have laughed, but the colors were too bright to look at and he was going too fast. Metal screeched and rubber burned and the car careened off the street and slammed into a telephone pole. He was propelled from his seat and his head slammed through the windshield and the pain stopped and everything went quiet. It was better now. It was such a relief. Ribbons of glass sliced through his head and stuck in his eyes and he didn't care.

The car behind him swerved, slammed into the fender of the car ahead. Traffic piled up. Cars slid to a stop around the wreck. People ogled and gasped and dialed the police.

A few cars back, a woman parked neatly at the side of the road and came forward. "I'm a doctor," she said, and pushed her way through the crowd. It didn't take a professional to see there was no hope for this man. Glass protruded from his face. His bones were shattered, yanked haphazard through his skin. There was nothing she could do. But she could hear something.

The excited chatter of pedestrians faded away. She moved closer.

His mouth gaped open, blood dripping on the pavement. Static. Must be the radio; something happened to it in the crash.

Around the glass, his eyes stared at her. Beneath the static, something hissed and whispered, and she leaned in to listen.

ROOT ROT

MARK WAS STARTING to wonder if she was on something. Brittany had never been into drugs before, she wouldn't even smoke a joint with him, but that was a few months ago, and he didn't know her that well, not really. Sure, they had a few drinks, hooked up a couple times, had that one movie date that turned disastrous. Her boyfriend had been a stoner, though, hadn't he? Jack or Jason or something? Whatever it was, she was sure out of it tonight.

Not his problem. He mixed an extra shot of rum into the Coke he poured for himself. Now that they were back at his place, he was starting to sober up, and he didn't really want to. Not now. Her drink he poured a little light. Get them in the same head space, maybe.

When he returned to the living room, her back was to him and she stared silent out the window. Her waist was a little thicker than it had back when they had been hooking up. Looked like she was one of those girls who let herself go once they got involved with someone. Maybe he should have tried his luck with Tinder instead, but he had been so surprised to run into her, and she had seemed willing.

"Hey, drinks are ready. I can put some music on or something. Why don't you get comfortable?" She didn't turn around. "You okay?" Just a little bit of an edge to his voice. Hopefully she didn't notice.

Brittany turned, her piles of curls moving as one tangled mass, eyes unfocused, blinking hard, looking past him. "Are you okay?" he repeated. The expression on her face was blank and stupid, like she had just woken up.

She mumbled something indistinct, wobbled over to the couch and sat down. "How did I get here?" Jesus Christ. Definitely high. All right then.

He tossed back half of his drink in one gulp. "We ran into each other after the bars let out. Dunno where you were before that. Listen, do you want a coffee or something? Or . . . ?" He held her drink out to her and she took it, stared into the glass. Meanwhile, the shot of rum was hitting his stomach and head, hitting it good. Yeah, let the booze chase away the annoyance. Get a drink or two in her and she would be feeling good too. They could still keep the party going. He could help her shake off whatever was going on, the boyfriend or whatever. She wasn't the kind of girl to stay with someone a long time anyway.

He tapped on his phone for a minute, brought up his hooking-up playlist, and let the music wash over him.

It had been a while since he had been with Brittany. She might not be the hottest chick he had ever hooked up with, but she was cute and she liked it dirty. It would be worth the trouble, he just had to get in the mood to get her in the mood. Besides, it was getting late, and if he kicked her out, by the time he got everything settled he wouldn't be able to get anyone else, and it was Saturday and he would be damned if he wasn't getting laid this weekend.

She was staring over his shoulder, towards the door. "You expecting someone or something?" He made himself laugh when he said it. The last thing he wanted was to be dealing with a jealous boyfriend. He had seen her ex, though, and the dude was no threat to him if worst came to worst.

"Someone's already here."

"Nah, it's just me and you, babe." A tangle of remotes and controllers were between them on the couch. Brittany was a thousand miles away, hands folded in her lap. She was stuck in her head, definitely on something, but that was fine. He just needed her to connect with him, get back into the moment. He knew how to do that. He moved the junk onto the coffee table and slithered closer to her so their legs were touching, and placed his hand on the small of her back. She shivered, and he pushed hair back from her face.

"You look good, Britt. It's been too long."

Her eyebrows knitted together, and her mouth worked as if it were dry. "What?"

"Me and you. We've had some fun before. I'm glad to see you again. I know it didn't end on the best note, maybe, but it's nice to give it another go." He leaned in, but she didn't turn to meet his lips and he ended up smelling her hair. It smelled off. Salty and damp. He plunged in anyway, licked the lobe of her ear the way she liked. She didn't lean in, but she didn't pull away either, so he wrapped his arm around her and pulled her closer, turning her face to his and tasting her lips. He couldn't smell any booze off her, nothing at all. She tasted like dust. She turned her face away slowly, pursed her lips, looked back out the window.

"Hey." He spoke softly, tried to smile. "Earth to Brittany, where are you?"

When she opened her mouth, her lips stuck together briefly. "I'm not sure."

He turned her back to him, and she let herself be turned. He caressed her cheek and she looked through him. He stroked her neck, then pressed on her shoulders, laid her back against the couch and rubbed his erection against her, ran his fingers along her collarbone. He moved to kiss her again, but she pulled away. Christ, what a waste of time. Why did women have to be so fucking difficult?

"What's the problem, Britt? If you didn't wanna hook up, why did you come home with me?"

A tear slid down her face. "I was scared."

He pulled his arm away, raked his hand through his hair. Stood up and slammed back the rest of his drink. "Scared of what, of me? That's fucking ridiculous."

"No."

"What?"

"Not scared of you." The tears were coming faster now. "I'm not sure what happened. I think it followed me. I think it's here right now." She wrapped her arms around herself. Her eyes were so wide and wet and dark, it was like they sucked in all the light in the room.

"What are you talking about? What are you on, anyway?"

She didn't answer, just got up, jostling the coffee table, stumbling back to the window. Trembling noticeably, she pressed her face against the glass. The street was motionless. There was a rip in the seat of her jeans, and it didn't look like an intentional one. That wasn't her style.

Mark glanced at his phone. It was past 2:00 a.m. What a waste of a fucking night. If he hadn't run into Brittany, he could have found some skank online by now, or Christ, he could have just jerked off and called it a night. "I don't have time for this shit, Brittany. I dunno what was going on with you and Jack, but I'm not getting involved in all that. I'll call you a cab. You still living at the same place?"

She turned around and looked at him, all those eyes, all that hair. "I'm not sure."

"You're not sure." He started to dial. "Well, you're not staying here. I'm calling a cab, you can tell him where you wanna go—"

At first he thought she was laughing, these awful barking noises, the insane cackle of a witch. But when he looked up, her eyes were bulging and panicked. Her hands gripped the sides of her neck, and the hacking continued, mean enough to rip her throat. "Hey, are you okay?"

She didn't answer; she couldn't. The coughing didn't stop, and now her face was turning red. Sweat stood out on her forehead as she struggled for air, a sound like *tearing*, no, like the flutter of bat wings, the screeching of the woods, loud, too loud, so loud it squeezed past his eardrums and into his brain.

"Can—should I get you some water—?" No. That wouldn't help. She shouldn't still be coughing, whatever it was should have passed, but she was falling to her knees, she was getting worse, she was turning blue, her hands at her neck her eyes bulging and oh, fuck, what the hell was he supposed to do?

His first aid training had been years ago, too long ago; he had never had to use it before now. He knew how to do the Heimlich, but not really, did anyone really know how to do it or did everyone just have the same faded memory of outdated first aid training? Any last traces of being drunk burned away from his mind and body and he was talking, rambling, barely knew what he was saying as he moved toward her. "It's okay, you're gonna be fine, calm down, I got you," and he lifted her up, wrapped his arms around her from behind, nestled his clenched hands beneath her breasts. His fists pounded against her ribs, and he knew it wasn't hard enough but he was scared, he didn't want to hurt her, but she kept making those awful sounds and he hit her again and again and it wasn't going to work, she was going to keep coughing until she died right here on his floor.

But then there was a different sound as something broke, as it spurted into her mouth and she stopped coughing, finally. She spat and there was a splatter, and then the much nicer sound of her gasping in a full breath. They fell to their knees together and his head was light and far away, but she was breathing, tears streaming down her face and so pale and so scared but breathing, thank Christ.

"Okay," Brittany said. "Okay, okay. I think I'm okay now."

Then he saw the incomprehensible pile of shit in front of her.

It looked like it still belonged inside her body. It was huge, Christ, it was the size of an orange, no wonder she hadn't been able to breathe. There was a visceral black sheen to it, like some cancerous organ that had been ripped out from inside her body, expelled by the force of his fists. Dozens of sharp brown protrusions jutted out from its innards, and matted clumps of hair stuck haphazardly to the whole thing. It leaked a thin black ooze onto his carpet. "Britt—what the fuck is that? What is going on?"

"Something happened in the woods. I think he saw it. I shouldn't have made him."

"What are you talking about?"

"I feel better now. I'm sure I'm better now." Brittany tried to stand up, but her legs didn't quite work. She slid back to the floor again, and Mark helped her up. He couldn't stop looking at the thing she had left on the floor.

"You gotta go. You really gotta go now, Britt. I gotta clean this up,"

Her eyes were flat. The wrong shade of green now. All wrong. "I'm fine. Don't worry. I just gotta lay down for a bit." She stumbled into the hall. Her legs kept crumpling beneath her, but she made her way to his room. She sighed as she collapsed into his bed.

Jesus Christ.

Of all the fucking luck. He still wanted to kick her out, but that suddenly seemed like too much trouble. He didn't even care about getting laid anymore. He felt hungover already, and this endless night wasn't even over yet. It was too early to feel like this, but the headache that pulsed behind his temples was an old friend, and the taste in the back of his throat was sickening. At this point, it was either start drinking again or hang his head over the toilet for the night.

The thing on the floor stared up at him. If he left it there overnight there'd be no hope in getting the stain out of the carpet. Brittany could pay to clean it; she'd have to, or pay for the damage deposit he'd lose. He'd kept the place in perfect shape up until now and this sure as hell wasn't his fault. He had just wanted to get laid and go to sleep, maybe get some morning head, and instead he ended up with whatever the fuck this was.

How had that been inside her? Broken branches and ... God, whatever it was, it smelled terrible. He was gonna throw up if he kept looking at it.

Just a shot of something. Beer was for enjoying; this was medicinal. He needed a drink and then he'd clean it up and then he'd kick her out of bed and pass the fuck out. The night was ruined anyway, may as well finish it off quickly.

He poured another double shot and was about to toss it back when something rippled outside the kitchen window. His temples tightened into a real headache now, one that twisted through his skull. There was nothing out there. Just the thin alley between his house and the neighbor's, the same brick wall, the same pile of garbage that was always there. An uncomfortable sensation burned deep in his guts, something flopped over, and it felt like something was brewing there, and he knew that when he went to expel it, instead of shit it would be blood and sticks and oil and he would be left on the toilet seat, screaming, while something moved all around him that he couldn't quite see.

No. Okay, no. That was a weird thought. It was late and he had been drinking and it was a bad night, just a bad night, so he pushed it aside, drank the rum, grabbed a roll of paper towel, and he didn't have any fucking cleaning supplies that would put a dent in whatever that was, so he'd just scoop up the worst of it and get Brittany to give him a twenty to pick something up tomorrow. Maybe he'd let her sleep after all. Waking her up sounded like way too much trouble right now. His headache was bad enough as it was. He dragged himself back into the hallway.

The mess was gone.

There was just a trace of a stain where it had been, like a skid in your underwear, oops, you hadn't gotten it all, embarrassing, an incrimination of your hygiene.

Did Brittany clean it up? The bedroom was quiet, he couldn't imagine she had gotten up and cleaned without him hearing her. It had to go somewhere though, didn't it?

Looking at the smear on the floor made him feel dizzy, but it was a welcome dizziness. Like being drunk again. He wandered back into the kitchen and this time he chugged the rum straight from the bottle, this time he let it sink like fire into his guts and all the bad stuff went away finally, his headache swam away, he tossed the paper towel in the sink and stumbled to bed.

He felt better. Yeah. Nothing to worry about. Hell, with the alcohol swimming through his head, this whole disaster almost seemed funny. What a fucking night. Maybe once Brittany sobered up she would laugh at it too.

He used the flashlight on his phone to light his way, shedding t-shirt and pants as he went. Brittany had shed her clothes too, a messy pile on the floor. She even took her underwear off. She was lying bare-ass naked on his side of the bed and he had to crawl over her to get into the corner. It was difficult to maneuver his arms and legs; the alcohol was definitely kicking in now. He felt pleasant, fuzzy, and she felt good under his hands, her bare flesh. She murmured something indistinct and all the previous weirdness of the night was easy to forget now that there was a naked girl tangled in his sheets.

Mark hoped his clumsy fumbling would wake her up, but her heavy breathing continued unabated. He settled into the corner of the bed, turned the flashlight off. The blinds were still open and the moon shone a dull glow over the room, highlighting her curves in the darkness. Some of the blood left his head and flowed into his cock, a dull throb that peeked out from his boxers.

He lay on his back, hands under the pillow, staring at her from the corner of his eye. His vision blurred a little when he looked at anything for too long, but her ass looked gorgeous. He remembered how it felt in his hands the last time they had hooked up, in his kitchen, her leaned over the counter, grabbing her fat ass and shoving himself inside while she made those quick little panting noises, clutched the sink, pushed against him.

ROOT ROT

She knew what she was doing, crawling into his bed naked. Mark rolled on his side, put his hand into the thick mass of her hair, caressing, more tender than he felt, hoping to gently wake her up. "Britt," he whispered. His hand trailed down her shoulder, slid over the curve of her breast, down her waist and generous hip, over her ass. He squeezed, and his erection was so hard it hurt. "Wake up." She had come home to fuck, and he had brought her home to fuck, and here she was naked in his bed. Was she trying to torture him or something?

He inched closer, pressed against her. She still didn't wake up as he poked his cock between her legs, but her cunt was sopping wet, he could feel the slickness even without being inside her, it drenched his cock and he moaned as he slid against her labia.

"You're so hot." He slid one hand up to clutch her breast. She moved a little, like she was pulling away, but his grip on her was too tight and instead she just brushed against him, smooth thighs against his hard cock, and then he was too hot to stop, he pushed her down, flat on her face. She murmured something that he didn't understand and he maneuvered himself between her legs and slid inside her hole.

Then a lot of things happened at once.

He thrust and moaned in pleasure, but the pleasure morphed to pain as something entered him, something small and sharp that splintered and sank into his dick, burrowed deeper, shards of glass that tunnelled through his skin and something opened its eyes inside him, outside him, everywhere.

And beneath his hands, Brittany crumbled: her skin tore in his hands, parchment-thin, flaked away, and beneath that thin skin were knots of wood and broken branches and something dark that stuck to his hands.

And the sticks were sharp and they cut him all over, they embraced him as he collapsed into his bed, they sliced ribbons across his face and the tiny insects that hid in the wood scuttled inside the tears in his skin.

And he screamed and shook and rolled to the floor.

His scream echoed, dull and far away, sucked into the dark corners of the room, and something about the sound of it was worse than the silence so he shut up. The light from the moon was gone.

Someone was here.

There was a shifting behind him, from the bed, the creaking of old bones or old wood and the thin whine of insects working their jaws.

There was a clicking as *it* clattered into the room. The shadows bled and he couldn't see it, but he knew. It could see him. Whatever she had coughed up, it was here and it could see him.

Eyes were opening everywhere. By some miracle, he pulled himself to his feet; he wanted to be smaller, he wanted to be hidden, but he moved and he didn't look at it, he wouldn't look at it, he stepped over it and he kept going and behind him something was shifting and creaking and reassembling itself.

No shoes, no clothes, but he would not turn around so he kept going, out the hallway, out the door into the grey dawn light.

It came too, branches breaking, bones creaking, the groan of old trees. Thousands of tiny legs rippled beneath his skin, millions of tiny mouths sang and *it* followed their song and grew and broke and reassembled and he kept walking. His cheeks were wet and he was afraid to wipe them because his tears felt wrong, they felt thin and oily and dark and the streets were so quiet and he just had to keep walking.

The buzzing started in his head, or maybe it never started, maybe it had it always been there maybe he had always been walking and this buzzing had always chewed through his brain, the same way it chewed through his muscle and fat and tendons until he wasn't sure what was left behind.

It hurt, but the pain felt far away and he couldn't think

because they chewed and chewed and chewed and he felt hollow and he felt sad and he felt nothing, there was nothing to feel because he was nothing he was no one, the chewing was all there was, the chewing and the fear of what he would see when he turned around.

There was nothing to hold on to out here, only cold air and tired feet and voices up ahead, laughing pretty voices and he moved towards them, blinking tears from his eyes because why would he be crying and why was he walking and why anything except this buzzing and chewing and there were girls on a bench and they stopped laughing when they saw him, one of them stood up and the words she said flew through him and behind him, back to where it was following, back where it could hear and she said, "Mark, oh my God, is that you?" and he fell into her arms and she kept talking but he didn't understand, they were just words, and something was caught in his throat and it tasted so bad.

POSTPARTUM

KEPT MY eyes on the television while I spooned pablum into Timmy's mouth. The horrors of the daily news were downright cheery in comparison to this dull horror in my lap.

I couldn't stand looking at him. It was his eyes. I had hoped he would have Tim's eyes, piercing and blue. Even mine, green and lazy, would have been preferable. But Timmy's eyes were brown and watery. Even all these months later, I found myself with the same old daydream where the hospital called, frantic to tell me a mistake had been made. A mix-up. The fantasy of relief was addicting. Not bonding with him wouldn't be my fault if he wasn't mine. If he wasn't Tim's.

But the call never came and so I did what I had to do, locked in my wretched little apartment, feeding him and changing him and picking him up when he squalled and putting him to bed when he was tired. He never smiled for me, but I kept one pasted on my face.

It would have been better if Tim were here. He would have found the thread of happiness and tied it together in a bow. But he was gone in a snarl of metal and fire and I was alone in this flat eternity of days.

Timmy whined and pushed the spoon away. A stream of drool dribbled down his chin. I set him back in his crib. Used, just like everything else in the apartment. He whined but didn't cry and the headache that was ever-present behind my eyes pulsed. I slouched back into the hard sofa

76

and rocked his cradle gently with a toe until he quieted. A few precious moments of peace. I closed my eyes but left the volume on, the news speaking to me like a dream.

Sleep retreated to the sound of Mom's car sputtering, making way for more pain. Keys jangled. She never knocked, even though the basement apartment was supposedly mine. But could I really complain? She fed me. Housed me. I didn't have to pay rent or utilities, just had to put up with constant "suggestions" on how I should be living my life. I should clean more. Read more. Paint more. *Be* more.

If Tim were here, I could stand it. I could have found a way to make this unplanned family my own.

"Hello, my darlings!" Timmy gurgled at the sound of her voice and I stifled a groan.

"He was sleeping."

"All he does is sleep. All you do is sleep." She lifted Timmy from the cradle. "He needs to be changed."

"Change him, then."

"I think we all need a change! This place is awful stuffy. Why don't you open the windows once in a while?"

"Because then you'd complain Timmy was going to catch his death of cold."

Silence but for the rustling of diapers. "You're awfully grouchy today."

I rubbed my eyes. Grey light streamed in from the window. A spring from the couch pinched my ass and the familiar smell of shit filled the air as Mom removed Timmy's diaper. The smile never left her face. "I'm sorry." I was. Sort of.

"I'm worried about you. I wish you would get out of the house more. All you do is sit in this stuffy apartment. It's not good for you and it's not good for the baby. I don't mind watching him more, you know."

I tucked my knees into my shirt, curled into a ball. "Where am I supposed to go? I'm not exactly invited to many parties anymore."

77

"Go for a walk or something. Get some fresh air. You can't sit in here all day, every day. Don't look at me like that. I'm taking Timmy upstairs while I make supper. I'll watch him. Get out, walk around the block a couple times, I don't care. Go to the store. I'm sick of you pouting around all day. It's not healthy."

"Ugh."

She scooped Timmy up. His tiny fists pounded on her back, grinning over her shoulder at me. I scowled. Mom left the door cracked open. I stretched out on the couch, closed my eyes again. The breeze that wafted in was cold and carried the scent of the outdoors. I would need to get a blanket if I wanted to sleep. I shifted, the couch uncomfortable beneath me. I sighed and pulled myself up. Fine. I would go for a walk and avoid another lecture.

I washed my face. Applied lip gloss. Smoothed greasy hair back into a ponytail. Who did I have to impress? Sneakers old and ugly, but they would do. I laced them up and locked the door behind me.

I'll admit it. The fresh air felt good. The sky was dizzying, clear and grey. Air washed away stale sweat on my neck. As annoying as she could be, Mom was right sometimes. I felt better. Not like life was suddenly worth living or anything, but I felt awake at least.

Tim and I had walked a lot, even after he got his licence, just for something to do. The best conversations we had were hand in hand, pavement beneath our feet. Now walking was something I did alone. And in the opposite direction, away from Tim's place. I didn't want to run into his mother, thank you very much. She always hated me, more so when I got pregnant. I hadn't heard from her since the baby was born. Tim's funeral was excruciating, and the silence that followed even more so.

So I walked away from the city, towards the fields. Mom's house was just on the outskirts of where city turned into farm. Twenty minutes and I would turn around, go back home, back to my mother's encouraging drone of conversation and my baby's lying eyes.

Or maybe I would walk forever. Just keep going and never look back. Wear these sneakers thin, all the way through, and walk until I only had bloody stumps to walk on, never see my fat stupid baby again.

I was fucking trapped. If Tim were alive, he would make me see the good things. He would be almost finished with school by now and he would get a job and we would be in our own little apartment with new things, not stale used furniture passed down from relatives. He would know how to handle Timmy. We could have done it together, instead of me, alone and cranky and worn thin on no sleep. Sustained on canned soup and Mom's generosity. It would still be hard, yeah, but if we were doing it together it wouldn't have been so bad.

I was approaching the Myette farm. Almost time to turn back before Mom was out bleating the horn at me, worried I'd been eaten by wolves. I should be so lucky. The grass beyond the farm was tall and snarled. The road beaten and gravelly beneath my feet.

I was just about to turn back when I saw it. The setting sun gleamed against something deep within the grass. I pushed the foliage aside with the toe of my sneaker. Bone. I paused.

Tim's mother had blamed me for his morbid pastime, but it was all his idea. The collection started when he got interested in veterinary school. First it was a cat skeleton, then a dog, and the collection just blossomed from there. He put them together with tools ordered online, spending hours on the perfectly articulated skeletons. He had been talking about getting into taxidermy next when the accident happened.

He would have loved this.

The grass moved aside to reveal more. It was a skull, a few ribbons of flesh still attached. A smile tugged at my mouth when I picked it up. Light as a feather and completely unidentifiable, at least to me. Not a cat. Not a dog. Nothing I had ever seen before. Deep eye sockets peered back at me. Yellowed bone slanted back from the brow at a strange angle. Small horns emerged, chipped at the ends. The whole thing was about the size of two fists. I turned it over in my hands. The fangs were small and sharp, curled into a wicked grin.

Mom wouldn't like it. Not at all. I pushed it into the wide pocket of my sweatshirt and walked home.

It felt good. The heat of the bone warmed my cold hands.

The skull stared at me from atop the television. Timmy stared at me too, perched in my lap, waving fat little hands at my face. I jiggled him and cooed at him and God, why couldn't he just go back to sleep? My shitty laptop wobbled on the TV tray while I scrolled through pages and pages of skull identification. Nothing looked right.

In the moonlight that shone through the window it was iridescent, mother of pearl. It could be a phony, a fake, but I didn't believe that. It felt real. More real than anything else felt. Tim would have loved it.

I plopped Timmy in his playpen and he started to cry, but the sound was far away. I held the skull, stared into those deep eye sockets, turned it over in my hands again. It smelled earthy. It smelled like secrets.

The rough texture softened in my hands. Pliant. My head spun, dizzy, but in a good way.

Timmy never stopped crying. I glanced at him. His face was red and bloated. Tears and snot streamed down his cheeks. Gently I replaced the skull and hefted him in my arms. He clambered awkwardly. He never sat right. He never fit.

I turned back to the computer.

What are you?

POSTPARTUM

~~

Thunder. Rain pounded down, soaking my hair and cheeks. The sky was alive with light and movement. A creature twisted through the air in front of me. A flutter of wings, black as night. It was beautiful. It was mine.

I woke to silence. The skull sat on my bedside table, grinning at me. My cheap nightlight illuminated soft curves and strange angles. The veil of sleep fell away. I had an idea. I moved quickly but quietly. Timmy was in the next room, all too easy to wake.

I opened the closet.

Everything smelled like Tim. My shrine to him. Tribute to love lost. Usually opening the closet made my knees weak and my eyes fill, but it was the bottom box I was after this time. I never bothered with that one before. It was his, not ours.

But now it was mine.

The boxes were dusty and collapsed and oh God, had it really been that long? Timmy was almost a year old and that meant Tim had been gone for a year and a half. It could make you sick, the way time still ticks by. I could have sworn I needed him to live and yet here I was, still alive, without him.

Never mind. Shift boxes out of the way. Timmy gurgled through the walls and I stopped, held perfectly still. *Please don't wake up*. Not the first time I've had that thought. How sick of a person does that make me?

This time he quieted, and I moved the boxes again. So slow. And yes, the box I wanted was here. Dusty, a few pieces broken, but mostly intact. I pulled out the bony remains of a cat. A small dog. A pig. Part of Tim's collection that he had left here. Even his little toolkit was buried at the bottom. I plunged my hands into dust and dirt and death. Mom kept telling me I needed a hobby. Maybe she was right.

It was like putting together a puzzle. I sat on the floor next to Timmy. I put on the shows he liked and disarticulated bones. He kept reaching for my tools, and I shoved the playpen closer to the TV. Puppets and cartoons shrieked songs at him and he giggled and snorted and shat his pants.

I felt better than I had in ages. I kept the computer nearby so I could look up what I needed as I went, but most of it came naturally. The bones slotted themselves together. Not in a way that made sense, but in a way that felt right, deep in my gut. Tiny sharp teeth smiled.

Tim would have thought this was so cool. He had shown me cryptotaxidermy stuff online once, imaginary creatures made from the dead parts of real ones. A little gross, but his enthusiasm was contagious. He would love this. Building a new creature from the inside out, bones and all.

They jumbled together in the cardboard box, cat and dog and pig and it didn't matter anymore. I attached a few together at a time and placed them aside to dig for more. Old bones transformed into something new. It was sort of like the way I used to paint, back when I cared about painting. Intuitively. No. Instinctively, that was closer to it.

These were Tim's bones. We were creating something together.

Timmy shrieked and I looked up from my work. He had his diaper half off and his hands were covered in shit and was there ever a time I didn't do everything through tears?

I cleaned him up and put my things away. Mom would be home soon.

I worked on it, whatever it was, for nearly a week. Days and nights, every chance I got. Slotting together bones as the skull watched. Its grin urged me on. It liked the body I was making it. Of course it did.

Mom was so encouraged by that one walk I took. She kept talking about it all week. She was just dying for me to go out again. Instead, I told her I was painting—no, you can't look yet, it's not finished—and that was good enough for her. She even watched Timmy some evenings to give me more time.

It came together beautifully.

The spine was incredibly long, twisting back and forth like a helix. One ribcage sat inside another, each rib sharpened to a point. The legs were many-jointed and centipede-like. Small shoulders, wide hips. A tail extended like a whip.

It was an atrocity and it was mine.

I finished late one night with Timmy snoring gently beside me. All that was left was to screw the head to the body and I did it with a flourish, my tired eyes curling into a smile. But when I stood back to admire what I had created, again with the tears.

It was so fucking disappointing.

What had I expected? Fulfillment? That was a laugh. I could throw up. All these long hours and just more letdown. How could this make anything better? It was beautiful, but it was nothing. Just a fucked-up skeleton with no one to show.

I let Timmy sleep in his playpen and collapsed on the couch. I just needed sleep. Forever. I sank into blackness and the skull ground its teeth, making small sounds that whispered into my ears.

I woke up and knew it wasn't over.

I hadn't failed.

I just wasn't done.

~~~

"Of course, I'd love to watch Timmy for a few hours! And you're getting out for a walk, that's terrific!" Mom shifted Timmy onto her hip. He spat up green. "Are you finished with the painting you were working on?"

"Not quite, I just figured, you know. Fresh air for inspiration."

"I think that's a terrific idea. Take as long as you need."

I took a different fork in the road this time, how experimental, how inspiring. Towards the highway. My backpack was light, but I hoped it would grow heavier. I didn't want to think through what I was doing. I just wanted to do it, wanted to keep moving forward.

Cars sped by. I clung to the side of the road, hurried forward when I saw what I was looking for. I slipped gloves from my pockets. Just a squirrel, but you never knew what you might need. The body was flat and stiff. I moved quick, back to the road, eyes averted.

I knew it was gross. I knew how weird I looked. But people did this all the time. I saw it online. Taxidermy is a thing. I wasn't doing anything wrong.

I unshouldered my backpack. The metal spatula helped. I peeled it off the pavement in almost one piece. I packed the corpse into a garbage bag and pushed it deep into my backpack. I kept moving. My cheeks were burning but I felt good. I was on a mission.

I needed a lot more than one squirrel if I was going to make this work. I filled my backpack bit by bit until the sun set red and I headed home.

I stuffed the ruined bodies deep in my freezer, wedged in next to cheap frozen pizzas and a freezer-burned chicken I had completely forgotten about. Mom had probably heard me get home, but I stank of sweat and death. Rivulets of gore dripped down my sweatpants. Death is messy, but hey, so is life. I tossed the clothes in the hamper and ran the shower.

The hot water was incredible. I never took long showers anymore. The water beat down on me, so much like the rainstorm in my dream. My heart was swollen and achy in my chest.

My idea was fucking crazy and I couldn't wait to do it. I still had to go through the routine, the wretched endless routine of life, get Timmy from Mom, make polite conversation and while away the minutes while Timmy slobbered and burped and spat up all over everything nice I had ever owned.

But at least I had something to look forward to.

Before I put Timmy to bed, I set the raccoon in the tub. I wanted it at room temperature before I got started.

Things got overwhelming and messy really quick.

I waited until Timmy was asleep before I got started. It's not like he would have known what I was up to, but I needed time and space to concentrate. I spent hours poring over taxidermy instructions online. The pictures were awful, but they didn't prepare me for what I was getting into. Nothing ever did, did it? The baby books didn't give me a hint of how I was gonna feel either. Nor did the comforting words of other young mothers assuring me how natural it was all gonna come. None of it was true.

Only death was true, and I felt like I could make something beautiful and strange out of it. Something special. The beast flew in my mind's eye while I set things up in the bathroom. I left the door open a crack in case Timmy decided he was hungry or wet or just felt like crying for a while.

I pulled on the same filthy sweatpants from the afternoon, why the hell not, and rubber gloves up to my elbows.

I didn't think it would be too bad. I was never a big animal lover. There are so many farms around here. Animals lived to work and to be eaten, not to be loved.

I thought I could be brutal.

The raccoon's mouth flopped open. His gut had been run flat by a car and it stank. I applied cinnamon lip gloss under my nose. Even with all the instructions I'd read, I was mostly winging it. I knew I was gonna mess up, but that didn't matter. I didn't need the whole body. It didn't even need to be that fresh. I was making something different here. Just for myself. It wasn't gonna be in a taxidermy contest, for Christ's sake, so it could be a bit messy. There was no way to create the thing I dreamed of without being a bit messy.

I slit flesh away from muscle and I only gagged a little bit. I worked gloved fingers beneath the skin to pull it apart and separate it. See, not so bad. His eyes stared up at me, glassy. Ticked fur was coarse even through the gloves.

It wasn't until I had made most of the cuts and tried to pull the hide away from the body that I got sick. I yanked the skin away and revealed the small meaty animal beneath and gagged, my guts twisting. My sharp knife slipped and expanded the hole in the abdomen. Black blood gushed out, reeking of death, and I turned just in time to vomit into the toilet. The mess of my gloves smeared on the seat. I threw up again.

Timmy started crying and I brushed tears from my cheeks with my forearm. I was weak and sick and awful and I was crazy, absolutely crazy to be doing this. No wonder I was doing it in the dead of night, I was insane. No one would be this insane in daylight. I ripped the gloves from my hands. I couldn't look in the bathtub again. The pelt dripped blood onto my floor. Lunacy swirled around me.

Dear God, my freezer was filled with dead animals.

Timmy cried louder and my guts heaved again. I couldn't deal with this right now. I would clean it up tomorrow and I would get my shit together. This was not right. This was not healthy.

I swaddled Timmy in a blanket, keeping his fresh clothes away from the gore on my sweatpants. I fed him and his dull eyes blinked at me. It was hard to believe there was a human buried in there. He shifted in my arms and I struggled to hold him steady.

Everything was terrible.

I turned my weary eyes toward the table. The skull of an impossible creature stared back at me.

Why was I so weak?

Its eyes were dark. Endless.

I wasn't the first person to get a little sick on their first try at taxidermy. So things got a little weird. Did that mean I had to give up? I knew I could make something really cool here. I just had to keep going. So what if it got messy? That skull . . . that skeleton. It was only half a project. It belonged inside of something. I could take my time and piece it together. What the fuck else was I going to do?

I put Timmy back to bed. I brought the skeleton into the bathroom with me. To inspire me. To watch me work.

It got easier after that.

Mom sniffed. Her forehead wrinkled as she surveyed the living room. "What is that smell?"

"Nothing."

"It smells like something died in here. It's not healthy for Timmy. You're throwing the garbage out on time, aren't you?"

"God, I had an issue with the toilet yesterday. Are you happy? I had to plunge it out and clean it all up. I Febrezed the shit out of it, sorry, I'm sure it'll clear up in a day or two."

"I'll take Timmy upstairs for the evening. Why don't you open some windows and air things out down here?"

"I think that's an excellent idea."

It had taken me days to get all the animals skinned. Disfigured pelts hung haphazard in my closet, hidden behind winter coats. Because of their messy deaths, I had only kept bits and pieces of each. But there was enough now to stitch together. The creature came to me in my dreams almost every night.

I was on the right track. I couldn't possibly be recreating something that had actually existed, but in some primeval part of my soul, it felt like it had. It didn't matter. It existed now. Sort of. And it was mine.

Mom took Timmy and he babbled on his way out the door and my gratitude was overwhelming, a physical force that made me lighter, like I was floating. I reached into the depths of my closet and spread the pelts out on my bedroom floor. No one would be fooled that this had been done professionally, but they were good. Good enough. They would do.

I stashed what was left of the bodies in my freezer, deep in the bottom beneath that freezer-burned chicken. Strange naked animals. I didn't know how to get rid of them. I got better with the last few I skinned, leaving their bodies nearly intact. Some of the first ones weren't much more than a bag of guts and entrails. At least when they were frozen they didn't smell. Much.

I was no seamstress, but the pattern assembled itself in my mind. Pieces stitched themselves together, layers of flesh and fur and feeling. The skeleton was all jutting angles in front of me. I drew. I arranged. I thought and rethought. I paced. The mania of creation overtook me.

Sometimes I forgot myself, found myself bent in front of the skeleton, just staring.

Hours passed in a dizzy haze. I referenced things online occasionally, but most of it came from somewhere deep within my head. Within my soul.

That night, I started to sew.

This part took longer. I pricked my thumb against the needle, bled on my floor again and again. I struggled with the sizing, but I pushed forward inch by inch. My pelts were amateur, but this part wasn't. Raccoon blended to squirrel blended to bird blended to cat magically, tail and hoof and beak.

POSTPARTUM

It was all coming together. After days of late-night revisions, dark circles bloomed under my eyes. My heart throbbed and burst from my chest. I got closer.

Days? Weeks? Later, I draped empty skin around the skeletal figure, inch by sacred inch, dressing it in the finest I could make. It fit perfectly, and somewhere in the distance, Timmy cried.

I knelt in front of it, waiting.

Why didn't I feel anything?

I had done everything right and I was ready to tear it apart. It *wasn't* right. I didn't know how to make it right. It was still empty.

Timmy and I cried together.

I groaned when the sun peeked into my room, hugged my filthy pillow to my chest. I wasn't ready to face another day. My creature hung back in the closet and rotted slowly away. Timmy would be awake any moment, ready for breakfast, and day after day of the same thing stretched endlessly ahead.

I couldn't live like this. I wouldn't. I opened the window and air streamed in, lifted tufts of fur from places I had missed in my sweeping. They floated lazy in the air.

Maybe I just hadn't looked hard enough. There was more. There was a piece I was missing. I had to go back to where I had found it. I had to walk. Think. Feel.

I fed Timmy quickly. He burped up a thick paste and I wiped it from his chin, brought him to Mom.

"I have to get groceries," she said, doubtfully, balancing Timmy in her arms. He grabbed at her nose. "Are you going to be gone long?"

"I just need half an hour. I'm trying to get out more. I thought that was what you wanted? You have all day to get groceries. I'll be back soon."

I couldn't remember where the skull had been, not

exactly. Somewhere past the Myette farm. I kicked through the grass with my feet, paced back and forth, over and over. The sun got hotter as the day droned on. I found nothing but dirt on my shoes, a new tear in my jogging pants. Fuck. My sweater was too warm and I was clammy beneath it. There was nothing here.

There was nothing for me anywhere. I walked back and something fluttered in the bushes. Small pained sounds. A flash of feathers.

A crow had injured itself, razor wire wrapped around its foot. It hobbled towards me, bleeding and disoriented. It was the wings that caught my attention. Fierce and black and oily. It must have been badly hurt, because it didn't take flight as I approached. Maybe Tim would have nursed it back to health, but I wasn't Tim.

"Here birdy, birdy." I crouched down. It cawed but didn't take off, just limped away. I shuffled forward and stroked its back, felt greasy feathers beneath my fingers. It sent a spark of electricity through me. I had found what I was looking for. The last piece of the puzzle.

I made it quick.

His head broke like a grape beneath my sneaker. A squelch and a pop and a burst of blood. I was used to blood by now.

I stuffed the broken body into my backpack, lingering over the wings, careful not to tear them. I stood up. Mrs. Myette was standing in her yard, staring at me. Her face was pale. I met her eyes briefly before I turned home.

Timmy slept as I sewed. The phone rang upstairs, a million miles away. I felt it pulsing within me. Something was ready to change.

I didn't hear Mom come down the stairs until the key jingled in the lock. She never knocked. Fuck. I could move fast when I needed to. My creation was light in my arms.

Bits and pieces of sewing tumbled to the floor. Nothing incriminating, I hoped. I shoved the creature into my room and pulled the door shut as Mom walked in, eyes searching.

"What are you doing?"

"Is it too much to ask for a little privacy? Why don't you ever knock? Jesus, I could be naked in here or something."

She looked at the bits of fur on the floor. Needles and scissors and strange sharp things, not far from Timmy's reach. Not like he had any interest in anything other than the blobs of screaming color on the television.

"I thought you were painting? What are you working on down here?"

"I am painting. I ripped something. I was just doing some repairs, if you must know. I didn't realize I was required to paint all the time." I swept up the supplies with an arm and shoved them into my sewing bag, out of sight.

Mom hefted Timmy out of his playpen. His eyes lolled in his head.

"He's fine, Mom. He can't reach it. I was watching him."

She held him, not quite looking at me. "How was your walk this morning?"

"Fine."

"Where did you go? You were gone a long time."

"I was just walking. I don't know. Trying to get some exercise. Get some fresh air. God, you nag me when I don't go out and nag me when I do. I can't win."

"Mrs. Myette just called."

My heart was thick and coppery in my throat. Nosy bitch. "Okay."

"She said she saw you today. In front of her yard."

"What a fascinating conversation that must have been."

I forced myself to meet her eyes. Her mouth twitched. "Are you feeling okay, sweetie? Really, truly okay?"

"I'm fine. What's the big problem? I'm not allowed to walk by the farm anymore? I'll make sure to walk into town next time."

"She said she saw you kill a bird."

My breath came out in a huff of air. "That's fucking ridiculous. What, do you think I'm a fucking sociopath or something?" I watched the way she held Timmy. "Are you people insane? Why would she say that?"

"I'm just worried. I want to know what's going on with you." Her eyes watered. Brown and stupid. That's where Timmy got it from. Mine after all. I had my dad's eyes, but Timmy had my mom's.

I sat down. "I'm fine. I'm just . . . I'm just tired all the time and sad and shitty, but I didn't kill a bird. I just like to walk. And think about Tim." My eyes watered, but that wasn't part of the lie. I felt like shit. All the time. Maybe I was distracting myself with some insane taxidermy thing that I didn't feel like I could talk about with her, with anyone, but it would all be over soon and I just wanted to be left alone.

"Maybe you should talk to that counselor again. I could call for you."

I sighed. I didn't want to argue anymore. I didn't want to listen to her. I just wanted this conversation to be over so I could finish sewing. "Sure, Mom. Let's call her tomorrow. That's fine."

Mental health services are pathetic around here. The appointment wasn't for two months, but at least Mom was comforted by my willingness to go. That was the most important part.

It was so close now. The bones were right. The fur and feathers and wings were right. But it was still empty. I wasn't frustrated anymore, though. I felt capable of seeing this all the way through.

POSTPARTUM

I woke from a dream of the rainstorm and dug through the freezer, searching. I knew the next step. I knew how to finish it.

But before the meat unthawed, I realized it wouldn't work. The flesh I had was falling apart. Dead for too long. I opened the closet where my creation hid.

It was so beautiful. Cryptic messages spelled out in snatches of fur. I stroked its back. Within this flesh, bones that Tim had painstakingly collected and I had repurposed into something mine and mine alone. The love that flowed through my body was pure. It needed to be finished. How could I back away now?

Timmy was sound asleep. I was wide awake, nerves jumping, energy pulsing through me. Outside, the sky crackled with electricity.

I walked into the night. Alone. I took my backpack. I took my baseball bat.

There are a lot of trusting strays in my neighborhood. Everyone feeds them but no one owns them, not really. Cats and dogs that come and go. They would be missed, but not much. They fell with a thud, their bodies fresh and clean.

I came home tired and bruised and dripping. Timmy was crying, but I had what I needed. I fed him while I planned.

Wide loops of thread to hold meat and organs together. I stuffed it full. I kept going. Days passed and it rotted slowly in my closet, leaking viscera and something strange and black and stinking. I knew it was crazy, but it was electric and right and real and beneath snatches of fur, the skull looked out and grinned.

Mom knocked. She had to. I had finally installed a chain and she could only open the door a crack.

I peered out at her. "I'm not feeling great, can this wait?"

"I brought you a flashlight. There's a storm coming, I don't want you guys to be stuck in the dark"." She tried to push the door open, but I wasn't budging. "There's that smell again. Are you taking your garbage out?"

"I don't smell anything. Must be Timmy's diapers. Babies stink. Don't worry about it."

"Can I come in and have a look around? I'm sure you must have left something out, I can smell it all the way upstairs."

I took the flashlight and pushed the door closed. "Leave me alone. I have a headache. We can talk tomorrow. You can clean the whole apartment if you want. Just leave me alone for now."

I was always working, but it never felt finished. I stuffed new flesh on top of the old. I filled it with organs and fat and meat and I was so close. It was not just a creature anymore, it was nearly a god. Beneath the rot there was the scent of something ancient and true. I could see constellations in the darkness of its eyes. The wings curved out, sharp and dangerous. The fur was a menagerie of insanity, but it fit like a glove around the double ribcage and the other secrets that lay within.

The great god of my insanity, etched from leftovers and death. But it still wasn't finished. It didn't have that final touch. Not yet a god; but built in the image of one.

The storm was coming. I could feel it beneath my skin. The sky darkened and the rain began. My heart beat out an excited cacophony. Timmy cried at each crack of thunder and I rocked him gently, humming a song I've never heard.

Midnight approached. My closet couldn't contain it anymore. I took my creation into the backyard, my son wrapped in a blanket in the crook of my arm. The moon was huge, a thumbprint in the sky. The rain soaked me through, so cold my teeth chattered. The rain beat against the creature and I was so close.

It wanted it to fly and I knew what was missing.

The empty eyes looked at me. The fur was plastered

down, nearly ruined, but the wings were strong and ready. Yes, I knew what was missing.

Life.

I pulled the blanket away. Timmy did not cry until the rain hit his face. I promise, I was quick. As quick as I could be. Everything else came from the dead, but the most important part needed to be fresh, full of blood and life.

This moment was sacred. I placed Timmy on the ground and leaned over him, protecting him from the rain.

My knife was sharp. I poised it just over his sternum and it slid through his skin like butter. I thought he would cry harder then, but he just made a strange strangled sound. I was experienced now. With my expert hands, I snapped ribs like twigs and carved out his heart. The life slid from his eyes so quickly and quietly that I didn't see him go. There was no time to waste.

His heart was smaller than I thought it would be. The tiny vital organ still pumped in the palm of my hand. I reached beneath fur and into rotting meat and slipped it deep inside. The blood pumped and flowed and the rain pounded down, so hard and fast I couldn't tell if I was crying.

Stiff bones stretched. The fur turned warm and soft in my hands. There was a creaking of bones as the tail twitched. Joy rushed into my heart, the joy I had been told so many times about. The true joy of motherhood. The wings fluttered.

My creature, my new god, turned to me with a mouthful of razor teeth. A grin, but not a happy one. Not for my benefit. Fear and pride and something else mingled together in my stomach and I grew cold.

Deep in the blackness of its eyes there was a green like my own. Not even a hint of Tim's blue. It was all me.

Powerful wings flapped and it lifted into the air. There was one perfect moment, just one, as it was highlighted against the sky. Lightning crackled. It was just as I had imagined. It was perfect and it was exhilarating and it was all completely wrong. Its mouth opened wide, too wide and thunder roared and I screamed.

And then it was gone.

My knees were weak. I was soaked and frozen and I don't know how I felt.

"What are you doing outside?" Mom's voice was shrill, panicked. I didn't look at her. I looked down. Even in the rain, my hands were covered with blood. Water pooled in the hollows of my son's eyes. His jaw was slack and relaxed, and for the first time, I saw how much he looked like his father.

THIS NARROW ESCAPE

I PRETENDED TO sleep for as long as I could, but my husband was persistent. He pushed against me and murmured in my ear, "Come on." Work was only hours away, but he would not be sated by reason. I would never get back to sleep if I refused him; I would be up for hours, worried about his feelings being hurt. I turned to him. He pushed his mouth against mine, rough and mean, and pulled me on top of him.

He felt different. Luke was a large man, but his body felt angular beneath mine. My thighs looked thick as tree trunks on either side of his hips. When I settled onto him, my legs fell awkwardly from the sides of the mattress and splayed across the floor. As I moved my body, my head brushed against the ceiling.

Afterwards he was snoring in moments, but I lay awake, disturbed.

Luke waited for breakfast, his face buried in the newspaper. He ignored me while I rushed around, manic in my attempt to cook and get ready at the same time. The day outside was cloudy and gray. I wished it were warm enough to open a window. The kitchen felt stale. Faded yellow walls loomed closer than they had before.

I handed Luke his bacon and eggs and sat down with my own. I had to balance myself carefully on my chair, the sides of my slender hips spilling over the seat. He put his newspaper aside to dig in, and I noticed again how much *smaller* he seemed. His shoulders had once rivalled those of a linebacker, but now they were diminutive, almost feminine.

The windowsill, usually a comfortable distance away, pressed painfully into my side. I ate slowly, my elbow banging into the wall with each movement.

"Are you losing weight?" I blurted out. My real thoughts were too insane.

He barely glanced up at me and rolled his eyes. "I don't think so. Maybe you're gaining some."

I didn't speak again through breakfast. I was hurt, and it was too much effort to talk to him in the morning.

Work passed in a pleasant blur. Weekdays always went by so fast. I was caught up in conversation with some of the girls in the office, and ended up leaving a bit late. Luke would not be happy. He didn't like that I worked at all, but financially it had become necessary. I dreaded the day he got a raise and decided I didn't need to work anymore. Then I would have to be my husband's substitute mother again, keeping the house in order according to his ever-changing preferences.

My mood worsened again when I saw the cars wedged in our driveway. Company, and I hadn't been there to greet them. Luke wouldn't be pleased at all.

My living room was packed with men who looked like Luke: dark suits poorly cut, hair parted to the left, the same half smiles that didn't quite reach their eyes. I squeezed through the doorway. Hallway walls clenched against my shoulders. I smiled warily. Luke removed himself from the crowd and pulled me aside. His motions were easy and graceful as he danced between the crowds of furniture and people that seemed to invade all available space in my home.

"Where were you?" he hissed.

"I had to work a little late, I didn't know we were having company."

"I left a message, you were supposed to have things ready. I invited some of the guys back for drinks. God, you're useless sometimes. Get some snacks ready, maybe we can still salvage this."

I went to the kitchen, side-stepping through the narrow doorway. Since I had been gone, the kitchen had grown smaller, more of a hallway than a room. The fridge and other furniture adjusted to fit. The table and chairs jostled rudely against me as I struggled to prepare something for the men to eat. I had to keep my arms near my sides in order to avoid banging against the walls. Finally, the snacks were ready. As I left the kitchen, it compressed again with a hiccup and squeezed me out. I nearly spilled my tray of goodies as Luke sighed in exasperation, but I righted myself and managed to keep things together.

I served Luke and his friends, bumping into slender angled shoulders. Conversation stopped as I struggled through the room, smile frozen on my face. It was no use. They watched me silently, their eyes unreadable. A heavy blanket of judgement settled on my shoulders. Between the shrunken walls and the quiet men, there was no room for me. I tried to imitate a gracious hostess, a lovely wife, but once the food was served, the walls closed in and squeezed me out. I didn't mind. My back ached from stooping over

I excused myself to the bathroom. No one noticed, not even Luke. I dug in a drawer for a tape measure and wrapped it around my thighs, my hips, my bust. No change. It wasn't me.

I woke the next morning, barely able to breathe, panic rising in my chest. The room surrounded me like a coffin, the ceiling and walls inches away from my body. My limbs flailed, slamming against the walls, leaving ugly bruises. I closed my eyes and counted breaths. When finally I calmed down, I began the difficult process of getting dressed. It was impossible to stand upright. I hunkered down in a squat to lift my shirt over my head and lay flat to pull my pants over my hips.

I crawled through halls like air ducts to the kitchen, where Luke sat, looking comfortable and serene, awaiting his breakfast. "Doesn't something seem strange to you?" I gasped.

"You always find a problem with everything, don't you?" He was perfectly at home in our compressed kitchen. The hateful look in his eyes was too much for me. Instead of trying to find a way to cook on the ridiculous rail-thin stove, I slithered through the hallway like a snake. I went to work with an empty stomach.

Work passed in a pleasant blur. Too fast. People smiled at me. People thought I was clever. People complimented me. I was good at my job, and I was appreciated. And then the day was over. It was time to drive home and face another evening with my husband.

At first I thought my house was gone, that it had disappeared into thin air. I got out of the car and surveyed the yard. When I tilted my head just right, I saw that it wasn't gone at all. It was just very thin. Two-dimensional.

I could open the door and squeeze myself inside. I could spend another evening watching television with my husband in our cramped living room, listening to his passive-aggressive complaints. That was my duty. I was his wife. I reached for the doorknob, but my wedding ring snagged against the house and tore away a thin strip of siding. I crumbled it in a ball and tossed it over my shoulder, like a piece of garbage. The next piece I tore off quicker, until I was frenzied. I tore it to shreds.

My hotel room is expansive. The pillows are plush. The bed is huge, large enough for me to stretch out like a starfish.

THE LANGUAGE
OF THE MUD

I MISSED HIM, yeah, and that was awful, but somehow the worst part was trying to find it again, those eight or ten inches of earth that stole my father. I knew if I found it, everything would make sense.

I needed to hear what he had been about to say. "I really—" what? I really fucked it up this time? I really miss her? I really miss you?

I just wanted to know the end of that sentence.

I just wanted to find the spot again.

I pored over the dirt and the mud and the grass over and over, nose to the ground, trying to find a hint—a wavering of motion, an echo of his voice, a whiff of that sweet-rot scent.

Was it here, or an inch to the left? Was his right foot right here, right where mine is, or was it tilted towards the trees?

I was seventeen. My dad was staying at some shitty hotel outside of town and my mom was refusing to take his calls. I dunno why he was driving around that morning, but he caught me skipping school and drove me home, an excuse to talk to her, or maybe an excuse to talk to me. Well, I wasn't saying much. He followed me into the backyard and watched as I lit a cigarette. He frowned but kept his silence because, hey, I wasn't the one with substance abuse issues, was I?

I wish I had been nicer to him that day. Every day.

We sat on the picnic table. The wind bit through my sweater. I was puffing away, watching him sweat. I wasn't even really mad. Mom was the one who was mad.

"Do you think she's ready to talk?" he asked, and I shrugged and said something, said whatever, said I dunno, why don't you ask her? He got up from the picnic table, stretched, took two steps into the backyard, shuffled his feet, said "I really—" and then he just fucking disappeared.

He didn't sneak away. He didn't leave. My eyes were on him the whole time.

Two steps. Shuffle. Gone. The grass rippled and that was all.

How did I react? I don't know. I really don't. A few minutes there just kinda escape me. I think I screamed. I probably screamed. I didn't black out. I didn't block out some traumatic event. I didn't lose any time before he disappeared. I remember that perfectly. My dad, tall and broad-shouldered and smelling only just a little bit like stale beer, stretching, walking, shifting his weight, "I really—"

And then just grass.

Mom got home a few minutes later and I was still staring at the lawn. I would have thought I was on drugs too, if I were her.

Life went on. Can you believe it? Boring old life went on. But days passed and there was no call and no money and eventually yeah, even Mom started getting worried. Their fights never went on this long.

She thought I was covering up for him. She thought I knew exactly where he was and just wouldn't tell her.

I didn't know exactly where he was. I didn't even know exactly where I saw him last. I almost knew though. Within a few inches. And whenever I could escape her notice, I was in the backyard. Trying to figure it out.

The ground was solid beneath my hands. Shouldn't it be softer somehow? Shouldn't it be changed?

Should I have been afraid? I wasn't afraid. It wasn't like

it was quicksand or something. I didn't think I would fall down there after him. I just wanted to know.

I kept looking and looking until his voice came on the wind. "The last time the grocery store was so busy." Just a fragment. The words floated by and I wasn't even sure I heard them.

I wanted to tell mom, but she was on the phone with Aunt Susan, bitching about dad, and was "not in the mood for your bullshit today."

They loved each other, you know? Even with all that fighting, even with all the times he left and came back and left and came back, they loved each other. She counted on him. She counted on the fighting and the apologies. It was part of their routine. She didn't understand why he didn't come back this time.

I sat out back smoking all spring, waiting for something to happen. I heard him every now and then. "The consistency is off." "Down here in the muck and slime." "Arcs of vision passed by." Nonsense phrases. Bits of things. I wrote them down, tried to piece them together. The worst thing was, the more I read over them, the more familiar they seemed, until I wasn't sure if it was something I heard him say once or if I had actually heard it there, and if I did hear it, was it because I was standing in the right place at the right time? Was it right here? Was it exactly right here, or was it a step to the left?

He was just gone.

I started waking up at night, snapping abruptly out of dreams, and when I woke up, I didn't go outside, even though I wanted to. I would wake Mom up if I walked past her room. But I looked out the window, and I looked at the spot, or near the spot, and I just kept playing those moments through my head.

"I really—"

I really wished he would come home.

So it was one of those nights, and our neighbor's fucking dog got off his leash again and he was bounding through our yard, and he was circling the spot and my heart was in my throat because what if, what if—but our neighbor came up behind him and grabbed his leash and pulled, but then the leash went loose and the dog was spinning and barking and alone.

Mom didn't believe me, of course she didn't, not even when the dog got hit by a truck and the newspapers starting piling up next door.

I was glad the dog got hit. He ruined everything.

I couldn't hear Dad anymore. Well, I could, but it was all twisted up with the neighbor's voice now, and the words were even more mixed up and I didn't know which ones were his and which ones were hers.

How had she found it so easily, without even trying? I couldn't find it, no matter how many hours I spent out there, inches from the ground, dirtying up my jeans.

Sometimes I skipped school to sit out there. Sometimes I couldn't help it. I shuffled into the backyard after math class once, and a man was there. He looked familiar, like a neighbor maybe, but not a close one. He was dressed in a suit, carrying a briefcase, like he was on his way to work, but instead he was in my backyard, circling my spot, a wrinkle of concentration on his forehead.

I was pissed. I didn't want more people here. I didn't want them to fuck up the voice more.

I didn't want someone else to find it.

"What the hell are you doing?"

He just looked at the ground, then at me, then back at the ground, his eyes big and round and wet. He shuffled his feet, stepped forward and back.

"Get the fuck out of here," all my teenage bravado. And he was reluctant, but he did step away, brushed past me, and I stumbled over to the spot and listened.

"Get the dog inside and wash behind your ears." Her words, his voice, someone else's cadence. I was furious.

I stopped going to school. Mom was never home to get the calls from the principal. I just erased the messages from the phone. I camped out in the backyard all day, and when people showed up with their wet eyes and desperate faces, I could tell them to fuck off before they even got started. Before they even had the chance to ruin things.

"Lots of feathers here this time of year."

But I couldn't keep them away all the time. I had to eat, at least when Mom was watching. I had to sleep, at least when I could. I didn't catch anyone else disappearing, but I knew when they had, because the words changed again. Dad's voice got further away; everything got all mixed together.

I didn't want to spend all that time out there, but I couldn't help myself. A bad habit, worse than smoking, and I just couldn't shake it. I would shower, get dressed, make my lunch, tell myself I was going to school, and then all of a sudden it would be hours later and I would be sifting dirt between my fingers, rubbing my face against the grass, watching ants crawl by and wondering if they would disappear too, listening for the voice that rarely came now, and when it did, it was all wrong.

Mom and Aunt Susan caught me one afternoon. I didn't even realize I was there until I heard Mom's tired voice. "Get out of the mud." She didn't sound mad, just tired. I stood up, brushed the dirt off my knees.

"What are you doing out here?" Susan laughed. "Aren't you a little old to be playing in the dirt?" I muttered something, but my gaze kept drifting back to the ground.

"What are you looking at?" There was something off in her voice, and she stepped toward me, and the spot I was looking at was way off, because she was still a few feet in front of me and then she was gone.

The sound that came out of Mom's throat was awful. And it's even more awful that my first instinct was pleasure. I'd told her. I was right. But the look on her face made me feel small and ashamed. Her hands fluttered by her sides.

"What did you do?" Tears were coming from her eyes. She'd never cried in front of me, and didn't seem to realize she was doing it now.

And then the voice, unsteady, "Get out of the—I wouldn't," my dad's voice, but all mixed together with Susan's and the neighbors and everyone and all jumbled up and I felt dizzy.

Then Mom was down on her hands and knees, digging with her bare hands, and her nice skirt was getting all dirty but the dizziness passed, and a jolt of energy burst through me because I knew, I just knew that she had it. She had the exact spot. I don't know how she got it so quickly, but she did and I had to help.

The grass was sticky like moss and peeled back smooth from the earth. The dirt beneath was black and wet and pungent. Mud smeared our hands like oil. We dug.

It takes a long time to dig, you know. It wasn't easy, but we didn't stop. My nails broke and my back ached and I didn't stop. Mom's skirt was filthy and she didn't stop. Dusk came and we didn't stop. We barely made progress—the dirt kept coming and we had only our hands, and they dove deep into the organs of the earth and we were so determined and we couldn't stop because we had the right spot.

I started to get tired. Mom's hands slowed down. Time slowed down.

I was suddenly very conscious of each handful of dirt, very conscious of the voices swirling around us with their nonsense phrases.

It accepted us, finally.

The muck slid away from our fingers and the hole tunnelled down and let us in. Just a few feet down, but it was enough.

Broken, rotted scraps of wood lined the sides of the hole, spreading it open, and the digging got easier. My blood pounded through me, felt too thick.

And then my broken nails hit something, sent vibrations reverberating through my hands. Mom reached in, and together we reached deep inside and the voices whisper-shouted and something burst.

A torrent of brackish water erupted from the hole,

covering our filthy shirts. It stung. I backed away, yanking mom's sleeve, pulling her back with me. The sickly-sweet smell hit and my eyes blurred with tears. I blinked past them, stared into that pool of water, my gut empty with despair.

My reflection gazed back at me with vacant eyes.

The stench of rot grew stronger and my throat filled with bile. A sickening yellow mist blurred my vision. I started coughing, and Mom started coughing, and voices all around us started coughing. I couldn't stop. I couldn't breathe. I couldn't breathe. I couldn't breathe. The air was too thick, too heavy, too wet. My mother wheezed and clutched my hand and for one merciful moment, the hole left my mind, replaced by the all-consuming need for air, and we stepped away, we pulled each other inside.

Dad was sitting on the sofa, smiling.

"I'm so happy to see you guys." His voice was not his own. Not at all. He stood up. I felt the blood drain from my face, but mom surged forward and embraced him.

He smiled at me and I couldn't breathe. I still can't breathe, not like I used to.

The muck covered the yard for a few days, sludgy, impassable. Slowly the ground sucked it all back up, and all that was left was dirt and grass. I could never find the spot again.

I kept digging. I dig and dig and dig and I can't find it. I can't even hear the voices anymore, but my dad is back, and Aunt Susan is back, and my neighbor is back.

None of their voices sound right. None of their clothes fit right. Not even their skin fits right.

I'm not the only one looking now. There's always someone else. Sometimes there are dozens of us, shuffling our feet, looking at the ground, sweating and pacing and running our fingers through the earth.

I wish I could find the spot.

I wish I knew what he had been about to say.

LONELY HEARTS CLUB

ON OUR FIFTH DATE, I ripped his heart out.

On our first date, we ate Italian. Heads bent over noodles, eyes locked over wine. He picked at his cuticles and I smiled. We traded cleverly selected stories and sweet spiced kisses. I placed my fingers on his lips and he nibbled, tasting me with a grin.

On our second date, I gave him a tattoo. A small one. A heart on his hand, hidden in finger web, where only he could see it. We sat on my dirty carpet, where I laid out fresh clean linen and my supplies. India ink. A brand-new needle. Alcohol. I took my time, drew my tiny stencil and leaned in close, smelling Old Spice on his sweater. Like my father used to wear.

He barely flinched. I held his hand steady. I felt his eyes on me as I stabbed the needle in, again and again, pushing in fresh black ink, wiping off blood. Stab. Stab. Stab. I took my time and it was perfect, the tiny imprint black as shadow.

When he kissed me, I bit his tongue. Tasted him.

On our third date, we exchanged angry words and found them to our liking.

On our fourth date, the tattoo had grown, creeping its way up the backs of his hands, his arms, peppering his back with evidence of our love.

On our fifth date, I ripped his heart out. I laid down the clean linen again and he looked up at me, trusting. With clinical precision, I sliced my way through muscle, fat, tendon. It fluttered like a bird in the cage of his ribs. Trapped. Ready to be set free. Blood stained my carpet, but I didn't care.

I pressed the scalpel into his hands. Sweat on his brow, he mirrored the incision, opening the plate of my breasts to reveal the meaty flesh that lay beneath.

Tender, exposed, we never looked away. I kissed him and he tasted like blood. Right hands entwined, our left hands reached deep into each other's body and pulled the prize. I held his heart in my hand, beating, sputtering its insane heart song. It felt heavy. Used. But now it was mine and I nestled it into my own empty cavity.

We sewed each other up. My stitches were neater than his. He pressed a thumb down the haphazard scrawl of thread on my chest, bumps rising to meet him. He read me in Braille.

We lay next to each other for hours, letting the rhythm of our breath and the pounding of our hearts sync. We made love, or something like it, breathlessly, our new hearts rattling unfamiliar in our chests.

When he fell asleep I walked barefoot to the bathroom, sidestepping the carnage that sank into my floors. I stood naked in front of the mirror, looking at the zigzag of scar tissue that made its way down my sternum. I liked it. I pressed my palm against the place where his heart now beat and listened to its whisper.

I lay back down next to him, placed a hand on his chest, where my own waylaid heart burbled. And then I slept.

The time spent apart in the drudgery of day-to-day life was shallow. Empty. On our fourteenth date, we carved off our hands. Just the left ones. We were both right-handed.

His went first. I always took the lead. With an old nightshirt I tied him off mid-arm, the knot as tight as I could make it. He barely flinched. The bowl of ice was nearby. The cleaver was heavy in my hand. I swung with all my strength, but it still took a few whacks to make it through the bone. He chewed on a hunk of leather to keep from screaming. It was the last slice that bothered him the most, separating the last slivers of skin and tendon.

It was worth it. He held the spurting limb above his head to slow down the bleed, but my kitchen was splattered with bright red dots by the end of it, caught up in the fan and sprinkling the ceiling and walls.

I liked it that way.

He did mine next, one-handed, always the gentleman, and my thin wrist broke and shattered and came apart with only two strikes. The pain was bearable when I looked into his eyes.

Our sewing was messier this time. More desperate. Passionate. We were clammy and pale as we reattached squirming limbs to each other. Dizzy. But we did it. That's how strong we could be.

I stretched out the hand that was his, and it felt good. Right. I wiggled his fingers. His heavy tan hand looked odd at the end of my thin pale arm, but it *felt* right.

I was more in love with him than ever the next day. It felt like he was beside me, even when he wasn't. He touched things with my hand. The smooth curve of an apple. The hard surface of his desk. The crumbling pages of an old book. There was a new fascination in objects that surrounded me. Things that had once held the weight of boredom and despair were new again as I juggled them in his hand.

Late that night, I slipped my blouse from my shoulders and with his hand I traced the scar down my chest, finally cupping my small breast, nipple popped out hard against the palm.

I felt the weight of his hard cock in my left hand and I sighed.

BETTY ROCKSTEADY

We explored the world through each other's limbs, but soon that was not enough.

On our thirty-second date, we sewed ourselves together. Siamese twins. I let him take the lead this time, passing the thick needle painfully through my side, pulling it tight and snug up against his body. This was an easier procedure. Not as messy. Our blood still stained my kitchen walls, making it feel like home.

This was the beginning of the end.

Even that night, I knew we had made a mistake.

He slept soundly beside me, but I lay awake hours after he did. His flesh tugged painfully at my side. I was heavy with sleep, but it was impossible to get comfortable. I couldn't turn. I couldn't move. Every movement I made pulled against tender skin on my hip, my thigh. The wounds were bleeding and left gentle dots of red against my sheets. My good sheets.

I lay back, his hand pressed against my forehead. It felt too warm and the hairs on his knuckles scratched my delicate skin. I found myself wishing for my own cool, delicate hand.

We took turns at work now. One day at mine, one at his. His job was boring, tedious. Long hours where I had to sit silent and still. He didn't like the distraction. He was different at work. Not the same gentle man I loved, he was controlling. Conniving. Sneaky. I hated it there. I hated him there.

He didn't like my work either. There wasn't room for him. I sat in the chair, sweetly getting caught on the missed days that were his fault. He knelt next to me, glowering and twitching and moving so much that it irritated my stitches, making them weep sticky white fluid.

I noticed it over dinner, Chinese food at home. He stared at his phone. I played with my food, ignoring him and praying he would notice. His left hand sat snugly on my thigh, no longer a novelty, accepted as my own. His right hand moved small and twitching, and I realized the heart was gone, soaked up by his skin, faded lighter each day, neither of us noticing until now, when it was already gone.

He was a sloppy seamstress. Day by day the stitches became looser, leaving crusty fluid in their wake.

I couldn't count the dates anymore. I don't know where we were. It was all one long day, separated only by the shadows of night and not by the ways we changed.

Was it our eighty-third date? A hundred and five? I was ordering coffee and he was staring at his phone again. The boy behind the counter smiled at me, a shy smile. His face was round and sweet. I didn't think about it, I just slid my eye from its socket and handed it to him with an assortment of change. He took it and I took my coffee and I didn't wait to see what he said.

It took my lover days to notice it was gone. He never looked me in the eyes anymore.

But he was furious! He suspected what it meant, and even as I protested his accusations, a tiny part of me stared up at the coffee boy. His face was soft, my lover's was hard. His smile was always hinted at, never obnoxious, just a smirk of a dimple on his face. I liked him. I liked that he kept my eye. Didn't toss it in the register like it was nothing. He cherished it, took it home, and I watched, distracted, even as we argued.

We made up, half-heartedly, but that night while he

slept I wiggled and moved and rolled over and tore those stitches apart.

We said we would sew ourselves back up. Soon. But days went by and it just didn't happen. Didn't seem urgent. I was enjoying my newfound freedom. Loved the feeling of being able to stretch both arms high above my head. His scars stayed red and ugly, but mine healed up fine. I babied them, washed them clean and bandaged them up again.

Then there was a night when he just didn't come back. He went to work and didn't come home and I was mad, but a part of me was fine, just fine.

I looked at the stump of his hand on my wrist and it was ugly. I felt his heart beat in my chest and the rhythm of it made me sick. It was all wrong. Days passed without even a text. The heart sang in pain but it wasn't mine. I covered the hand in a mitten so I didn't have to look at it, and that helped.

I stared at the scar on my chest. I still liked it there. It was something. It showed that something had happened. It was real. But what beat within was not.

It was on the seventh day without him that I finally got up the nerve to see him again. I went to his apartment and the door was unlocked. He wasn't home, but my things were waiting for me. My hand in a melting bowl of ice and my heart in a cage, beating restlessly. Scrawled in the blood, words: *I don't care if I never see you again.*

We had pushed too hard, too far. My remaining eye watered, but did not shed a single tear.

I had brought my own tools. I removed the hand. That was easy. I dropped it in the melted ice. Who knew how long he would be gone? Not my problem. Let it melt. I slid my hand back into place and flexed my fingers. I had forgotten how beautiful they were, long and pale and tapered to points.

A brand new scalpel slid through my chest. I cut carefully at first, but watching my heart pounding out its own rhythm made me desperate. With both of my hands, beautiful as doves, I tore his rotten heart out. It had grown black and ugly in my chest.

The emptiness of my chest was huge, a mean thing, gaping wide open, full of sour feelings. He had never been who he said he was, had he? Had I?

No matter. I took my heart back and sewed up my chest and felt warm for the first time in a long time.

I was whole now. Complete. I went home on my first day in my own body and lay in my bed. My strong heart beat its own rhythm and I laid my left hand over my chest. Somewhere, not so far away, I batted the lashes of my eye.

It would be different this time.

OUR FERAL SKIES

THE CLOUDS WERE swollen and the sky was bruised. Kent's knuckles clamped white on the steering wheel. Had he remembered to close the basement windows? The rain would start any second now. They shouldn't have dawdled over the groceries. His jaw ached from being clenched for so long.

Megan laid her hand on his knee and some of the tension drained from his shoulders. Okay, so some stuff in the basement might get wet, but Megan's lips curled into a smile, and their own private storm might be over. Going for groceries together was a small thing, a silly thing, but the sense of peace it brought was enormous.

Swirls of pink and orange danced above their house. An incredibly beautiful sunset, especially compared to the usual dusky grey of their small-town nights. They stepped outside the car and the air crackled with electricity.

Kent loaded his arms with groceries. Megan took the lighter ones. She smiled at him. "Do you think we've got everything we need?"

"I'm sure it won't be that bad."

A warm wind whipped hair around her face. Kent swallowed, the taste of iron in the back of his throat. Were these nerves from the storm, or from the thin line of hope that Megan had extended? Either, both?

They trudged toward the front door. Clouds dark and angry, plump with rain ready to spill. Smudges of red ink leaked across the sky. Megan's eyes dilated, huge and dark on her pale face. His hands were too full to touch her. Something twisted deep within him. He felt the urge to crawl into the basement, hammer thick boards over the windows, crouch safe in solitude.

A cloud covered the thin light from the sun and bathed their doorstep in shadow. Something small and dark writhed near the stairs. Kent's shriek sounded womanly, even to his own ears. Heavy bags fell from his arms. He pushed Megan back, protective.

"Kent?" A wail wound deep into his eardrums, tapered into her laugh. "Are you afraid of that little cat?"

The dark stain unraveled and stretched. Copper eyes blinked open. It was just a cat. An *ugly* cat. Thin as a rail, with bumps of spine that protruded through matted fur. Bright eyes too big for its head, making it look almost alien. His heart still pounded against his chest, but now heat lit his cheeks. He busied himself picking up their groceries. Hopefully nothing was broken.

"The poor thing is starved," Megan murmured. The cat wailed, stretched out thin legs. "Are you hungry, little kitty? Kent, open one of those cans of tuna."

The warmth from earlier in the evening had dissipated. A cold, tired feeling settled deep in Kent's bones. There was a distant rumble in the sky. He wanted nothing more than to go inside and crawl under the covers. But yeah, he could open a can of tuna for the cat. Sure. Then they could go inside and get on with the night. Get on with their reconciliation.

Megan took the can, cooed gently to the cat. The thing was so skinny and poorly maintained that it must be wild. It looked nothing like the cats his parents had kept. Those cats were civilized, well bred. This one would look more at home deep in the woods somewhere, reclusive and half mad, spitting with rabies. Kent expected it to spring away when Megan approached, but it leapt toward her, making Kent's heart pound hard in his hollow chest. It didn't attack, just wound around her legs and screeched.

Megan stroked its back. It ate ravenously, keeping its eyes on her. It was just nervous, of course, but something about the eye contact was unsettling. Did cats make eye contact? He couldn't remember.

The first true rumble of thunder sounded like something massive clearing its throat. He heard the rain before he felt it, a screaming of sleet. "We better go inside." A gust of wind nearly took the little cat off its feet.

Megan's hair tangled, branches in the wind.

"We'll have to bring him in. We can't leave him out here in the storm." Her forehead creased, the way it always did when she was ready for an argument. It made her look old.

He didn't want the cat in his house. Their house. The ratty thing was probably covered in fleas. He itched just thinking about it. But this was the kind of thing Megan had been talking about. He was afraid to be spontaneous. Afraid of change.

"He probably belongs to someone. We can't just . . . " and he was defeated already. It was the wrong thing to say. This cat obviously had no home.

"I doubt that, but even if he does, we can still take him inside and keep him safe."

Huge orange eyes winked at him. Dismissed him. The cat turned back to Megan and rubbed against her. She stroked its head and it made a sound, a mumbling, something deep beneath the ground that groaned and shifted.

"He's purring," she said, and the fight was over before it began.

Their little house creaked and groaned, but the power stayed on, so they distracted themselves with television. It was easier than talking to each other. Kent sat upright, rigid. Megan leaned against him, curling hair between her fingers.

The ceiling creaked.

"I don't like it wandering all over the place like that. He could be peeing all over everything. Can't we just keep him in the spare room? I don't see why he has to be crawling all over our things."

Megan smiled, amused. "He's just getting used to the place. He'll settle down, and I'm sure he won't make any mess that's impossible to clean up." Then her lips were against his, soft and welcoming, but brief. She turned back to the television. He didn't even know what they were watching.

She was right. He didn't need to plan everything. Didn't need to micromanage every aspect of their lives. He could just enjoy the feeling of his wife curled up against him. She pulled the blanket beneath her chin and he stroked her shoulder.

A subtle shift in hallway shadows. The alien reflection of wide almond eyes peered in. Kent looked away. Claws ticked against hardwood as it made its way into the room.

"Oh, hello, you've decided to join us, have you?" Megan extended her hand towards the cat. It kept its eyes on Kent but allowed itself to be stroked. That awful rumbling again. Could you really call that a purr? It was hideous. Mossy fur brushed his arm as it struggled into Megan's lap. How could she stand to touch it? It moved in tight circles, stiff joints creaking as it snuggled in.

Just one night. If it made Megan happy, he could stand it for the night. Tomorrow, after the storm, he would let it outside and probably never see it again. Hell, if it came back, he would do whatever he could to chase it away. As long as Megan didn't see. One night. His arm still felt greasy from where it had brushed against him.

The cat closed its eyes, a tiny black hole in their living room. Megan smiled, looked up at him again.

"What do you think we should name him?"

Kent bit his lip until he tasted blood.

Disorienting dreams. The sky spilled unnatural light in colors he had never seen. Rain and wind and sleet and pain. Where was Megan? Breathing was difficult. The air was too thick. The night was alive with staring eyes. His clothes were soaked and heavy, slowing his movement.

Long sticky moments between sleep and awareness. Kent opened his eyes. It made no difference. He heard the storm rage outside, but saw only darkness. He needed to check the basement, see if water had seeped in, ruining old boxes of nothing. Was the power still on? He reached across Megan to check the light.

No, he didn't.

He didn't move at all.

The dark disoriented him. A croak escaped his throat, but that was all. Was he awake? He couldn't see *anything*.

The first thin taste of panic. His chest was heavy. Breath too slow. He couldn't move. *Paralyzed*? He tried to scream but there was nothing. His mouth didn't move. He couldn't see anything. He couldn't *feel* anything, just that heaviness in his chest, pinning him to the bed.

Slowly, his eyes adjusted. Shapes crowded in, his own belongings frightening and unfamiliar in shadow. Twin globes of shining orange, incredibly close, inches away. It was the damned cat sitting on him. That was the feeling on his chest. It was just the fucking cat and he wanted to throw it off but *he still couldn't move*.

Its eyes were all he could see, orange and penetrating. What was it doing to him?

The rain sounded like laughter.

The eyes shone. Everything else disappeared into darkness. Megan snored beside him, her breath slow and heavy, comfortable.

Thunder rumbled, shook the house.

Through the crack between curtains, the sky lit blue and green, casting a sickly glow in the room. The fear that quaked through him was primal. He wanted to run but he *couldn't fucking move.* Maybe he'd had a stroke. Maybe he was dying. Maybe he was already dead.

Finally, it blinked. It stood. It stretched, too tall, too thin, casting impossible shadows. Then it leaped from the bed. Its paws squelched on the floor and it nudged through the door and finally, finally, Kent's toes and fingertips tingled and his mouth cracked open in a scream.

He didn't want to feel irritated. He didn't want to start in with the arguments again, but Megan cocked an eyebrow and he hated the look on her face. "It wasn't a dream," Kent snapped. "You think I don't know when I'm dreaming?"

Her lips tilted slightly, half a smile. "What then? You think Storm put a spell on you, or, like . . . what? I don't know what you want me to say."

The scent of tuna wafted towards him and he pushed his toast aside. The cat ate with gusto, chunks of food flying from its mouth. "We're going to have to pick up some real cat food," Megan added. "I don't think it's good for him to just eat tuna all the time. Something about taurine."

"Why on earth do we need to buy anything for it? I don't remember agreeing to adopt him." He couldn't keep the exasperation out of his voice. Megan glanced at him but didn't reply, just started tapping at her phone. "It's not that I'm against having a pet. We can get a pet if that's what you want. But I'd rather pick one out together. This cat creeps me out. It's awful."

The cat looked at him, narrow slits for eyes. He found he couldn't meet its stare.

"Sleep paralysis."

"What?"

"That's what it's called. Sleep paralysis," Megan held up the phone, too quick for him to read what was on the screen. "I've heard of it before. Did you ever have night terrors when you were a kid?"

"It wasn't a dream. I told you that!"

"I know it didn't feel like a dream, but come on. What's more likely? The cat hypnotized you, or whatever you think it did, or you were experiencing this real, honest to God, well-known phenomenon? Even the fact that it was sitting on your chest is part of it. It happens to lots of people! The Old Hag syndrome." She passed the phone to him. "Read it."

"I don't need to read it."

Those wrinkles in her forehead again. He sighed. He read it. It made sense.

The cat muttered to itself, twining between their legs. "See, he likes it here. He's always purring."

If you could call that purring.

She scooped the cat up and it allowed itself to be held. "He needs us. I wish you'd give him a chance. You promised you'd be more flexible. Isn't this a good place to start? Once he's had a few good meals, and he's all cleaned up . . . " She nuzzled against the cat, and finally it wriggled out of her arms. It hit the floor and skittered away.

Megan smiled at him, but the wrinkles were still there. She held out her hand and he took it.

She was right. He was being ridiculous. And he did promise.

The storm had sounded worse than it was. Aside from a few cracked branches, their yard looked mostly the same. A low whine sounded from somewhere nearby. A line down somewhere? He'd have a walk around the neighborhood later and check it out. He would relax a while first. It was a bit cold to sit out on the deck, but it reminded him of better days.

The whine droned on. The longer he looked at the yard, the uglier it seemed. There were branches to pick up, and some of the trees needed to be trimmed back. The hedge, especially, was in need of some care. There was a lot of work to be done after all. There was always a lot of work to be done.

She was right. He didn't know how to relax.

Especially with that noise. It was getting louder. Unpleasant. Guttural. A radio somewhere? But it couldn't have been left out overnight; the rain would have destroyed it.

He left his coffee on the table. It would go cold quickly, but it was barely drinkable as it was. The grass crunched beneath his feet. Brittle. Dead. He followed the sound.

It quieted as he approached, turned to a whisper. A hiss. Just the rasp of breathing. It was coming from the hedge.

Kent pushed aside tangled branches. There was a deep growl and he drew back.

They came out hissing. A pale ginger cat with red eyes, pressed low to the ground, and a grey one, too large, almost a dog, balding in strange patches. They moved past him, slow, not afraid, but disturbed. Angry.

Kent breathed deep. Just cats. Ugly cats, but just cats. So why the fear in his throat? Why did he want to run?

What had been making that noise?

The branches parted again. Storm crawled out, dusty fur rippling in the grey light. He slid past, sleek and quick as an otter. He was gone.

Silence.

When he caught his breath again, Kent dug into the hedge. Thorns rippled thin cuts on his arms, blood trickled out, absorbed by the moist earth, and there was nothing there. Darkness, tangles of grass. Nothing. Just the cats.

A stinking puddle of blood soaked into their bed. It was too much blood for such a small creature. The mouse was very dead. Not eaten. Eviscerated. Its belly yawned open, revealing tiny rearranged organs. Empty eyes stared into the void.

"It's pretty gross," Megan admitted.

"Yeah." Kent said. His throat felt full. He didn't trust himself to speak again.

"It's not that I don't think Storm did it, I just think you're overreacting. That's what cats do, they kill small things. It's good, means we won't have any mice around the place."

"Are you kidding? Does this look like what a cat would do to you?"

"I don't know, I mean, yeah, it's weird. But I don't think cats *always* eat their kill. Part of hunting is keeping their reflexes going. Just because it's not eaten . . . " She was already typing something into her phone, looking for a Wikipedia article to back up her position.

An oily stain dribbled across the floor. Kent turned. Storm gave him a dirty look and began washing his paws.

"You! Get out of here," Kent pounded his foot against the floor, clapped his hands. The cat didn't budge.

"Oh, Kent, stop it."

"Is this how you want to live? Dead animals everywhere?"

"It's hardly everywhere. I know it's gross, but..." Megan lifted the cat into her arms and frowned. Those wrinkles again. God, he hated them. "He's just being a cat. He thinks we aren't any good at hunting, he's trying to show us how."

Storm leaped from her arms. Blood glistened in his whiskers.

"Grab some fresh sheets," Megan said, "I'll clean it up." But her face paled as she approached the bed.

Kent stopped her. "No, I'll do it." Megan looked relieved, so he went on, "But I don't want him in our room anymore. We're going to have to replace these sheets." Kent gathered them up quickly, trying to avoid looking at the corpse.

"They weren't the good ones anyway." Megan forced a smile.

Kent kissed her, briefly, over the bundle of bloody sheets.

Rain pattered into the doorway. The cat stared at him.

"In or out?" Kent demanded. The cat was like a statue. Kent pressed his socked foot against the cat's behind. Not cruel. Just giving it a nudge in the right direction. It hissed, but only a little. Ears twitched, eyes widened. It was distracted.

Kent heard it too. Outside. That sound again. The cat darted out of sight. He should close the door, go back to his hot coffee and warm chair, but there was something out there.

God, let it be a fox. A growling fox that was fast and mean and ate cats.

It didn't sound like a fox.

What *was* it? He stepped onto the porch.

Their dead end street stretched into a small copse of trees, thick and brambly. That was where the noise was coming from. He didn't see Storm anywhere. The grey rain was giving way to dusk. Megan would be home soon. He should start supper.

But what was that cat up to? What was *making* that sound? He had to know.

He tried to be careful, but he was clumsy. He slid in slippered feet, tumbled down the incline, scratched his arms up again. There would be bruises tomorrow. He sat in the tangle of bushes to catch his breath. Sticks and damp grass poked into his thin pant legs. What did he think he was doing out here?

The moon rose in the sky, a sliver of light. It made him feel lonely.

Something growled. He could smell himself, sweaty and afraid. The long grass moved around him.

"Storm?" Another growl, too loud for a cat. He held his breath, and the sound broke into a cacophony of murmurs.

The grass erupted. Dozens of cats spilled out toward him. The moonlight distorted them, changed them, and oh God, this was a mistake. They hissed and scrabbled and ran. Fur brushed his arms and he shrieked, a thin girlish sound that he hated, but *their eyes*. There was something wrong with their eyes. The storm of cats writhed and screamed and he staggered up, tried to run, but he stumbled and fell, tearing a hole in the knee of his pants and soaking himself with mud. Nimble bodies raced over his back. He groaned and the woods answered him. They groaned too. He covered his head and curled around himself until the grass quieted, settled. He sat up.

Something moved next to him and rage pounded through his head, red hot. He reached out, caught a handful of tail. He wanted to shake it, to break it, to hear something else be afraid for once and the shrieking spitting thing turned and oh God *what was it*?

It was Storm. It was just Storm, but it was all wrong, something had gone wrong and it turned on him and its mouth was too big and *oh God its eyes*. It howled, tore a bloody chunk of flesh from his arm. He let go and the cat scrambled away.

Kent trembled, gathered himself up. His legs were rubbery and weak, but they carried him home. He brushed away tears with mud-caked hands that left dirty smears on his face.

"I think we should go to the hospital. You probably need stitches. And a tetanus shot. There's raccoons out there sometimes, and they have all sorts of diseases." She wrapped the bandage tightly around his arm. Blood oozed through.

"I told you what bit me, it was that fucking cat!"

"Kent, it's not a cat bite! Did you even look at it? What the hell were you doing wandering around down there anyway? Jesus Christ."

He didn't have an answer for that. On top of everything, he was getting a headache. "I'll go to the hospital tomorrow. It's too late to drive back into town now."

She rolled her eyes. Almost as bad as her furrowed brow. "Oh, perfect. That'll be a great time to get stitches. And I'm sure you'll be in a brilliant mood tomorrow when it's all infected and full of pus."

"You could be a little sympathetic here, Megan!" He was the one bleeding all over the kitchen floor.

"You could stop being such an asshole, Kent! God. I'm fucking sick of fighting with you. I'm going to bed. Do whatever the hell you want."

Kent's face was hot, his temples tight with pain. Anything he said would only make it worse. He let her walk away. Listened to her footsteps pound up the stairs and the bedroom door slam shut.

"I'm getting pretty sick of it too," he muttered. He ran the tap and grabbed a bottle of aspirin. He swallowed two with a swig of water. The window above the sink looked into the backyard, where glowing eyes peered back at him. The cat could stay out there all night for all he cared. He certainly wasn't letting it in.

It was impossible to sleep on the couch. Every time he closed his eyes, he pictured it watching him, waiting to pounce.

He checked each room again. He even checked the locks on the doors, as if the cat could open them itself. He lay back down but didn't close his eyes.

Nothing in this house felt like his own anymore.

Maybe he could go stay with his parents. Just for a few

days. To collect himself. Figure out what he was going to do. He couldn't think here. He kept hearing things. Soft paws padding across the floor.

He just needed a few hours of sleep. He couldn't get that here, not in the wide open living room where that fucking thing could attack him at any minute. He wanted to be in his own bed. At least up there he could close the door. It was his bed as much as hers. Let Megan take the couch if she didn't want him next to her.

His bruised hips complained when he walked up the stairs. He closed the bedroom door softly and stood in the darkness, waiting for his eyes to adjust before he crawled into bed. Megan muttered something, rolled over.

He rolled onto his side, turned away from Megan. He listened to her breathing, tried to slow his to match. He needed to sleep. He couldn't think if he didn't sleep. Maybe he would stay after all. He could talk to Megan tomorrow. They could go on a vacation or something. Get back in tune with each other. Get the neighbors to feed the fucking cat for a few days if they had to. He wanted to make this work. He *needed* to make this work. She was all he had.

He shifted his weight, tried to get comfortable. Maybe he should leave. Maybe it would be easier to think without all this pressure. He could leave her a long note, so she knew he wasn't really gone, just . . . just for now.

Or what about therapy? For them both. Even if it was expensive, it would be worth it. Teach them how to communicate again. Find some common ground. It couldn't *all* be his fault. They could make it work together.

His leg cramped and he turned over. Megan lay on her back, eyes gently closed, lips pursed. She looked like she was getting ready to kiss someone. In sleep, she looked young again. Like the person he had married. Before all this . . . all this nothing, really. Nothing had happened. They just needed to connect.

The door creaked and a thin beam of light broke the darkness. Kent went still. The fear churning through his stomach was irrational. The cat wasn't in the house. It couldn't be the cat. He had closed the door tight.

It landed, soft as silk, on the bed. Kent tensed up. Liquid darkness moved. Eyes shone at him, then blinked away. It must have been in the room the whole time. It couldn't unlock doors. He was afraid to move, didn't want to startle it into attack. His arm still throbbed from the bite.

He needed to get up, shake the bed, push it away so he could run, but he couldn't convince himself to move. The cat's eyes flickered over him and his limbs went heavy. Sweat broke his upper lip. He was dreaming. He was dreaming and he had to wake up. He couldn't stand this again, he couldn't stand the feel of the cat climbing over him, sitting on his chest, staring at him.

It didn't.

It ignored him, padded softly up Megan's sleeping body. An acid taste filled Kent's mouth. The cat perched on Megan's chest and stared at her.

Storm moved in fits and starts, all wrong angles and shining pools of black. It touched its nose to Megan's. Her eyes blinked open, just for a moment, sleepy. A soft little sigh escaped her lips and the cat pushed its snout inside the gentle parting there.

It pushed further.

Whiskers shone as they angled back. The cat shoved its entire head inside Megan's mouth. Her jaw strained around it, and there was a groan from somewhere deep inside. Her eyes sprang open. Wide. Panicked. She met Kent's eyes and he struggled. He pushed and thrashed inside but he couldn't move. A scream built in his throat. His fingers twitched lightly, and that was all.

The cat pushed its way further in, opening her mouth wider, ignoring her strained choking sounds. Kent's breath stayed slow and calm, but inside he was frantic.

Her jaw cracked as the cat's shoulders pushed through.

The cat climbed deeper, inch by impossible inch.

Megan's eyes bulged and wet tears glistened in the dim light. Her throat tented out like a well-fed snake.

Hips and hind legs scrabbled inside. The horrid O of her mouth began to close. All that was left was a sleek black tail. It slipped inside easily.

Kent screamed. His whole body thrummed with pins and needles. His limbs moved, slow and awkward and clumsy. "Megan!"

He clawed sheets away. He took her face in his hands, pale and round as the moon. Peaceful.

Her eyes fluttered open. He didn't know what to say. Sweat dripped from his face on to hers. Her forehead wrinkled, then her face softened and she touched his cheek.

"Baby, did you have another bad dream?"

The cat didn't come back. Whatever had attacked Kent had probably gotten Storm too. At least, that's what Megan said. He wanted to believe that, so he told himself he did. He felt better. They didn't fight anymore. Megan was happy, and that made him happy.

His arm would heal. The doctor had given him antibiotics and a concerned look. That had been weeks ago, but it felt better every day. It still throbbed sometimes. Especially with this bad weather coming.

Megan padded down the stairs, stretched. Her face was clear, her skin better than it had been in years. Kent put down the newspaper. "This storm's supposed to be worse than that last one."

She smiled, a glint of teeth. "I'm not worried." Her hand on the back of his neck. Cold. She stared out the kitchen window. "The storm is beautiful." Throbs of red and violet swirled as dark clouds moved in. She took his hand. "Come outside with me. Let's watch the sky together."

They stood on the deck and watched. Ink splotches filled the sky. Trees shook and trembled. Kent held Megan tight against him. Her hip felt good beneath his hand. When the rain started, something darted out of the trees. A strange, rippling shape, running low to the ground. Familiar. Kent opened his mouth. Closed it. He didn't want to say anything. Not yet.

It slithered up to their step. The ginger cat from the hedge. Horrid eyes, so orange they were red, coat paler than flesh.

"The poor thing," Megan purred. It was far too thin, torso long and disjointed, as though it had two sets of ribs. It groaned up at them, revealed rows of vicious teeth.

The cat pushed its nose into Kent's pant leg. Knobby bones ground against his shin. Bile rose in the back of his throat. He swallowed, looked at Megan. Her eyes were soft. A good, calm feeling radiated from her, and he allowed it to settle through his shoulders. He pushed a strand of hair from her face, rubbed his thumb over the spot on her forehead where wrinkles used to form.

He just wouldn't look at its eyes. If he didn't look at its eyes, it wasn't so bad. "I'm sure we still have some cat food left in the cupboard. Want me to go get it?"

"Let's all go," she said, and opened the door. The deformed cat looked up at him. He didn't meet its eyes. Instead he watched the sway of Megan's hips. She was worth it. She always had been.

He followed her inside. He would follow her anywhere.

The cat trailed behind. It wouldn't stop looking at him.

THE TASTE OF SAND ON YOUR LIPS

FIFTY-FIVE 55-WORD SHORT STORIES

YOU SHOULDN'T BE HERE

Maybe if you got here sooner. But you're here *now*, aren't you? There's nothing I can do about it. You keep turning pages, greedy, eating words like berries, red juice spilling down your chin. It's disgusting. It's obsessive. You should stop. Leave. Don't come back.

I guess it's too late.

You really shouldn't be here.

THE PLANET IS AN OCEAN

The ocean is dead. Rumors say it was never alive at all. The water reflects black skies, deep and dark and thick. The sea is still as a tomb, but for the occasional lapping wave that licks the island, a vicious tongue, swallowing grains of sand, kissing the shores with its poison.

No one swims.

THE ISLAND APPEARS

It might be a mirage. When you blink, it seems to disappear.

For now, it is fiercely alive, writhing with motion, with things that play and scream and fuck and devour and sleep. Beginnings, middles, ends.

THE TASTE OF SAND ON YOUR LIPS

The island gives way bit by bit. Soft sand dissolves to ocean. It has been here forever. It endures.

THE EYE

Huge and throbbing, blinded in a long-ago war. Milk-white, buried deep in the forest. You walk by, so quiet, afraid it can hear. It blinks and squints and tears drip silently to the ground, burning grass and weeds, turning insects to muck.

Once all-seeing, once all-knowing, now afraid. You pass, unobstructed.

THERE ARE NO FISH IN THE OCEAN

Clouds spill to feed the island. Pink-stained fog coughs and spits out a fish. He lands on his feet, his breath coarse and ragged.

A child offers him a glass of water. He dives in. She places him on a bench and forgets.

His memory lasts 55 seconds, then he forgets, too.

He is content.

AT THE CROSSROADS

The King leaves the castle. He has heard those distant rumblings. It is dangerous, but he goes alone. His court no longer listens to him. He wants more than this. There are answers to find.

The cats sit at the crossroads, cleaning their paws. They have no advice for him.

He makes the wrong choice.

THE SIAMESE-SIAMESE CATS

A single tail that twists and winds. Flashing eyes. Whiskers flicker with impatience. Rough tongue reassures.

"How long shall we stay?"

"Until it's over."

"And when will it be over?"

"Soon, brother, soon."

"And how will we escape?"
"A way will open."
"It always does."
A yawn. They curl together. No point in losing sleep.

THE TEETH

Chattering clattering teeth, gnash and spit and chew. Pearly whites made of clouds; what they eat is left behind.

Just stay still. It doesn't hurt. Let them pass you by.

Watch them! They tear at your heels and gnaw their way through, but you don't feel a thing. They go on and so do you.

MOTHER

Her belly expands and contracts. She feeds it handfuls of dirt, crunchy beetles. She gulps puddle water. There is no one left to ask for advice.

She has no idea how long it takes.

It has been years. It has been longer.

She has torn off her face and sewn it to her gut, waiting.

THE HAPPY CLOWN

No one has seen the clown for years, but you can visit him if you want. He's in the Queen's dungeon. She doesn't know he's there. You don't need a key, the door is open. He is not trapped. He just remains.

Melted face, white and red and dead. He smiles.

He is not missed.

THE SKY GROWS STRANGE

Don't look up. Don't look up. Don't look up. Don't look up. Don't look up. Don't look up. Don't look up. Don't look up. Don't look up. Don't look up. Don't look up. Don't look up. Don't look up. Don't look up. Don't look up. Don't look up. Don't look up. Don't.

Something is coming.

134

THE EARTH IS SHAKING

Don't look down. Don't look down. Don't look down. Don't look down. Don't look down. Don't look down. Don't look down. Don't look down. Don't look down. Don't look down. Don't look down. Don't look down. Don't look down. Don't look down. Don't look down. Don't look down. Don't.

Something is coming.

THE HUNT FOR THE KING

Where did the King go? He has been gone for a long time, and something distant is rumbling.

We send armies of ants to retrieve him. They scatter across the island, tiny legs stiff but fast. They find nothing. They find no one.

Everyone wakes up at once. Everyone looks. There is nothing to find.

LONG LIVE THE QUEEN

The Queen is dead. She was sewing her mouth together when the needle slipped and plunged deep into her heart. Out spurted a ribbon, jagged and purple and thick. She grew light-headed. There was no chance to save her. She fell from the tower, tangled and strangled in her own blood.

We watched it happen.

THE WORM WAKES

Beneath the earth it churns. Each undulation shifts tiny cities of sand and lays them to waste. A timid head pokes out from the ground, unseeing, seeking, not finding.

Something about it bothers you deeply. You pluck it from its hole and throw it to the fish.

The fish eats and forgets. You do not.

THE HUT

Rock and clay and moss sunk deep in the muck, far past the desert, where no one goes.

Rumors say an old god lived there, back when rumors said anything at all. Now the gods are dead. Only we remain.

The door cracks open. Something dark and low and oily slithers out. No one sees.

THE ADVERSARIES

Their battle dragged on for five hundred and fifty-five years. They grew bloodied and bruised beyond repair, but still they fought on. Legs quivered but held.

The sun turned black. They were distracted. They looked up.

They were not blinded, yet it was the last thing they ever saw.

One reached for the other's hand.

THE SAD CLOWN

He is crying. He never stops crying. Hidden beneath the castle, he felt when she died. We all did.

Melted face, soggy candle. Wax and blood and greasepaint stain the concrete. The door yawns open. He can leave anytime. He stays. He cries.

He would escape if there was anything left of him to run.

HE KEEPS ON MOVING

The King journeys to places unseen. The woods part to take him further and close behind him. The trees display new colors, vivid and impossible on this grey island. Miraculous visions appear to him, clarifying nothing.

He is confused. He stumbles forward. He stumbles back. He is pushed along, a swimmer in a dangerous current.

THE TASTE OF SAND ON YOUR LIPS

HOW MANY LEGS DOES THE OCTOPUS HAVE?
He lurks on the top of the mountain. Bulbous head extends into the sky, shimmering clouds obscure his view.

His legs are long and tapered, branching off into twists and thorns, reaching to all the secret places of the sands, touching everything. They caress and pinch, squeezing blood from stones. He knows all, says nothing.

THE MAN IN THE CLAY HOUSE
He's almost done, so he starts again. He won't finish. What happens after you finish? It worries him. So when the end comes, he stops, rips it up, starts over. It's easier to begin and begin than it is to start something different. He works quicker each time. He tears up. He tears it up.

THEY TORE EACH OTHER APART
When news of her death came, neither sister shed a tear. The older arched her brow. "I'm next in line."

"But I'm the smartest and prettiest."

"Perhaps, but I am the oldest."

"I am faster."

"I am stronger," and she was upon her little sister. She lied. They were well matched.

There was no winner.

IN A THIMBLE
The water is still, not even a ripple, until the mermaids rise. They are not beautiful. They are full of teeth, each scale a mouth, and each mouth starving. When they wake, they scream. They used to sing, but their voices are hoarse. The King hears them and he stays away.

He is still lost.

THE CATS GROW WORRIED
They prowl and pace, unable to assuage their fears by grooming. They don't know what is coming, just that it is strong and fierce and comes and comes.

"I think I'm hungry."
"You just ate."
"Did I? Perhaps."
The fish closes his eyes and they pass him by.
"We must keep walking."
And they do.

EVERYONE WAKES UP

At exactly the same time. No clock strikes, but our eyes all blink open. We are blind for a moment, unaccustomed to the light.

A heavy sense of dread fills your heart, and mine. The taste of blood floods your mouth. It is time.

You look to the sky and see nothing.

I'm so sorry.

WORD HAS SPREAD

The wind is whispering. The leaves are falling. Everyone knows, but no one remembers how they heard. Somewhere in the distance, a dog screams. The eye falls from the sky, careens through the sand. The clown is laughing and laughing and laughing. I am picking flesh from my thumb. I told you not to come.

A DOOR APPEARS

A rough sketch appears on the horizon. Hazy brushstrokes are refined, it bursts into three dimensions. Lines are sketched, finalized, inked. Next, a wash of color is applied. Plain mahogany shifts and changes into something exquisitely carved. With each moment that passes, new details come into view. A brass door knob bulges. A keyhole gapes.

THE OCEAN STIRS

These waters have always been dead and dark and empty. But now, leagues and leagues below where the water meets the sky, something massive wakes.

THE TASTE OF SAND ON YOUR LIPS

It yawns, stretches, and adjusts its bulk into a more comfortable position. Eyes blink shut. It falls back into a dying dream.

Above, the seas are rough. The waves climb.

EVERYONE WANTS TO BE THE QUEEN

Bushes rustle, trees fall. Everyone is dying. We are all out for blood. Some of us rage and run and scream. Some of us sneak, lay traps, move in shadows. Something grinds against the sky.

Days pass and the dead are walking.

They chew and chew and chew and chew.

Everyone has a master plan.

MAPS DON'T WORK HERE

The girl rips hers apart, piece by piece. Faded mountains, crusted rivers, beloved homes: a mess of jagged melodrama. She wipes tears on dusty plains. The wind picks up. She scatters it to the sky.

She starts on herself. Paper face, paper fists, paper heart drift into the breeze.

A sliver of mouth whispers, "Goodbye."

STOP WHAT YOU'RE DOING

Jam your fingers into your eardrums. Deeper. Ignore the pain. Hum. Concentrate on your breath. Close your eyes and start counting. Think of a safe place, somewhere far away. Farther. Keep humming. Keep counting.

When you feel my hand on your shoulder, it's safe.

If you count to fifty-five and don't feel my hand, run.

THE SISTERS

A nose, an eye, a lock of hair.

A hand, a cheek, a hunk of lung.

Blood attacks vein. Bone attacks nail. A tongue strangles in intestine, a toe is severed by teeth. Eyeballs roll like dice, fingers fall like dominos.

A puzzle of body parts, each scrap of flesh in its own private war.

THE RAGE OF STARS

Night falls, then falls again, darker. The sky swirls with crimson, an inky Rorschach.

You can't see them, but you can hear them. Each star has a tiny mouth and they are screaming.

Black waves are churning, building tall and fast and strong.

You pick stardust from your hair, so sharp it cuts your fingers.

BREAKFAST

He refuses and pushes the bowl away.

"Eat your porridge, it's your favorite kind."

He frowns, pale face solemn.

"If you don't eat, you won't grow big and strong."

His voice is static, out of tune, not human. "There is no survival. This is the end."

His mother shakes her head, then bites his off.

THE WITCH ON THE HILL

She is singing a song you haven't heard in a long time. Her voice hurts something buried deep within you, forces you to remember. Hearts pulse, wings tear, vocal cords sever. The thing inside you dies.

Even the hill shrivels away, a sunken valley. The witch becomes stone, then dust.

I don't like this song.

A KEY IS FOUND

"It's coming."

"Of course it is. I told you that."

"How much time?"

"Barely any."

"Then what shall we do?"

"We wait. First, we eat."

Ears slant back. A rustle, a pounce, a spray of blood. Hunger sated. Within the belly of the mouse, it glitters, plucked free with razor teeth.

"Well, that's a relief."

THE WOODS

The trees carve eyes into their trunks so they can watch. Gnarled folds hiss. Ropey branches twine together like the king of rats. They clench and release, clench and release. Something whines. Blood drips to the forest floor. On the breeze, the scent of burnt flesh.

The squirrel slices his belly open and sacrifices himself.

THE SALT PICKS AWAY AT EVERYTHING

The sky opens and showers us with salt. Our voices are too hoarse to scream. Stinging grains exfoliate as they peel back the surface of the land. Twin cats press close together beneath a mountain of garbage, listening to the sizzle of slugs.

It rains for a time, then stops.

We all display new flesh.

PUSH BACK

The warriors stamp their feet, tear down walls, open gates. Glass overflows, water splashes, fish goes belly up. The clown is exposed to the elements. The mermaids eat; something silky stains their teeth. The pregnant gut explodes, the baby crawls, the mother screams:

Where is the King where is the King where is the King?

THE WAVES

The ocean is black and oily and thick. The water beneath the surface is chaos. The water above the surface is a war. Waves crash together like angry thunder. The stars fall and sink and fade.

The ocean is dead the ocean is dead the ocean is dead.

The waves scream and shake and growl.

DON'T LOOK, THE MOON IS SMILING

Fat and heavy, hanging low enough to touch. Wicked teeth extend past cheeks, chewing stars and clouds. The lemmings look up (the sky is falling). They are destroyed in flame. The moon laughs, a cold breeze, and even their ashes disappear.

He turns his head, crumples the sky.

Close your eyes, he wants a kiss.

DIZZY SPELLS

They are spinning and spinning and spinning. Each mouth is agape in rictus grin. The sickness makes their eyes bulge wide.

They dance in tandem. Their shoes wear thin. Soft, delicate feet bleed where the leather frays—a trail of blood that leads back to a shattered home.

They are spinning and spinning and spinning.

ROCK MOUNTAIN

A child sits on her swing set. Deep in shadow, her mother plucks weeds.

The swing stops. "Do you hear that?"

"Yes." Her mother turns in slow motion, her face is not her own. A puppet string lifts a shell to her ear.

Beneath their feet, the earth opens. The mountain crumbles. They are gone.

THE MAN WITH THE SUITCASE

He is crouched beneath a tree, cradling a tattered suitcase. His long fingers are tied in complex knots around the handle. Black blood drips from his ear and stains his white suit.

He shakes. He gathers his nerve and opens the case. The wicked winds blow; the contents escape.

There is no hope. Not here.

TOO FAR GONE

The seams of the sky groan. Trees pull away from the ground and march off on broken branches. The earth patches itself up, but soil falls through the cracks.

Everything is falling apart. The armies of ants sew it back together, but their needles are dull and rusted. Their thread is too thin. It tears.

A DOOR IS USED

At last they arrive.

"I was beginning to think we wouldn't find it."

"Where shall we head to next?"

The key slides home. "An excellent question, brother."

The door sighs open. They hesitate on the threshold, but the wind hisses a melody, and even a cat must decide quickly.

The door shuts behind them, disappears.

I HEARD SOMEONE CRYING

Cover your ears. You'll thank me later.

The banshees are out. They circle the sky like vultures, snatch children from the sand. Their necks are brittle, heads twist off with a snap.

Many have already given up. All through the village, face down in the sand, they take their fingers from their ears and bleed.

TOO LATE

The King stumbles through the sand, sees a familiar curve of tree. Everything clicks. He knows where he is; he knows the way home.

No one cheers for him. The beach is empty.

He turns to the castle, to where it should be. A dark, oily stain hangs in the sky.

He hears himself whimper.

BETTY ROCKSTEADY

I SMELL SOMETHING ON THE WIND
Do you smell it too? Salty. Rotten. Meaty. Dead and burning. A pyre of garbage and spoiled flesh.

Nothing looks the same anymore. The sun is a scribble. The sky is a mouth. Everyone is on fire, but it blinks in and out.

Ashes, ashes.

I am so afraid for the fire to go out.

THE HORRIBLE SOUND OF SILENCE
Everything stops dead. A distant hum cuts off abruptly. Hundreds of eyes look to each other for comfort. Pupils dilate, enormous holes that lead to the sky. In that darkness, unholy stars swirl.

Your mouth is moving. I can't hear you. All our mouths are moving, thousands of teeth grinding silent.

Tears are razor sharp.

CRASHING WAVES
The storm started so long ago that it became commonplace.

The water crashes against the sand, no longer sated by just a taste, hungry for more, licking faster and further up the shore, taking great gulps of people and the places they called home. No one screams. Not anymore.

The ocean is dead and starving.

TSUNAMI
The entire ocean sighs. The Great Wave is coming. It eclipses what is left of the sky. It eclipses *everything*.

It is so fucking beautiful.

Everywhere I look, all I see is ocean.

I smell death in her waves.

Everyone left standing sinks to their knees.

No one prays.

This *is* God. God is here.

THE TASTE OF SAND ON YOUR LIPS

THE FORCE OF THE OCEAN

Rock, paper, scissors, the sea. The ocean always wins. Greedy, she swallows us whole. Everything is death.

I don't know which way is up. Wicked waters displace and destroy.

The taste of blood in your mouth mingles with the taste of sand on your lips.

Everything sinks slowly in these black waters.

Goodbye, goodbye, goodbye.

THE DROWNING

No one can swim.

There is nowhere to run, there is nowhere to hide. The island is devoured. We are devoured. Waves scatter our remains.

Time passes.

Eventually, the waters smooth. Not a grain of sand is left untouched. For a short time, bodies bob on the surface, then they sink.

There is nothing left.

ALL IS QUIET

All is still.

It's just the two of us. I'm sorry I can't meet your gaze, but you could have stopped this at any time. *I* could have stopped this at any time.

We have to live with our choices.

We will go on. We will try to forget.

Please, just turn the page.

DUSK URCHIN

HER FIRST INSTINCT was to not answer the door. Her first instinct was *always* to not answer the door, to hide out of sight of the windows and wait for whoever it was to go away. What kind of person just stopped by and expected you to greet them, anyway? There were so many other, less intrusive ways to get in touch with someone.

Ashley perched on the couch, folded over a corner of her book, and listened. *Jon?* Her first nauseating thought, always hopeful, always disappointed. But the knock came again, more insistent this time, and just in case, she glanced in the mirror. Her hair was hopeless. She could have at least washed her face today. It was probably just some kids selling something. It certainly wasn't Jon, leaving his new wife and his new son on a sudden whim, racing back to her empty womb.

She opened the door. It was Mr. Peterson from next door, staring at the sky, chewing his lip. She barely noticed him, the little girl beside him was so striking: glossy black hair, and the darkest swirl of blue eyes. Ashley couldn't help but stare. Mr. Peterson turned from the sky, offered Ashley a thin-lipped smile.

"Hi, Mr. Peterson." Whoops, there it was, a guilty memory. She had promised to come over for tea after she was all settled in. That had been months ago, and she had only seen him in passing since.

"I'm sorry to stop by. I'm sorry to do this." He spoke

slowly. The girl slid past Ashley, liquid quick, leaving a scent of rotted leaves.

"Hey, where are you going?" What was this, an impromptu babysitting request? So much for her relaxing day. She looked back at Mr. Peterson. "Is that your granddaughter or something? I'm not really set up for kids here." Or anywhere. Irritation squirmed through her gut.

"You don't have to worry about that. I'd better come in."

She wanted to tell him to go away, but she couldn't make herself say the words. Instead, she forced a wobbly half-smile into place. She looked down the hallway, didn't see the girl. What was she doing?

"Please?" Mr. Peterson's eyes were watery. How could she say no? He looked older than she remembered. Maybe he was getting sick. She realized she hadn't seen him out in his garden for days. "I don't think it will take long," Mr. Peterson said.

Ashley had lots of breakables out in the living room, collections she had begun when she realized there weren't going to be kids around to break them. She didn't want them in the hands of some stranger. "Yeah, come on in," she said, finally, and Mr. Peterson shut the door.

The girl sat on the couch, statue-still, silent. Her features were so delicate they barely looked real. Black bangs skimmed her eyes, deep blue, shining like mirrors. She didn't smile, didn't blink. Ashley realized she was staring, and tore her eyes away.

"Uh, so, do you want me to make tea or something? I think I have some soda for your granddaughter."

"I don't think she's my granddaughter," Mr. Peterson said, quietly.

"What?"

Mr. Peterson pressed his lips together and shook his head. "Nothing."

The living room smelled musty. "So, can I get you anything, uh . . . ?" Her voice sounded brittle, its brightness false. "What's your name?"

The girl didn't say anything. She just looked back at Ashley, hands folded in her lap. Her pale lips curved slightly, a hint of a smile. The room was smaller than it should be. Ashley wasn't used to having company. It made her feel claustrophobic.

Mr. Peterson coughed. Ashley turned in what felt like slow motion, saw him wipe something black away from his mouth with a handkerchief. "I'd like a glass of water, please," he rasped.

"Uh, sure . . . does she . . . have a tablet or something to play with?"

Mr. Peterson chuckled and coughed again. His shoulders hunched forward and he shrank into himself.

The girl tilted her head slightly. Ashley wished she would stop looking at her. Why were these people here? She shouldn't feel so awkward in her own home. "Well, the TV remote is right there." She pointed and noticed that her hand was shaking.

Mr. Peterson followed her to the kitchen and sat at the table. She poured him a glass of water and when she turned around, his head was in his hands. She felt a twinge of annoyance, and flushed with guilt. She couldn't help it. She didn't want to spend her day talking to people she barely knew. Jon was right; she never would have connected with an adopted kid. She hated strangers.

"Mr. Peterson?" She set the water next to him. He barely glanced at it.

"Sit down, please." His eyes were so serious. She sat and he pulled his chair closer, close enough that she could smell his stale cologne. The bags under his eyes looked bruised.

"Is everything all right?"

"Have you ever seen that little girl before?" His voice was barely a whisper.

"Uh, I don't think so. Is she a relative of yours?"

There was something like amusement in his eyes. "She says she's my daughter."

"Your daughter?" Mr. Peterson was in his seventies. That girl couldn't be older than ten.

He laughed. "It hardly seems likely, does it? An old man like me . . . my kids are all grown up. None of them live around here. They can't stand me, and I guess I can't blame them. They're all grown up. My wife has been dead fifteen years, and I've only been with her memory since." His hands shook in his lap and his knee beat out an agitated rhythm. "But last week, she showed up, and I can't seem to get rid of her."

Ashley pressed her lips together. He was going senile. Whoever the girl was, he was hardly in any condition to take care of her. "Is there someone I can call for you, Mr. Peterson? Some family or something?"

He shook his head. "I tried to call them, but something's wrong. I called them all. No one answers anymore. There's no one there. I called them every day. There's just her now."

Ashley stood up. "Let me try." Her words came out sharper than she would have liked. "Can you give me a phone number to call?" She knew she shouldn't have answered the door. God, she shouldn't think like that. If she hadn't answered it, who would help Mr. Peterson?

"There was never a problem with my memory before. It's her."

This was exhausting. She was hardly equipped to unravel this mess. She had just wanted to enjoy her weekend and try not to think about her failed marriage, and now she had to rescue a senile old man and some kid.

"How about your doctor?" she pleaded. "Who's your doctor?" She didn't want to call the police, because she just knew it would be Jon's brother who showed up and that was a whole other pile of bullshit she didn't want to have to deal with. Mr. Peterson kept shaking his head. The silence in the house grew thick. The girl hadn't turned on the television. What was she doing in there?

"I killed her last night. It didn't help."

"What?" Ashley's breath stuck in her chest.

"I couldn't stand it anymore. She wouldn't stop looking at me. I felt like I was going crazy. *I don't know her*. But I couldn't leave. There was nowhere to go. There was nothing but doubt." He grabbed Ashley's hand with his dry, bony hand. "She wasn't in any of the pictures. I was starting to believe, but she wasn't in any of my pictures, and no one would pick up their phone and she kept calling me Daddy, and she wasn't in any of the pictures." His eyes were full, desperate.

Now she had to call the police. This was too much. This was crazy. She started toward the phone, but his hand tightened, his nails dug into her wrist.

"Mr. Peterson, please, you're hurting me." She didn't like how shrill her voice sounded.

"I filled up the bathtub. I made it a nice temperature. Isn't that silly? It wouldn't matter if it were hot or cold, but I made it just right and I put her in and she didn't struggle. She just looked at me. Did you notice her eyes? They're not blue, they're black. They're the night sky. I held her and she didn't struggle and she died." He let go. He was crying, the tears weaving through his wrinkles.

Ashley was frozen, her throat thick. He was out of his mind.

"I buried her in the backyard. She was back this morning. I killed her and buried her and she's back. I didn't dream it. I didn't imagine it." He stood up and Ashley stumbled back, but he was just going to the window. He pointed a trembling finger. "Can you see it? I didn't imagine it. I didn't."

Something moved in her stomach, something vast and expanding and painful. In his pretty little backyard, right next to his pretty little garden, a pile of earth was raw and torn. Just the right size for a little girl.

Then there was the acrid stench of urine, and she thought perhaps he had wet himself.

"It's time to go home." The girl stood in the doorway, her eyes on Ashley. He was wrong. Her eyes weren't black. They were a color Ashley had never seen before, set deep in a face that was china-doll perfect, not even a hint of a freckle. She held out her small, pale hand to Mr. Peterson and he took it, shoulders slumped. She led him to the door.

"Wait . . . " Ashley said, following them. "I need to call someone. I need to do something. Little girl, what's your name? Where's your mom?"

"Don't worry," he said, "I'm not going to hurt her. Not again. There's no point."

She didn't know what to say. "Are . . . is there someone I can call for you? You haven't . . . why did you come here?"

The little girl stopped and Mr. Peterson looked back at Ashley. "It was *her* idea. I'm sorry." He smiled without teeth. His mouth was a rancid hole.

Something pressed on Ashley's throat. She slammed the door behind them.

The house was too quiet. Ashley sat at her kitchen table, chewing a fingernail. She had to call someone. She had to do something. The poor old man was going batty all by himself. Whoever the little girl was, she was probably in danger. But she didn't know who to call. The police? The last thing she wanted was Jon's brother over here, looking at her sad little house, asking her questions and smiling and making small talk and pretending like he had been rooting for her all along.

She looked out the window, at that little patch of earth. She was being indecisive. She was being weak.

The house was so quiet. How did she spend day after day in this quiet house without going insane? The silence was hollow, like there had been a cacophony of voices there just moments before and now they were suddenly gone, sucked into a black hole. No. It wasn't like that at all. That was just a weird thought.

She had to call the police. She couldn't just let whatever was happening over there happen. Her purse and her phone were in the living room. She forced herself to get up. She had to make the call before too much time passed and she looked even crazier for just sitting around, doing nothing.

Her living room smelled of rotting fruit.

There was a dark stain on the sofa, where the girl had been sitting. It licked across the cushions, shimmering black and blue like an oil slick, like *her* eyes.

Don't touch it. Something fluttered in her chest. The colors bent and swirled and Ashley felt dizzy looking at them. She couldn't stop looking at them. *Just don't touch it.*

Behind her there was a sharp intake of breath. Ashley turned, in slow motion. Tiny dots blurred her vision. There was no one there.

She curled into the chair farthest away from the couch and fumbled her phone from her purse. She tried to keep her eyes away from the couch. Her fingers stuck to the buttons as she pulled up the number for the police station.

The phone buzzed and clicked and the numbers disappeared from her screen. The feathery hairs on the back of her neck shivered. She could feel someone watching her, their eyes on the back of her skull. Impossible. Her back was to the wall. There was no one there. She shuddered and turned, a river of nausea in her gut.

A cockroach skittered silently up the wall.

She turned her phone off. Turned it back on. Everything was fuzzy. She dialed again and listened to silence. There must be something wrong with the battery. There was a landline in the kitchen; why hadn't she used that in the first place? She peeled her legs from the chair.

She wouldn't look at the couch. She would only look straight ahead.

Tears prickled at her eyes, and she didn't know why she was crying. Her chest felt full, and her steps were slower than they should be. The phone was next to the window, and the window looked out on that fucking pile of dirt. It stretched away from her, wriggled in her hand, but she caught it and dialed and was rewarded with static.

Just as she was about to hang up, there was a knock at the door.

The phone slipped, made a dull thud against the floor. She didn't want to answer the door. Her instinct was not to answer it. Everything in her gut and her head and her heart agreed. She didn't want company. She just wanted to be alone but the knocking wouldn't stop and it wouldn't stop and it wouldn't stop. Everything was silent except for the pounding on the door and the pounding on her brain and she had to answer it.

When she touched the doorknob, the déjà vu was so thick it was disorienting.

She would only open the door a crack.

Her brain told her it was the same little girl, but her eyes weren't so sure. Something about her features had changed. Hadn't it? She was different. It couldn't be the same little girl. She couldn't make out what she looked like. There was the impression of those sharp features, Ashley could *feel* those sharp features, but her face was a white blur, floating, soft as a cloud.

Her blue-black eyes hung in the sky.

"What do you want?" Ashley was surprised at how her voice sounded. It sounded old.

"Mommy, let me in." The girl held out her hand. It was smeared with something, a Rorschach blotch of filth. Ashley couldn't let it touch her. She slammed the door shut, locked it, backed away.

The door shook and the knocking began again, louder, angrier. *She just needs help. You have to help her.* The voice in Ashley's mind was tinny and unfamiliar. She stumbled into the hallway, into the scent of decay, and she ran up the stairs, fell to her knees, climbed up with hands and feet. The panic that pounded through her brain was reptilian, ancient, and the pounding on the door and the walls and the windows was older still.

The walls were knocking, the ceiling was knocking, everything trembled and shook and Ashley wouldn't look, she just wouldn't look.

Her bedroom was safe. Your bedroom always had to be safe. She just couldn't shut the door because then if someone came up the stairs she wouldn't see them and they would want her to let them in.

The room smelled like piss.

Ashley couldn't breathe.

The closet door bent. Something tapped on it and a small, sad voice called, "Mommy?"

The rest of the sounds stopped. Her house was quiet again. Just that voice. "Mommy, let me out."

Ashley didn't feel right. She didn't feel right at all. She closed her eyes and she could see her daughter's face. A perfect blend of her and Jon. Fine soft hair like Jon's, thick in the hips like Ashley, and her eyes . . .

Where did she get her eyes?

"Mommy?" Underneath the sweetness of the voice there was something slick and thick and oily.

Did she have a daughter? She must have a daughter. Her daughter was talking to her. Her daughter couldn't be talking to her if she didn't have a daughter. The knob to the closet was cold. She shouldn't open it. She had to open it. Everything felt fuzzy.

Something about Mr. Peterson.

Why did Jon leave her if they had a daughter?

Something in her stomach tore. She backed away from the closet.

She shoved her window open. The fresh air that streamed in diluted some of the piss smell. The sky was full of indigo stars. She crawled out the window, onto the roof of the porch. She wanted to climb all the way down, she wanted to feel the ground under her feet, she wanted to run, but there were things moving in the yard. She could see their shadows as they crept behind the trees.

Mr. Peterson's house was dark. There was a patch of ground that had been dug up, a dark rectangle, big enough for a man.

The night sky was the darkest blue, almost black. Where had the day gone?

"Mommy, what are you doing out here?"

"I'm just watching the sky," she mumbled. Something crawled out and sat next to her. Her daughter. She had a daughter. But where was Jon? *If she had a daughter, where was Jon?* There was a pain in her stomach, a nasty, chewing pain.

She didn't want to look into her daughter's eyes. She didn't know why, but she didn't want to do it. Instead she ran her hands through her daughter's hair, and they came away sticky.

LARVA, PUPA, MOTH

I.

IT SLID BENEATH my toenail, razor-sharp.

I slept snug against Melissa, my chubby tummy and breasts squished up against her smooth curves. Pain startled me awake. The sun streamed through the window and I blinked it away, confused.

The sharp pain dulled to a hum. Just an unpleasant twitch. I sat up, stretched, not alarmed, and passed fingertips across my toes, absent-mindedly rubbing the sensation away. A shimmering of motion pulled me awake.

I clicked the light on and curled my legs up, examining my flesh carefully. Melissa, always a light sleeper, turned to me. "What are you doing?"

"I think there's a bug or something in bed. It bit me." I fluffed out the blankets, swept my hand across the bed and saw nothing. I bent closer to re-examine my foot.

The pins and needles sensation continued and my skin burbled. Swollen? I prodded gently with my fingers to check for pain and my skin rippled as something skittered away.

"There's something in me," I choked.

"What?" Let me see."

We both peered down at my foot.

Her long hair created a curtain around us, intimate. "I don't see anything."

I pressed my hand against my foot again. The itch remained, but Melissa arched a skeptical eyebrow and I didn't say anything.

We got up together. We showered together. Got dressed together. Ate breakfast together. Applied makeup. Kissed soft lips goodbye. Melissa left and I stayed behind. My unemployment insurance trickled through my hands as she worked and improved and was successful. I tidied and cooked but there was only so much to do in our small apartment. I said I was working on my art but mostly I scribbled mustaches on the newspaper and watched television. It droned on and on and I droned on and on. The computer glared at me. I circled want ads and pretended I would email them. I pretended I was waiting for a call from a potential employer. I plucked my eyebrows.

I watched the clock with bleary eyes. Lunchtime approached and I looked forward to the possibility of Melissa coming home. A tickling on my leg, and I brushed it away. It intensified to an itch. I peeled off my sock. The skin was clean and pale, and I scratched bitten nails against it.

The swelling was bigger. My skin tented out around it. A cyst. It must be a cyst. Some kind of reaction. Something *had* bitten me. I knew it. It felt strange—not tender, not exactly, but I could feel it there, pushing against my skin. Timidly I pressed a finger against it. I wanted to know if it hurt. I had barely grazed it with a fingertip when a shape darted away from my hand, a small bulge that rippled and crawled across the thin skin of my ankle. The sensation was unbearable and the thin screaming I heard was *me* and I was screaming and slamming my foot against the wall, *crush it kill it smash it*. Tiny hairs tickled deep inside me, places that were incredibly tender and had never been touched before.

"Beth, what the fuck?"

I came back to myself slightly at the tinkling sound of

my girlfriend's voice. She had come home for lunch, after all, and stood in the hallway, staring at me as I battered my foot against the wall. The concern on her face was tempered with disgust and I felt insane.

"There's something in me. I need to see a doctor."

I sat in the sterile room and I clutched Melissa's hand as she scrolled through her phone with the other, bored. My stomach churned as fast as my skin crawled. Each movement it made set off a deeper level of nausea. The bulge was rounding my kneecap now. I could *see* it. A curving mound of skin, skating in an S-shape as it meandered its way around my kneecap. It didn't hurt, not exactly, but I couldn't look at it for long without gagging.

I swayed gently, my feet tapping against the exam table, breathing deep.

"So is that all right with your parents, next Tuesday?"

"What?" I gulped. It was hard to put together the threads of what Melissa was saying.

An exasperated sigh. "The dinner party thing? So our parents can finally meet? You did mention it to them, right?"

I had, and I gulped and nodded and wavered and she took that as agreement and went back to staring at her phone. The doctor was taking forever. The office had been nice enough to squeeze me in. Melissa had been nice enough to come with me. Maybe her lack of concern should have been calming, but instead it made me more nervous. My thigh twitched with movement and I stared at the walls, teeth clenched.

Whatever it was, the doctor would help me. Would he excise it today? I stared at the lineup of scalpels on the counter nearby.

He came in abruptly, startling me. Melissa barely looked up over her glasses. "What seems to be the problem?" Smile too wide on his face. He was old and fat and looked rather like Santa, but it didn't make me feel any more comfortable.

"Um . . . when I got up today . . . I think a bug got in me." I gestured to my leg. The bulge writhed. The doctor leaned down close to take a look at it.

"Hm. I see. Does it hurt?"

"No . . . not really. It feels strange, though. Like pins and needles."

He nodded, considering. "Well, that makes sense. Something moving around in there. But it's not bothering you any?"

"There's a bug inside me, of course it's bothering me!"

Melissa glared at me. She hated outbursts.

"Fair enough," the doctor said. "So, what can I do for you?"

I stared at him for a moment. "I . . . what can you do? Can't you get it out?"

He rocked back and forth on his feet. "No, nope, seems to be in there pretty deep, and it's not doing any harm, so I wouldn't worry about it too much."

"What are you talking about? It's got to get out of me, what the fuck?" My voice cracked.

"*Beth*," Melissa hissed.

He frowned. "I'm afraid I'm going to have to ask you both to leave."

"But . . . "

Melissa squeezed my hand. "If the doctor says it's fine, it's fine." Her voice was honey. Her eyes were steel. I could feel my face turning red, but I swallowed it down. Melissa was already angry enough.

On the way out, I swiped a scalpel.

Melissa treated me to stony silence and went to bed early. I pretended to watch television for hours. Mostly I watched the twitching thing travel up my thigh. I was not letting whatever it was live in me.

When I was sure she was asleep, I went to the bathroom. I washed my hands. I set up some clean towels. Tweezers. I cleaned the area with peroxide. I waited.

It was getting bigger, growing rapidly. It moved quickly, but in a pattern. My eyes grew heavy and sleepy as I watched, but finally it slowed. Settled. I struck. The scalpel slid through skin like butter. Black blood poured out and I stabbed and stabbed and thought I got it but instead there was a sharper, deeper pain as it burrowed deeper inside.

I kept carving, desperate now, but there was too much blood.

I passed out.

II.

Melissa bandaged my wounds. She helped me back to bed, kissed my forehead, brought cool water that I sipped gratefully. She said nothing. A smile played on her lips, but I was too tired and weak to wonder. She said nothing.

I drifted off to sleep, my thigh aching, but within all was still. I was sure it was gone. It had to be.

I didn't feel better.

Days passed and Melissa didn't bring up the incident. Neither did I. There was no point in arguing about it. The blood was gone, the bathroom pristine again. If it weren't for the healing wound in my leg, I would have wondered if it had happened at all.

After dozing in and out for a few days, I was able to hobble my way to the kitchen for breakfast with Melissa. I couldn't look her in the eye, but I felt her watching me. "Are you feeling better?" She pushed greasy hair out of my eyes. Freckles danced on her cheeks.

"Yeah, I think so. Mostly." It was hard to choke out words. I was certain she must be mad at me, but there was nothing.

She ate and talked easily while I stirred food around my plate. I wasn't hungry, and each bite I forced down felt like straw.

"Our parents are still coming over Tuesday, right? You'll be up for it?"

"Oh right, yeah, yeah. I'm sure it will be fine. I'm feeling a lot better." I swallowed another piece of bread. It tasted brittle and sat uncomfortably in my esophagus.

Melissa went to work and I went back to my place on the couch. I did feel better, everything except my stomach. I watched daytime television and sipped delicately at water that I could barely keep down. I had barely eaten anything, but I felt uncomfortably full, my belly too tight.

I lifted my dirty t-shirt to gaze at the expanse of my stomach. It was distended, pale and round as a moon. I pressed against it, but there was no pain. It was nothing. Nothing was wrong. I must be getting my period.

That night the coughing fits started. I coughed and coughed and Melissa just frowned, her mouth a small slash mark across her face. She brought home lozenges and asked me if I wanted to go see the doctor again. I refused. It would go away on its own. My wound was almost healed.

Monday evening, we watched television together, our arms pressed side to side. I was getting better. I was sure I'd be better tomorrow. I had to be; our parents were finally meeting each other. I didn't even have the energy to be nervous. My hair was pasted down with sweat, and when I dared to look in the mirror my skin was pale, but I was sure my morning shower would refresh me. Just a respiratory tract infection or something. This whole thing felt like a fever dream. My belly loomed smooth and round beneath my shirt. I'd have to find something to wear that would fit over it.

I coughed and pain racked through my body, dislodging something deep in my gut. My stomach clenched and unclenched painfully. I couldn't stop coughing. Tears poured down my cheeks and I fell to the floor, that awful dry taste in my throat. I couldn't get any air in. I couldn't breathe. Melissa's eyes widened. I felt absurdly grateful to see her concern.

"Beth, get up, get up." She pulled me to my feet. My legs felt rubbery and weak. She knotted fists beneath my ribs, thrusting hard, but it didn't help.

The mass shifted with each cough. My throat felt too full, too tight, too dry. Melissa let go and I sank back to the floor, sweat pouring down my face. My vision blurred, spots dancing before my eyes. Melissa's footsteps pattered to the phone in the hall, but it was too late. I couldn't breathe. I coughed and coughed and finally it loosened. It was coming up.

I crawled across the floor, limbs out of control. It was too much. It was way too much. My jaw seemed to unhinge and suddenly, with a single great heave, it came. My mouth filled with the taste of blood, phlegm, and something else, something foreign and deep and oily, and it all came out, a huge mass of *something* that pasted itself against the floor.

I gasped in massive, welcome breaths of fresh air and Melissa raced back into the room, phone in her hand and relief on her face. I heard her voice, far away beyond the rush of crisp air I took in. She knelt beside me, holding me tightly, kissing my forehead with light sweet kisses. I cried a little, overwhelmed, unable to help myself.

I was the patient again, light fresh sheets around me, cool sips of water for my aching throat.

The mass was still there the next morning. I padded out of bed, headed to the bathroom when the sight of it stopped me in my tracks. It loomed in the living room, thick mucousy strands pasting it to the corner. How could that have possibly come out of me? It was huge, at least two feet long. A thick off-white sac with strands of phlegm, green and deep red, running through it. I tasted blood and realized I was chewing on my lip.

Melissa came up behind me, wrapping her arms around my waist. "How are you feeling?"

"What is that? What the fuck is that? How did that come out of me?" I tried to keep my voice even, but I could hear the panic creeping in.

"Don't worry about it, I'll clean it up later. Let's just relax today."

"Melissa, that thing—what the fuck?" I couldn't catch my breath. How could she act like this was normal? My thoughts spun out of control, but she just looked at me. Her eyebrows knotted in displeasure and I swallowed heavy, my throat still tender.

I had no choice. I slumped in the kitchen chair, head in my hands. My body felt too empty now. Weak. Hollow. I moved around the house on stick-thin legs, trying not to look at the thing in our living room. Time ticked down and Melissa kept finding other things to do, fluffing her hair and getting dinner ready.

"Shouldn't we clean that up before our parents get here?"

She shrugged. "I don't think it's a big deal. It's fine there. I'll get it tomorrow."

I opened my mouth to say something but I hated the way she was looking at me, and I closed it again.

III.

My parents were bound to say something. They always spouted whatever was on their minds with no regard to being polite. For once I looked forward to it. I danced around anxiously when they came in, waiting for them to see it, to say *something*, but they barely spared it a glance.

"Hm. Couldn't have been you that did the decorating, Beth." My mum eyed Melissa's tasteful paintings and I sighed, resigned into my role for the evening.

Melissa's parents were beautiful. I had been so busy thinking about my . . . the *thing*, that I hadn't even had time to be anxious about this dinner. My father hadn't bothered to change out of his stained work clothes. Now that we all sat around the table together in heavy awkward silence, I remembered why we had been putting this off for so long.

Melissa's cooking was fantastic. She and her parents did most of the talking. My father looked bored, and my mother was silent, picking at her cuticles and pushing food around her plate. It wasn't so bad. I had expected things to be awful, but instead they were just awkward. Awkward I could deal with. Awkward I was used to.

I had barely eaten the last few days, and I made up for it now. My stomach was empty, gaping, and I was suddenly desperate to fill it with anything—steak, cheese, salad. Everyone else was finished eating and I still felt empty. Only the disapproving glare from Melissa's mother was able to stop me.

"Let's go into the living room for our coffee," Melissa said, breaking the silence. "Beth and I can clean up later."

"Are you sure that's a good idea?" I murmured.

"Oh, it's fine," she spoke. Too loud.

While I had napped that afternoon, she had cleaned the entire house. Nothing was out of place. Except for the giant misshapen *thing* in the corner. No one else seemed to notice, and for the first time all evening, conversation flowed easily. I barely heard it. I couldn't tear my eyes away from the pulsing mass in the corner.

I could hear something inside it, scratching.

It was in there. It had to be. Whatever the hell had been inside me had grown, and now it was in that thing . . . that shell . . . that cocoon.

"Melissa." I stood. I could see it clearly now. It was moving. Stretching. The outer shell was cracking.

"Not now." She leaned forward, speaking closely with my mother.

"Melissa, look at—"

And with a great tearing sound, it burst open. A thick tarry substance soaked the walls. It splattered my face, making my eyes stick together. I clawed at them, sending fat thick droplets soaring to the floor. I couldn't see it yet, but I could hear it.

Never had I had felt so empty, so flat.

It scrabbled against the ceiling with wings made of translucent flesh. Plasma and thick blood sprayed as it shook free of its encasement. Its body was thick and meaty, broken shards of bone tenting out of hunks of flesh stitched together with tendon. Its head was a throbbing heart, and antennas like arteries stretched out, exploring, rivulets of blood spraying out as it beat an insane heart-song.

I looked towards my girlfriend and her eyes filled with tears, but they were the wrong kind of tears.

"Oh, it's beautiful." She reached out her hand. The mutation of flesh perched on her pale skin, staining it with thick black blood. Our parents oohed.

"Help." I sank to my knees on the floor, my breaths shallow and deflating fast. I looked to my father, and his eyes were shining as he looked upon the thing. A faint smile played across his lips. "Dad." He took my hand and patted it between his own, the sense of joy on his face impossible to contradict.

"Well done, well done." Melissa's father pulled out a cigar.

Melissa's laughter tinkled as the thing circled around her head, wings flapping, clean now, sparkling shiny skin that danced in the light.

"Beth," my mother said, hesitant. I looked to her, hoping for the light of sanity in her eyes, at least. Instead, her eyes were shining. "Do you think I could hold her?"

ELEPHANTS THAT AREN'T

EVEN BEFORE THE critiques started, Lindsay was ready to run. She'd been ready to quit almost since she began. Art school. What a joke. Not even really art school, just community college. A way to build her portfolio, chase after her big dream. But already it was obvious she wasn't cut out for this.

Her portrait looked ridiculous up there next to the others. Amateur. A cartoon. She had worked on it for hours, but the colors still weren't blended; the eyes still looked fake, looked even worse next to elegant charcoal portraits and abstract acrylics.

Her guts clenched as Chad (not Mr. Brooks, just Chad, so chill, so relaxed, so middle-aged cool) went through their work. Pretty, barely nineteen-year-old students, already vastly more talented and accomplished than she was after twenty-eight years. One girl had just painted her eyes, dark and wet and incredibly detailed. The prettiest girl in class had done this insanely unflattering, distorted version of herself, painted directly on a mirror. The guy who sat next to her had done an abstract that was still somehow instantly recognizable as himself. Stylish, meaningful. Not like the hot mess it was when Lindsay tried that style.

Finally Lindsay's, she was next in line, and it looked like a kid had drawn it. She had tried so fucking hard and it still looked wrong; the proportions were all off, and she was mid-grimace when Chad looked at her.

167

"Okay, now we move on to Lindsay's piece. Lindsay, can you tell us a little bit about what you were trying to accomplish here?"

She had notes in front of her but her hands were sweaty and her eyes were blurring and the words were so weird and formal. Mom had been able to rattle off deep introspection of a piece from the top of her head. Yet another talent Lindsay hadn't inherited. "Just . . . I was just trying to make it look like me. Um. I used some old pictures, plus a mirror, and I did a bunch of sketches, but it just . . . I don't know. It didn't come out how I wanted it to." The girl next to her tried to smile comfortingly, but it just made Lindsay feel worse. She wanted this class to be over. The whole semester, in fact.

"Okay, it's great that you used a mirror, and there's nothing wrong with going with a literal interpretation of a portrait, but I think what went wrong here is what we talked about before. It's a good effort, but you weren't really drawing what you see, were you? You were drawing what you expected to see." He pointed to the eyes. "We can really see it here. This is something a lot of girls—sorry, women, do. They idealize the eyes, make them bigger, prettier than they really are." Cartoonish. He meant cartoonish. No one had eyelashes like that. "When you're doing a literal portrait, what you want to do is really focus on what you're seeing, or, conversely, if you wanted to do a stylized graphic portrait, that's fine too, but you have to really know what style you're going for there, or you end up with something muddy and in between, like this."

He moved on to the next picture and her cheeks flamed. She should know better than this by now. She should be working harder. This was pathetic. Tears slid down her cheeks and it was ridiculous, a grown woman crying, it was *really* ridiculous, a grown woman taking this class, thinking it would do anything for her future. A waste of fucking time. A waste of a perfectly good inheritance.

"All right, we'll finish up the rest of the critiques

168

tomorrow morning. Remember, tomorrow is the final day for midterm project pitches. We've got some really interesting stuff coming in so far. A short film, an illustrated book, photo exhibits . . . if you haven't touched base with me yet, tomorrow's gotta be the day. And make it cool. Dig deep. I wanna see the best you've got."

The best she's got. Jesus. What if he had already seen it? The class dismissed, some of the kids stayed behind chatting, but she slinked off. She had a hell of a lot of work to do if her pitch was going to be ready for tomorrow.

References spread all over the table. Illustrated fairy tales and comic books and other people's DeviantArt printouts, and pages and pages of loose paper, tight dark sketches that all amounted to the same thing: garbage.

A triptych of fairy tales, that was the vision. Red Riding Hood and the wolf on the left, Sleeping Beauty on the right, and Alice in the centre. Her own *personal* triptych, the ones that had meant the most to her as a kid. The ones Mom had read aloud, over and over. Exquisite detail, beautiful colors, somehow pull it all together into three paintings that interwove with each other.

Sounded like a great idea. Looked like a great idea, in her mind's eye at least, but when she tried to sketch it out? Oh man. The proportions were technically not too bad, but the anatomy was stiff. The detail in the background, the things that interwove together—the forest, the thorns and roses and mushrooms—looked perfect in her mind, but on paper, not so much. Oh, someone else could have pulled it off. Easily. But in her hands, it looked more like a junior high art project.

Junior high. Hell, elementary even, when she had been considered advanced. Precocious. But everyone had caught up with her and she had neglected her skills and now here she was, up past midnight with class at 8:00 a.m. the next day and nothing ready for her pitch, just a bunch of half-assed sketches, the best of which looked like she had traced them, because she had. Nothing original. Nothing unique. Nothing special.

Her face was greasy in her hands. The later it got, the worse her interpretations got. Her eyes kept blinking closed. She may as well go to bed. Lick her wounds. Face Chad in the morning and hope he could somehow guide her. Yeah. Be willing. Don't be embarrassed. Be willing.

It was so frustrating, though. It was inside her, she could feel it; the desire was there, but she just didn't know how to get it out, how to translate it into something she could use.

Her blankets smelled sweaty and unwashed, but she sank into bed gratefully. She closed her eyes, but her brain wasn't ready to shut up. Not yet. *You'll never pull it off. This is a waste of time, a waste of money. A waste of what Mom left you. Just because she had a successful career in the arts doesn't mean you can. If you really had what it takes, don't you think you would have done it already? What are you gonna do when the money runs out? Back to the call center, back to a miserable, uninspired life. This was your chance, but you took it too late, and you blew it.*

Lindsay rolled over. Too hot. She couldn't get comfortable. What difference did it make now? It was past one and she was going to be exhausted tomorrow no matter what. Toss the blanket off. Okay. Just a few hours of sleep. Just a few hours of quiet.

You had so much promise when you were a kid but you wasted your time and now you're wasting it again. Twenty-eight! It's too late to be going back to school, especially for an art class. Do you know how tough the business is?

Her eyes popped back open, stared into the swirling darkness around her, at blinking clock lights. Almost one-thirty. Goddamn time flew at the worst times. Okay. Just a couple of hours. She was gonna look like shit in the morning, the only person in class with bags under their eyes and, God forbid, even the beginnings of wrinkles.

Okay.

Deep breaths.

Count to ten.

Don't cry.

Count to ten, back down to one, back up to ten.

Mom would be so disappointed if she saw this.

Okay.

No sleep. Not like this. The room was too quiet and her thoughts were too loud and awful and it just kept getting later, or earlier, whatever. Turn on the TV, volume down really low, just to have a little bit of white noise in the room. Cartoons. Something comforting. Like Mom used to put on while she was working in the other room. Those old ones. Mom grew up with them, but Lindsay hated them. Hated the way the characters moved, like they were made of rubber. Like they had no bones.

She closed her eyes again, and lights flickered against her eyelids. She couldn't make out what the voices on the television were saying, but she could hear them just enough that they blurred into a low murmur and that was perfect.

Okay. Breathe in and out.

Up to ten, back down again.

Drawing when she was a kid never felt this stressful. Dad didn't encourage it much, not after he and Mom split up. Didn't want to her to turn out like her mother, he said, but he was just angry. Everything he hated about Mom after the divorce was what he used to love. Her independence. Her dedication to her work. Every second weekend, that's all she got with Mom, but it was special. Lindsay always brought her sketches, and Mom was so fucking proud, told her she would be as good as her someday, and back then it seemed like it could be true. She framed almost all of them. Treated them like they were special. The orange tabby with a few blades of grass across his cheek, the lighthouse copied from the cover of a book, the pencil crayon portrait of Mom . . .

Oh, what was that game she used to do to try to fall asleep, when she was a kid?

Something about the pictures.

Yeah. That was it. A weird little thing. When she was sleeping at home, at Dad's, she would pretend she was at Mom's. Close her eyes and picture herself there. Picture it so well, fill in all the details, convince herself so much that when she opened her eyes, she would be surprised to still be at Dad's.

Yeah, she used to have a real imagination. The coarse blanket pulled up under her chin. The glossy black end table piled with comic books, the stumpy little lamp. Then the walls. The pictures. The cat with the grass. The lighthouse.

God, she hardly thought about that apartment anymore. Mom moved, then she died, and somewhere in there, years had passed. Whatever happened to those drawings?

She could still picture it.

Fill in the details. Coarse blanket. Knitted by her grandmother. The room was oriented differently than the one she lay in now, the bed in a different direction. The big window along the left wall. The little table. The pictures. More. Stuff she thought she had forgotten. The dark green rug, little catches in it from the dog's toenails. The sound of the television, downstairs, background while Mom prowled back and forth, making wild notes on loose paper. That pleasant drone that let her thoughts drift away.

Tobacco drifting up the stairs. Mom pretended she didn't smoke, only did it late at night when Lindsay was supposed to be long asleep. The sounds from the television were bright and cheerful.

That smell. Smoke. She could definitely smell smoke.

Her eyes popped open, and the cat was leering at her between blades of grass, the lamp was close enough to knock off the table and she gasped, and the air was dry and dusty, but she blinked hard and it all disappeared.

It was morning. She was exhausted. It was time to go to school.

Chad's office was small and oppressive. His decorating didn't help make it appear any bigger—dark blinds closed and every available surface cluttered with books and magazines and cut-outs and half-used pans of paint. The space he cleared off for her notes spilled over, papers cascading to the floor.

Lindsay tore the ends of her hoodie to shreds while she waited. Why had she brought all her sketches? He didn't need to see *all* of them to get the point. Some of them were barely even sketches, just a few shapes and lines, scratches where she had gotten frustrated. But he looked at all of them with equal measure, giving ample consideration to each.

"The vision is there, or almost there, isn't it?" Chad said finally. "I can tell you're getting at something with these, almost certainly the idea is there, but you just can't get it out yet." He leaned over the desk, meeting her eyes. "What are you trying to say with this project?"

She chewed her lip, tasted blood. "I want to work with fairy tales . . . like . . . like illustrative kind of art. But more."

"The triptych is an interesting idea, but I think you need to go deeper. Illustrative art was what your mother specialized in. You don't necessarily have to follow in her footsteps." He gestured to her drawings. "These are all very stiff. Restricted. You're thinking too hard about it. You need to be freer. Pull it from somewhere deep inside yourself. I want this project to really represent you." His finger tapped one of the drawings. "Stylistically, these are very conventional—you're trying to copy too much. You're doing what you think is expected. But what I expect is for you is to pull it out of here." He jabbed his finger at his own chest. His heart.

"How?" That was what she *wanted* to do. He was right. That was exactly what wasn't there. The heart. That connection—she could see it in other people's work, and she knew she wouldn't advance until she could find a way to rip it out of herself.

"It's different for everyone. You have to find who you are as an artist." He shuffled through her papers again. "Your drawing skills are rudimentary, but that will come. And that's not the most important part, at least not for this project. I wanna see the stuff I can't teach, not from books or lessons. Pull it out. Why are you here, Lindsay?"

He was being nice. He was trying to inspire her, but tears were prickling at her eyes. "I don't know," she mumbled. Looked at her shoes.

Chad sighed. "Well, see if you can figure it out. If you can't shake loose, maybe this isn't the right place for you." He glanced up, and at the sight of her tears, his eyes widened. "Hey, I'm not trying to discourage you. You've gotta build up a tougher skin. Art is hard. It takes time. Relax. Don't push yourself so much."

Lindsay rubbed her eyes with her sleeves, slouched down in her seat. "I want to do better. This isn't what I want to be doing. I'm sorry." She was almost as old as Chad, for Christ's sake, closer to his age than the other students, and here she was, crying like a baby.

"Okay. Okay. Okay. Don't feel bad. It's alright. How 'bout this? Take the weekend, think it over. Come up with some new sketches. Relax. Take your time. Have fun with it." He reached over to pat her hand, draw her attention back to him. "Don't be so afraid. Let your imagination come out. I want to see *you* in this. Go deeper. Go darker. Go wherever it takes you. You don't have to do what you think I expect. Do something that's you."

Lindsay gathered up her things, muttered a thank you on the way out the door.

The whole weekend.

Great.

She should have just quit.

Get past it. Move past your fear. Dig deep inside yourself. Let it out.

What does that even mean?

The drawings didn't get better. It all looked the same. Think out of the box? She *was* the box. Her pencil just traced over the same tracks over and over again. Looking through her books and printouts for inspiration just made it worse. Was it this hard for other illustrators to pull it out of themselves? Not the good ones. There was no way.

It was impossible to draw with tears dripping from her eyes. She wasn't making any progress. Forget it. Get a good night's sleep. Try again in the morning.

She lay back in bed, didn't even bother washing her makeup off. She was so fucking tired. She wished she was someone else. She wished she was somewhere else. Anyplace else but here.

She closed her eyes. No more thinking. No more worrying about the stupid fucking project, those stupid pretty girls in their pretty frames, what was so unique about that anyway? What was so personal? She liked fairy tales. Who cares? There was no artistry to that.

Stop thinking.

Go somewhere else.

Pretend you're floating.

Oh, like last night. That had helped, hadn't it? Back at Mom's place. The pictures on the walls. The

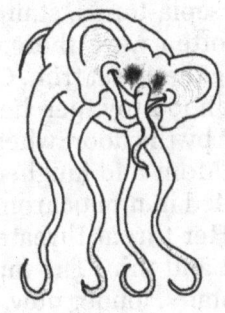

bed at a different angle. It wasn't so hard this time. The room came flying back to greet her. She *wanted* to be there. Back when she was comfortable in her skin. Back when it didn't feel so disgusting to just exist.

The lamp next to her. The covers tight beneath her chin.

The television playing downstairs, a distant drone. The smell of tobacco. Mom's feet padding back and forth.

The room expanded around her, not her small one-bedroom apartment now, the higher ceilings of Mom's, the window looking out at the moon, the sounds of the streets dull and far away, but there.

The tap of lighter, the smell of a cigarette freshly lit.

Lindsay opened her eyes, just a crack, and the vision didn't change. She blinked hard. The ceiling stretched above her, and the cat and the lighthouse and the pencil crayon portrait stared back at her. She peeled back the blanket, and it wasn't a dream, because she felt its itchy weight against her hand.

This wasn't possible. Of course it wasn't. But that sensible voice sounded far away. The truth was clear in front of her. Even the fear that bubbled in her chest felt distant.

Not a dream, no. Something else.

Things weren't quite the same. The whole room was covered in a layer of soot. Her finger against the lamp came away filthy. No matter how much she blinked, everything was sepia-toned, stained with brown. But details she had forgotten were there. The delicate carving that swirled along the closet trim. Charlie the horse, her mom's favorite childhood toy, perched on the dresser. The stain on the floor by the door, where she had tracked paint on her foot and Mom had laughed. All there, but swirled with dust, painted in monochrome.

Her throat threatened to close over, the air came so tight and thin. The music from the television trickled up the stairs, louder now.

I think I want to wake up.

The first pinch was gentle, too gentle; the second one tore the skin, sent deep brown drops of blood to the floor. It was real.

No. She obviously hadn't transported to Mom's. That was crazy. A dream. But not a regular dream. Something else. Like a lucid dream. Something where she was in control.

Maybe this was how she broke through into her subconscious.

A light flickered in the hallway.

Of course. The rest of the apartment. There was more to see outside of this room. There was nothing to be afraid of. There couldn't be.

She couldn't decide what to do. Stepping out of the bed was like stepping into a river. Her limbs felt buoyant and light. Each step away from the bed made it seem further and further away, the room tunneling away from her.

The pictures on the wall didn't look quite right. Not hers. Better? Oh, much better. Richer details. Better anatomy. Fully realized.

This was where her imagination lived.

But she couldn't ignore the rat-tat-tat of her heart. Frightened little mouse.

Don't be afraid.

The air crackled with static.

This was good, wasn't it? Or had she just cracked, gone completely insane, gone into some kind of stress disassociation or something?

Well. There was only one way to find out.

The hall was cloudy, a haze of smoke blurring out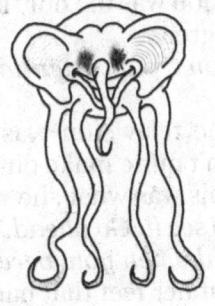

the finer details. The upstairs of the apartment was small, just the two bedrooms, one on either end of the short hall, and the stairway leading downstairs to the main floor. Mom had painted right over the stains on the walls, beautiful ladies, faeries, and Lindsay felt a surge of fear at seeing them—why fear? Why not pleasure? They were changed, subtly, and without their bright colors their smiles looked forced.

This wasn't what she would have pictured her inner landscape like. She would have wanted it to be colorful, beautiful. Lush and growing. But this made sense. Old dusty hallways full of claustrophobia and fear.

The light was coming from Mom's room. The door was closed, but in the inch of space beneath, a dull glow and dripping shadows. Hands damp with sweat, Lindsay clutched the doorknob. This was hers to explore. The doorknob twisted back and forth, but it didn't open.

"Hello?" Her throat was thick and dry and the words came out cracked.

Behind the door, a murmur.

Mom?

Downstairs, the crackling static of the television rose in volume. Saxophone music, slow and disjointed, called to her. She drifted.

The living room was the same as she remembered. Wasn't it? The plaid-backed chair, thick carpet, wood-paneled walls, shadows writhing in the corners. The television was the only light, and it pulsed, turned the sepia tones green.

Don't pay attention to that empty feeling in your chest.

The television was speaking, saying something she couldn't quite make out.

This was what she was here to see.

So see it. Go ahead. Go sit in front of the television like you did when you were a kid. Go ahead. Go ahead.

But her feet that had been so light a moment ago sank

178

into the floor and this felt like her last chance to turn back and she wanted to, she wanted to wake up, but she didn't know how.

So instead, she sat down in front of the TV.

Cartoons. Like Mom used to watch. The old ones. Black and white, not quite white, tones of grey. Grainy flaws in the paper spackled over the screen.

A beach. Animated waves crashing, punching the shore. Faces in the waves, not faces, eyes leering, frames skipping too fast, like they were in a hurry. The sun spun crazily in the sky.

Bile in the back of her throat.

Something sticky writhed across the screen. An elephant. No. Not quite an elephant. Emaciated, with legs too long and wriggling. It lurched across the screen, rubbery trunk pulsing, quivering.

There was nothing to be afraid of, just a cartoon, but the panic squeezed her chest like a vice. Her eyes were starting to hurt. She didn't like this anymore, and she tried to stand up, but her legs gave out beneath her.

More elephants, fleshy trunks gripping the withered tails of the ones ahead, the saxophone screaming, they spilled across the screen, movements exaggerated, somehow nauseating.

Their eyes weren't right.

Just a cartoon.

They were spirals, they were moving and insane, scratched out smears of ink.

The ocean's mouth opened, sucked them into its depths, spat them back out, more distorted, crumpled.

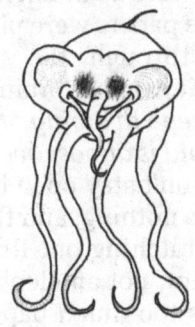

Dizzy. She was so dizzy.

The headache was *textured, palpable, crinkling, the elephants looked out of the screen and something in her brain opened, pain like a nail driven into her skull, opening a space, gaping like a mouth, she was screaming not screaming and the elephants' voices were garbled and when the tears had cleared but her head still went thump thump thump, the screen had changed, the elephants were slumped over, empty, sun gone, blacked out by the moon.*

The moon's eyes wobbled in its skull, fell to the beach. The moon flickered behind the sun the sun flickered behind the moon.

The waves turned to smoke, black smoke that churned and covered the screen, turned it black black black, staining her skin with soot.

The music stretched.

Everything was heavy, her breathing was slow slow slow, didn't feel right, didn't feel good, she wanted to wake up now, the screen was black and she couldn't see anything.

Could hear them.

Wet chewing sounds.

Wet wet wet.

Oh, her head hurt.

No bones, long legs, no bones. She didn't wake up or didn't remember waking up but she was drawing, her hands were a million miles away, the sketches were blurry, but the papers were piling up. It was hard to keep her eyes open through the migraine, through the elephants tramping on her brain.

Keep drawing though, just keep drawing, the weekend is almost over, she's breaking through finally, her eyes won't stay open but she's moving through the paper like it's nothing, and that's real, that's inspired.

Scratching out Red Riding Hood and the wolf is an elephant, not an elephant no, she wakes up drooling and there's too much paper to look through it all but thank

Christ, her hands keep moving and she can feel it, she can feel it, she's on to something. Finally.

Monday brought painful sanity. Lindsay flipped through her sketchbook while she slammed back a coffee. Went crazy all weekend and nothing to show for it, just bags under her eyes and more of the same uninspired sketches.

What the fuck had happened to her? She had felt like she was on to something. If that's what diving into your imagination feels like, she didn't want it anymore. Channeling her muse or channeling her mom, it just hurt.

The day was grey and flat but she slid on her sunglasses anyway. Felt like the kind of day where you need a disguise. Dry-swallow a couple of aspirin; the thought of a glass of water to go along with them was vomit-inducing. Even a coffee had been too much for her shaky stomach, especially once she got on the bus. The wheels rattled beneath her and brought a filthy taste up into her mouth.

Maybe today would be her last day. If this midterm project didn't go well, there wasn't much point in struggling through the rest of the year. It wasn't like she was gonna get a job out of this anyway. The whole point was to build her portfolio, go to real art school, just like Mom, network with more artists, and then what? This wasn't the life for her. She wasn't built for it.

Looking out the windows made her feel even more nauseated. The scenery they passed looked shallow, cardboard. In her lap, her hands were stained with ink and her sketchbook was falling

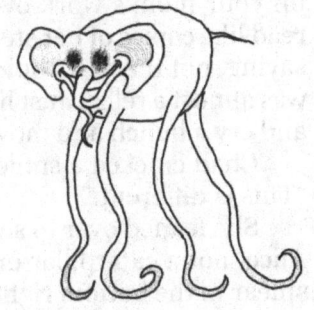

apart. Why was she going to class today at all? She shouldn't be embarrassing herself anymore.

But the bus pulled up to the school and there was no way she could tolerate another bumpy ride back, so she slithered inside.

Her heart hurt. She hesitated in the hallway, torn between cleaning out her locker and going in to get it over with.

"Hey, got something new to show me?" Chad's voice was an ice pick in her brain. Too cheerful for this early in the morning.

"Sort of . . ."

"Come on back to my office."

She followed him. Didn't bother taking her sunglasses off. Had she even put on deodorant today? Her teeth were fuzzy and sour. Chad cleared off a space on his desk and reached out for her sketchbook, and something got stuck in her chest. "I don't think—"

But he took it and she let him, watched him flip through, his skin rosy and well-rested and how the fuck could anyone be so bright in the morning? God, weren't artists supposed to be more damaged? She slumped into her chair. Braced herself. Waited for the news that she wasn't cut out for this so she could quit gracefully and get on with the rest of her shitty life.

Chad nodded. "These are a little better. A little looser. You're still not thinking outside the box, though. I looked up your mom's work over the weekend. These really do read like copies of her stuff—and I hope you don't mind me saying, not the best copies. They lack the life hers had." It was almost a relief. Just listen for a while and then go home and cry a bunch and move on.

Chad cracked a smile, tapped his finger on the paper. "This is different."

She leaned over to see what he was pointing at. Below Alice, not a caterpillar or a rose bush or a Mad Hatter. A smear in the bottom right corner of the page, black ink, an elephant. No. Not quite an elephant. The headache throbbed again, a scream near the bottom of her occipital bone.

"I don't remember drawing that."

He flipped to the next page. "Really? Here's another one. These are interesting. Do you do much work like this?"

She was shaking her head no, she could feel it, but she was a thousand miles away, a million miles away, on a grey beach somewhere. Chad turned the page. "Hey, there's more," more black smears danced below last week's fairy tale drawings. He turned another page, his left eye twitching. "It's a flip book, isn't it?" He flipped back to the cover and thumbed through the pages.

She wanted to reach out and stop him, but her hand was heavy and numb in her lap. Her throat felt thick, gritty.

He flipped through the pages rapidly, watching the smear flicker and move. Reflected in his glasses, the elephants marched across the page, writhed and flopped, boneless in the sand.

She would remember drawing them, wouldn't she?

He closed the sketchbook, opened it, flipped through again. His forehead shone with sweat and his jaw slackened, just slightly. When he spoke again, his voice was strangled and hoarse. "I think you should work on this. There's something here. There's something unique here. This is yours." He handed
the sketchbook back to
her. She wanted to slap it
from his hands, but she
didn't. She took it back,
clutched it to her chest.

"They're not quite
there yet, but keep
working."

"I don't know . . .
something doesn't feel
right." She was on the

ceiling, looking down at the pair of them, talking, something beneath chattering and moving, a song playing off-key somewhere. The colors in the room dulled, went grey. She blinked and she was back in her body.

Chad's head was in his hands. "Are you okay?"

"Just a headache. Go home. Work. Come back when it's done."

"But what about class—what about—"

"Come back when it's done."

The porcelain glared up at her, too white in her dim bathroom. She heaved again, emptied her guts. The sick was dark and gritty, felt like it was *tearing* something as she expelled it. The headache came, pulsing and writhing, lengthening and shimmying—

No.

That didn't make sense.

She was feverish.

She had tried to pick up her sketchbook when she got home, and the pages were as warm as flesh, and before she could see what Chad saw, whatever it was that made him believe she was an artist, the sickness flooded through her and now here she was, throwing up black moss and she should go to the hospital, but she was so, so tired.

When everything was out of her, everything that would come, she let her head hang over the toilet for a while. She had flushed several times but the scent was still there. She just wasn't ready to move yet. Time passed in pulses and finally, she pulled herself up the walls.

She opened the window. It was cold, but it cleared out her room. The breeze caressed sheets of paper loose from her sketchbook, pasted them to the walls. She couldn't keep her eyes open, so she collapsed onto the bed. Lots of time to work. First, sleep.

And almost immediately she was there. Mom's

apartment. From downstairs, the saxophone blared louder, urging her awake. Insistent. The walls shook with the sound of it, the pictures on the walls bulging towards her. Grey-green light poured into the room, casting crazy shadows with long legs. The floor rippled angrily, a grey ocean. She stumbled out of bed.

Across the hall, the door was open. That was where the light was coming from.

Instead of Mom's piles of half-used paints, instead of the references and mess taped up to every corner of the room, there was just a drawing desk. A chair. Clean white walls, white as paper.

"Oh."

An inkwell, reams of clean white paper. And equipment she didn't understand. A projector, reels of film, and that crazy light. An old memory turned over in her head, Mom explaining how they had done the movement in those first cartoons. Tracing reels of film, frame by frame. Turning jazz singers into crazy dancing walruses for Betty Boop.

"It's called a rotoscope." Her mother's voice. "It's a gift."

Lindsay started to turn, to see what she had been looking for all this time, but hands gripped her head like a vice, set the headache flaring again. "Don't turn around." And it didn't sound like her mother's voice this time. Not even a little bit.

The fingers were wet. Sticky. Not fingers at all.

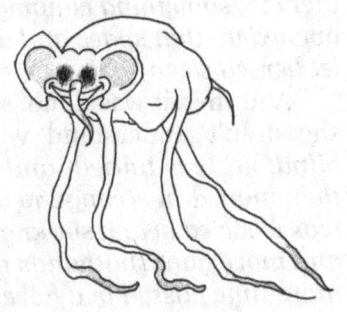

"I need to close your eyes." The damp appendages touched her eyes, and something gummy sealed them shut.

"What's happening? What's going on?"

"Shh. You can't see yet. It's a surprise. Stay where you are."

Something brushed past her, adjusted the equipment, then wrapped around her arm. Click click click went the rotoscope, and it moved her arm, and she started to draw.

Her mouth was dry and her eyes were heavy but slowly they blinked open and she was drawing elephants, she was drawing the sea, she was drawing things she didn't know how to draw and day turned night over and over again and she kept drawing.

And it helped her.

The limbs that helped her draw moved her hands and advanced the film so she didn't have to see, and they worked together because they had no fingers but she did, and she had no eyes but they had so many.

Her hands got tired but she kept drawing. Her headache screamed but she kept drawing. Pain replaced time.

click click click as the rotoscope advanced to the next frame and she kept tracing and the rush of creation was manic and sometimes she might have been screaming but the blindfold covered up the worst of it.

Every time she opened her eyes more drawings were added to the pile and how many drawings did it take to make a cartoon? So many. So, so many.

They never got tired and she could sleep while they drew and that sounded so good, sleep and create and let them in, something clawing at her brain, something that opened up that space and wedged itself inside and so she let herself sleep

And then it was done, she could feel that it was done, she didn't understand what she had drawn but *her blindfold was untied, and her limbs were rubber now, they moved in strange new ways and more machinery was wheeled in and she knew not to turn around this time and more handsnothands moved her, controlled her and more time passed in a haze of pain but*

Finally, the film reel was in her hands.

She'd never seen one before, not an old one like this, not in real life. It felt . . . not like she would have expected it to. Too soft. But it fit in her hands so well.

And it was hers. She made it. All hers. Not her mom's. This was *Lindsay's,* scratched out of a deep place inside her brain, her true self, her true calling.

She couldn't wait to see it.

And if she couldn't remember just exactly what it was, well, that was part of the mania of creation, wasn't it? That was what it was supposed to feel like.

Like a child, she cradled it gently to her chest on the way to the school.

She was late, but she entered the classroom with confidence. One of the other girls was at the front of the class, next to a blurry abstract. She was talking, but Chad wasn't listening. He looked older, slouched over his desk, unshaven. No one turned to look at her, but Chad's eyes flickered up and he cut off the student in mid-sentence. "Lindsay, finally." He stood up. He was wearing the same clothes he had been the last time she had seen him, only they were ink-stained now. Filthy.

"Uh," the girl next to the portrait stammered.

Chad waved Lindsay in. "Lindsay has something important to show us." The door clicked shut behind her. This was it.

Everything was ready for her. There was a reel-to-reel projector tucked behind his desk—she had never seen it here before—and he wheeled it out to the front, pulled down the blinds. "It's ready, isn't it?" His eyes were wet, bloodshot. Lindsay's mouth wouldn't work to

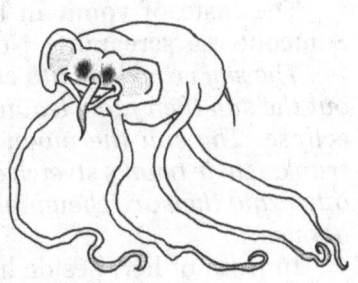

reply. It didn't matter. Chad continued the business of setting up the room, pulled down the dusty screen that she would play her film on. Then he looked at her. Lindsay stepped forward. The class shuffled uncomfortably. She ignored their whispering.

She had never used a projector before, but it was comfortable in her hands*nothands*. They seemed to know what to do all on their own. Chad's chair screeched as he pulled it forward. She could smell him. A damp, animal smell.

She loaded the film.

This was it. The moment was pregnant. She had done it. She had *made* something. Her pride shook, though, left a weird taste in her stomach. How had she even gotten here? The room was soft around her, flimsy.

She played the film.

She had gotten it right.

A creature was moving across the screen, dragging its legs. Its trunk trailed behind it, crumpled and sore. Its eyes were scratched out. The music was slow then fast then slow. The beach was in the distance.

Foggy. The murmuring in the classroom was far away. Where was the music coming from? Lindsay was very tired. Each slow blink was a rest, a silence, a relief.

the elephantnotelephant was joined by something tall, very tall, it stretched up into the grey sky, a tower with legs that have too many joints, or maybe no joints at all everything is moving very very slowly then very very fast

The taste of vomit in her throat. The taste of ink. Someone was screaming. Not her.

The sky crackled with electricity, black dots that blot out the sun then fade, leaving impressions in the sky. An eclipse. The sun the moon the sun. The elephants join trunks, their trunks stretch out long and writhe into each other and they are chewing and everything is moving all at once

In front of her, beside her, her classmates slid out of

their chairs, twitching to the floor, the smell of salt water and sand. Their frothing mouths.

The elephants the elephants the elephants

"The door won't open!"

Everything was so fucking beautiful.

The chaos around her was easy to ignore. She could relax into the film. Enjoy the aftermath of creation. Chad was beside her, and everything that was moving was slow and liquid. The sounds of vomiting, the sounds of screaming, it all faded away. She was weightless. She was boneless. Even if she wanted to move, she couldn't.

The day turned to night to day to night the sky was churning, the ocean was churning, the black smoke burrowed out of the water, so thick she could smell it.

Something was leaking out of her mouth but she was not afraid, she could never be afraid.

No, she was satisfied.

The ocean swallowed up the tower and the elephants and her mouth opened and it was all coming out, it tasted like ink and sand and salt and everyone was screaming, they opened the window and the outside was sepia-toned and the elephants—

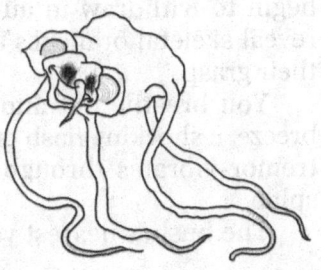

FIRST, A BLINDING LIGHT

THE HEADACHE IS brief but leaves you dazed. Floaters dance across your vision, disappear.

You breathe in, step onto the path. Uneven gravel crunches beneath your feet. The trail winds a slow wave up and down hills, bracketed by overgrown weeds and rotten leaves that pulp beneath tangled trees.

This road leads home, or if you turn around, it leads everywhere else. You could walk it with your eyes closed, and you have on occasion, blurry-eyed after some endless party, bushes shifting in the wind, guided by instinct around curves that may as well be the curves of your own hand. It's wide enough for two people to walk comfortably, but you've rarely ever passed anyone on your solitary trips home.

You've never seen whoever maintains the path, but every spring the trees and bushes are mown back to allow your passage through. When the long days of summer stretch on, the trees claw across the stones, reaching for you, tearing your clothes and grabbing fistfuls of hair. They begin to withdraw in autumn, when the foliage falls to reveal skeletal branches and whatever lay twisted within their grasp.

You breathe out and a red-violet leaf twists on the breeze, a shocking flash of color against the greying sky. A tremor vibrates through your tailbone, creeps up your spine.

The bushes nearest you rustle. Between their shaggy

leaves, movement. You peer into the configuration of rotten berries and broken branches and it moves again, the shining flank of something much too large to be contained here, something that growls and the muscles in its neck twitch and you glimpse sharp sharp teeth and you barely catch yourself from falling and that's when you see her, coming up the path behind you, her pale face, a smear of dark hair and the sunken green glow of her eyes.

The girl approaches and you didn't see anything in the bushes and you force a smile and you use the halfway smile you use when passing a stranger. She doesn't smile back. Not quite. She looks familiar, her movements strangely liquid as she closes the distance between you.

"Hello," she says, and then she speaks your name.

Her eyes flash from green to yellow, something alive in the irises.

"Do I know you from somewhere?" Your mouth doesn't open all the way. Your voice is not your own.

"Yes, you do." She nods ahead. "We're going the same way. Would you like to walk together?"

You don't say yes.

You fall in line with her, the rhythm of her feet. She tilts her chin up as she walks, as though she is watching the sky. You still feel the presence of her eyes on you, the way they saw past your skin, past muscle and sinew and blood and meat and all the way down to the cold hardness of bone. Something boils in your gut, expands, contracts, you can't take your eyes off her, the way her skin is shadowed grey by her dark hair, that tangled cloud that moves to reveal only a sliver of cheekbone or the pale cracked edge of a smile.

Her features are single puzzle pieces that you can't coalesce into a whole. You can't place her, you've never known her and it makes you uneasy to hear your name on her lips. She did say your name, didn't she? She keeps her head tilted to a sky where no sun shines. You follow her gaze and you don't see anything, nothing at all, and gravel fills your throat and when you swallow it your insides cramp.

You wish you were home, your chair, your books, your bed. It hurts to be here. It hurts. It hurts.

You're almost home. Echoes of your own footprints scuff across the path, each step one you've taken hundreds of times, thousands of times before. You feel your feet press away from the ground and a nameless fear wakes. "I'm sorry," you hear yourself saying, "but I can't place where I know you from . . . "

As if in reply, her mottled hand brushes through the pine needles of an encroaching tree. Does something else move in its branches? A cloud blots out the dim light of the sun and in the flutter of her fingertips you find a memory.

Her name hangs on your lips but your throat is too full to speak. Your neighbor, or maybe she lived down the street. Dark hair, pale skin, those glowing eyes. Rainboots splashing water, caterpillars accidentally squashed before transformation, a purple sunset, a smile at recess, and then nothing. She was gone.

They plastered dozens of posters of her face downtown, on every pole, in every window of every corner store. They used her school picture and photocopied it over and over, so many times that eventually her darkened eyes looked scribbled in charcoal and her face distorted into a horrific caricature of the girl you knew. Your parents ushered you from the room for weeks when the news came on but that didn't stop the fear from boring into you, a new fear that was too big to be contained within your body, so it leaked out and moved through every shadow in your bedroom at night. You had nightmares for years. How could you forget?

You speak her name but don't hear your voice. Everything trembles a little looser. You want to touch her, you want to turn her face toward you, you want to look in her eyes, but you are afraid to know and already you are certain.

She was dead. You always believed she was dead.

Your feet keep moving, keep crunching gravel, crushing errant leaves. The trees stretch taller here, reaching overhead, bony fingers that touch a sky where no birds fly, where nothing moves at all.

The girl is smiling. Even if you can't see her mouth, you can feel how sharp her teeth are. You want to ask a question but your tongue is thick and slow and something deep in your throat is pulsing and ahead there a turn in the road, a fork in the path, a different way home.

You think this is the perfect time to step away. The rightward fork leads back to the street, a safe street, just a few blocks from home, a street with houses and fences instead of bare trees and dark eyes.

You could walk away from whatever is happening here.

You owe her nothing. There's no need to say goodbye. You turn, you take a step, and your feet seem fuzzy but finally you make them move, and then her cold, small hand brushes your arm and it feels like all your muscles are stretching out at once when she whispers "It's not safe, stay with me," and that's when you see them.

Sharp angry bushes surround the exit of the trail and within those brambles you catch a flash of teeth. A hot huff of breath releases the stench of rotting meat. Huge eyes blink yellow, they stare through you, and a forked tongue hisses through the air and though foliage shrouds its face you can tell what it is but you won't say it out loud.

"Don't go that way," you hear, and it's unclear if she said it, or if it's your own voice in your head.

You listen.

You've made your last choice.

"Shouldn't we . . . get help?" The words tumble from your mouth, splash like raindrops on the stones, and you realize you don't have your phone. Or your wallet. Or your clothes. You don't have anything at all. You are just a body, but even that feels so far away now. You are just a soul, a flash of light, a thrumming vibration of energy following a woman up a path you have walked a thousand times before and really, truly, you are almost home.

You keep walking.

The sun peeks from behind the clouds and the hazy light bleeds to a warmer hue. Something cracks open at the crown of your head, spreads with a pleasant tingle down your neck, through your shoulders. It curls down your biceps, past your elbows, into your wrists, your fingers, and something seems to leave you. You realize the girl is speaking. Something about how you never kept in touch.

A shudder moves through your shoulders and creeps down your spine and you wonder if you're really still walking, and though the crunch crunch crunch of your feet is reassuring, it is not enough.

The girl is smiling. You want to ask what happened to her. You should ask her where she's been, and you try, the words are halfway tumbled out of your mouth when you remember and your voice shrinks.

Sometime last year maybe, maybe longer ago, wrapped in sweaty sheets, unable to sleep, sunken shadows under your eyes reflected in your phone, you saw her familiar face in your suggested friends list. That same golden glint in her eye, that tangled mess of hair. You clicked on her profile, amazed she had survived, amazed to see her grown up even if you couldn't quite make out what she looked like from her photos. You intended to friend her, to catch up but instead you scrolled through cryptic updates and then, finally, the videos.

You followed the bread trail to her YouTube profile and under the covers, your headphones projected her voice directly into your ears and you don't remember anything she said but you remember how you felt. You remember the damp tangle of hair stuck to the drool on her chin when she spoke of us.

We took her and we helped her and then her skin started to melt like the sky is melting now.

Every word you don't remember was the truth.

The trees droop like candles, the path turns slow and orange and liquid and the girl turns and her smile is a slash across her face that tumbles into the dirt and her teeth shatter and break. Her skin writhes with translucent worms and then they too disappear, leaving only her eyes that hang in the sky, distorted, scratched out, burnt in charcoal.

Then there is nothing.

You've always been walking this trail.

Alone.

You want to run. There is nothing here to run from but still something inside you insists and then there is a tugging on your spine, a yank that makes you feel sick and this time when you wrench your chin to the sky there is no sky, there is something massive and shining and you see yourself mirrored, at a distance, bathed in ultraviolet light.

You can see that you're at the beginning of the path.

You think maybe it is time to let go.

You think maybe you don't need to hold on.

Let these new thoughts come.

You've been holding so tight. The vibration rumbles through you and your body feels too heavy and you want to let go. You should let go. The light is so soft and it is pulling but it is gentle and insistent and the vibration intensifies and you are thrumming with light and you forget what you were trying to hold on to.

You don't have to be afraid.

You are not afraid.

You open your eyes and see nothing.

The vibration settles in your forehead. You relax. You notice how it slows, how it ebbs and flows, how it seems to breathe and you relax and it thrums but it doesn't hurt and you relax and it peels open and now you can see.

Your mouth opens. The light fills you, this holy song.

Loosen your grip. Let the tingle spread again, from your forehead through your throat, down your spine, through your hips, your thighs, your knees, shake your toes free, one by one. Let yourself rise.

Your body peels back, ripples of flesh swallowed by the earth.

You are almost home.

LULLABIES FROM THE FORMICARY

I THINK IT was my fault. Dan didn't think so, but it musta been me. I musta brought them home that day on the hill, one or two, tangled in my skirt, and it all started from there. Where else could they have come from?

My idea to go for the hike, my idea to stop spending so much money, my idea to bring the wine and it wasn't even fun, it was hot and sweaty and awful and I brought them home with me.

Can you hear me over the singing? You can't hear it? Never mind.

We should have called an exterminator right away. If we weren't so broke and stupid we would have. But our credit cards were maxed out and we had like five bucks to last until Dan got paid and the rent and the groceries were more important. Well, now what's more important?

The home remedies don't do shit. The ant traps don't do shit.

We just killed the first ones, smushed them in Kleenex and under our shoes and with rolled-up magazines and we didn't even notice what was wrong with them, not at first. Then there were more. And more. I could see them out of the corners of my eyes constantly, scaling my walls, trailing along my counters. Sometimes they weren't even there, but I just felt them. Or I'd glance down and they were crouched in my lap, five or six of them gathered in a circle on my knee, like they were planning something.

We kept killing them and they kept coming. A couple dozen smashed in the bedroom, then five swirling in the bathroom sink, two in the cereal bowls and more and more and more.

"Where are they coming from?" Dan kept asking. It didn't really matter though, did it? All that mattered was that they kept coming. We were counting down days until payday, so we could buy some better bug spray or ant traps or something with our "fun" money that never seemed to get used for anything fun. We certainly couldn't afford an exterminator. And we certainly couldn't kill them all ourselves.

It got worse. I woke up with them crawling all over me. I thought I was still dreaming. I hoped I was fucking dreaming. Dan was asleep beside me and they skittered across his face, his hair, his eyelids.

We didn't even *notice*. How often do you really look at insects? You kill them and you swat them and you avoid them but you don't look at them, not really.

On Tuesday, we were hysterical. They were everywhere. Crawling through our sheets, crawling across our skin, crawling into nooks and crannies in our floor that we would never be able to reach. We kept killing them and they kept coming. I wanted to scream, but the sound died in my throat because we have neighbors upstairs and they hate loud noises and they would pound on the floor, and then we would probably have ants falling from the ceiling. So I went to the bathroom to wash my face instead and one dripped from my hair into the sink and this is when I noticed they didn't look right.

They were big. I mean, not huge, but big for ants. I don't think they were big the whole time. I think they started small. I don't remember them being big at first . . . They had the impression of blackness, but they weren't black. The longer you looked at them, they changed. The colors moved. They shimmered like a scarab, like an oil slick.

The weirdest thing, the worst thing, was the legs. Ants are supposed to have six legs, right? It's like a rule. Are there any bugs that don't have six legs? Like centipedes or whatever, I know, but . . .

I thought they had six legs, but when I looked closer, each leg was like . . . doubled up, two sprigging out right next to each other. Twelve legs each, all together. I never heard of an ant with twelve legs. Neither did Dan. Yeah, we could have Googled it, if we were able to afford our internet this month. I couldn't stop thinking about it. Twelve legs. Dan thought it was weird too, but he was more concerned with how we were going to get rid of them.

Are you sure you can't hear that? Here, let me hold the phone up. No? No, it's okay. It's okay, never mind.

There was nothing we could do but keep killing them. Dan had all these ideas about picking up borax or something to kill them, or more traps, or Raid, or whatever, and I didn't mention an exterminator because really, where was that money supposed to come from? Either way, we had to wait till he got paid, and until then just keep splatting them. After a while I just let them crawl on me. What was the point? We had two more days till pay day and no matter how many we killed, they just kept coming.

I picked them out of my hair and swatted them off the table and tried not to complain. It was awful, but the look in Dan's eyes was just . . . such shame. I felt guilty too. It was my fault—oh, I'm sure he didn't blame me, but I was the one who spent our last couple of bucks on a bottle of wine and got too tipsy and accidentally pissed on an anthill. They crawled up my calves and my thighs and we brushed them all off but now we were fucking infested, so I guess we didn't get them all.

I heard them in the walls. I think it was their legs. Don't grasshoppers do something like that? That's how they make that sound, rubbing their legs together? Well, ants do it too. Or these ones do.

I couldn't sleep. I tossed and turned and I couldn't shake the feeling they were all over me but there was just another day to go, one more day of work to get through, and then, finally, pay day and a solution, but I don't think anything would have worked anyway. It was too late. Maybe it had been too late the whole time.

I heard them singing. I was falling asleep, finally, and that strange hum of legs twitching through the apartment turned to words as I floated between reality and dreaming. "Mud and blood and earth and seeds, tearing teeth, tearing teeth." Voices echoed in my head, sickening visions, cryptic words. "Snakes eat snakes eat snakes."

I woke up and my hand was covered in them, writhing, unfamiliar. I shook them off, and they splattered across the floor. Some of them burst with yellow blood as they hit the tile. Some of them skittered away to unseen cracks. How would we ever get rid of them?

Dan wasn't in bed.

I stumbled to the bathroom. Ants swirled dead in the toilet. I flushed it before I used it, but when I got up, the bowl was thick with them again. More of them were stuck in the wet soap sludge and I didn't wash my hands. I was afraid if I turned on the faucet, the water would come out choked with shimmering black legs.

I called to Dan and he didn't answer.

The living room floor bulged with a pile of sand. Ants cascaded in and out in orderly lines, their hides gleaming. The house was theirs now. What could I do? And where the fuck was Dan? I didn't even scream, didn't cry—it's amazing how quickly your mind can break, seventy-two hours, a few sleepless nights, a few thousand insects, that's all it takes.

I didn't have time to deal with it. I had to work. I had no sick time left and no work means no money, so I shook the rotten creatures from my uniform.

Dan was nowhere. I figured he got called into work early. No I didn't, I didn't believe that, he woulda woke me, but what else could it be? I called his cell phone. Called it again. I was late. Yeah, I was worried, but what could I do? I left our apartment to the bugs and called Dan again and again on my breaks while a knot tightened in my chest. His phone was probably dead. It had happened before. He would be home when I got there.

He had to be.

I barely made it through my shift. My coworkers kept looking at me sympathetically and I tried to ignore the twitching in my throat. I tried not to think of my poor apartment crawling with bugs and what the fuck were we gonna do and where the fuck was Dan?

By the time I got home, my brain was pounding out of control. I knew it would be worse. I knew it was too late. Anything we could buy would barely make a dent on the infestation. We needed an exterminator. We needed money. We needed to make it happen.

Too little, too late.

There were more ant hills. They were singing. My living room was covered in dirt and misshapen hills and thousands of shimmering ants with too many legs ran incomprehensible missions across the walls. More of them, bigger, stalked in orderly lines and swoops, marching dizzying symbols across the sand. They were singing. "The rift is open, the stars bleed red."

I felt something moving in my throat.

I kicked a hill apart and the ants scattered, their leagues stuttering in occult formations. "Dead and dead and dead and dead," I thought I heard, but it couldn't be. It was just their legs. Their horrible legs scraping against each other, and my sleep-deprived brain turned it into words. "Gaping mouth, yellow eyes and mud and mud and mud."

I boiled the kettle and when it was hot and screaming, I tiptoed back into the living room. I don't know why I felt like I had to sneak up on them, but I did. I poured the boiling water over one of the hills and I boiled the fuckers alive, and the hill melted to mud and I was laughing and laughing until I saw what was inside.

His skull was picked clean.

Can you hear them yet?

I can still hear them. I think they're in the phone.

CRIMSON TIDE

YOU WERE TWELVE years old when you got your period. It was the last summer you spent at the cabin, the summer before your parents split up, long after you had forgotten how to talk to either of them. They were drinking and fighting and going grey early, so you spent all day on the beach. Alone. You spent as much time as you could in the ocean, far away from people, lost in a universe of buoyancy and lightness. When you weren't swimming, you sat on the muddy shore, letting the tide wash over you, and when you were sick of being wet, you flopped on the sand and let the sun bake salt into your hair.

When the blood appeared in your underpants, it didn't even occur to you to ask for help. You knew what it meant, you had heard all about it from the girls at school, and so you padded the bottom of your bathing suit with toilet paper, gulped dry toast for breakfast, evaded your father's bruised eyes.

You slouched your way down the beach, sunglasses your protection from concerned glances at your emaciated frame. You walked past the families, past the laughing, past the other sullen teenagers, until even the nearest strangers were ants in the sand.

The water licked cold on your ankles. You walked in slowly, inch by inch. When you were up to your neck, wads of toilet paper drifted beside you, pulpy jellyfish swirling tendrils of blood. You floated. You drifted. You wished the ocean would swallow you whole. You closed your eyes to the blaring sun.

You weren't supposed to go so far from the crowds, but you did. You weren't supposed to go in so deep, but you did. Gentle waves turned harsh. Your peaceful moment turned to disaster when you found yourself struggling against the current. The beach was miles away, the water was thick and salty in your mouth. Your nostrils stung as you sank. You came up screaming for air, and sank again. No one heard you scream.

Except her.

It doesn't matter where she came from. You were drifting, and then your arms were tight around her as she fought the waves and dragged you both to shore. You vomited a torrent of water onto the beach, a tiny river in the sand. You shook and cried and she wrapped an arm around your shoulders, pressed you close to her side until you caught your breath.

Her skin was so pale it was looked blue. Her eyes were the greenest you had ever seen. You loved her instantly.

"Hi," she said.

She was there for you every day that summer, waiting for you in the sand with her sharp smile.

Everything was better with her. You no longer wandered the beach lonely; now you walked and swam and spent late nights beside her. Instead of curling up in bed with a book after dark, you snuck back out to the beach, to her laugh, to her smile.

She was a terrific swimmer, better even than you. She taught you to hold your breath under water, but you could never do it like her. Each time she surfaced, she showed you something new. A microcosm of the ocean cupped in her hands: tiny, iridescent squid; a family of crabs as small as a fingernail; bright beautiful shells; a fortune in sand dollars. When you tried, the water contained only sand.

She set them all free.

You didn't have to keep trying to think of what to say next like with your friends at school. You could sit beside her, swirling indecipherable pictures in the sand, and not say a word for hours, just listen to the crashing of waves and the screaming of gulls.

The heat of the summer was still blaring when August came to a close. You felt it coming as the long days became shorter. September loomed, no matter how hard you tried to ignore it.

That last night, you both cried. The sky was charcoal ash, the ocean lapped at your heels, and she held you close to her side again. Her arm was cold against your sunburned skin.

"Don't forget about me, okay?"

"Never!"

She pressed something into your hand. "This is for you, so you can always hear my voice."

You didn't know what to say. So she kissed you. Her lips were wet and tasted like salt. She glanced at you fast, then averted her eyes and ran. You unfurled your fist. A beautiful conch shell, pierced with a tattered cord of rope. You looped it around your neck and it rested against the flat expanse of your chest.

Your parents drove back home, back to your little town so far away from the beauty of the ocean. You pressed the shell to your ear the whole way. You never heard her voice, only the waves. You could still taste the salt of her mouth.

Your parents argued all that fall, right up until Christmas, late into the night almost every night. It was impossible to sleep unless you pressed the shell against your ear and listened to the sounds of summer.

They divorced in the spring. There would be no trip to the ocean that year. Or ever again.

When you were fourteen, a girl from school asked to see your necklace. She sneered when you showed her. It was nothing like the dainty jewelry the other girls wore. When you got home, you stuffed it deep into your dresser. That summer seemed long ago already. Your memories were fading. You had real life to deal with now: school and homework and boys and alternate weekends with your parents and trying to make friends *now*. You would never see her again. It didn't matter anymore.

Sometimes you would wake up in complete darkness and hear the sound of the ocean pulsing through your room. It made you feel like you were on a raft, adrift at sea.

When you were sixteen, you kissed a boy. Max was not that nice to you, but he was cooler than you were, and all your friends thought he was cute. So when he invited you to a party you said yes, and your stomach twisted with something you couldn't identify, nervousness or happiness or something in between.

He didn't pay much attention to you. The party was boring. You sat on a lawn chair in your black one-piece bathing suit, not meeting anyone's eyes. When he finally came and sat down next to you, his eyes were glassy with beer. He asked you if you had been in the pool yet. You shook your head no. You weren't expecting it when he leaned forward to kiss you. His lips were dry and tasted like nothing. He took your hand and pulled you into the water.

You dove in, blushing, and sat on the bottom of the pool. You opened your eyes and tried to gather your thoughts. The water smelled chemical. Legs kicked above you, watery, unfamiliar from this angle. You broke the surface to laughter.

"Oh my God, *she got blood all over it*," someone said. Everyone was laughing. Your chest tightened. Everyone was looking at you.

"I think I'm going to throw up," Max groaned. He was not in the pool anymore; he was dripping water all over the lawn. His face was twisted in an ugly sneer. The chair you had been sitting in was smudged with blood.

The water broke in waves around you as everyone clamored to get away from the blood that swirled from your swimsuit.

"Haven't you ever heard of a tampon?" Max hooted.

You hated him. You hated yourself, too.

That night, the sound of the ocean was deafening. You woke up seasick, your bed buoyed by rough waves.

You crawled across the floor, hauled the drawer out of your desk, dumped out papers and trinkets and notes and teenage debris until you wrapped your hands around the shell, remembered the only thing good that had ever happened to you. You said out loud, "I miss you so much."

You got back into bed to untangle the cord. As you turned the conch over in your hands, it spilled out a torrent of murky water, a clump of hair, a swirl of blood, so much liquid, more than the shell could possibly contain.

The sound of the waves stopped.

You pulled the necklace over your head.

BETTY ROCKSTEADY

Max's parents found him face-down in the pool. He had been drunk, and it looked like he had kept drinking after everyone else left. He got sloppy. He must have been running. You were never supposed to run by the pool. He cracked his head open on the concrete and left a smear of blood that would never wash completely away. Then he slipped into the water. It filled his eyes and his ears and his mouth and his lungs, and that was where he stayed.

You were scared. You didn't know how to talk to anyone, much less your mother. You couldn't tell her about Max. She was yelling at you about your grades and the sullen look on your face and you snapped back at her, said something mean. She hit you, just like she used to hit your father. You snarled. You were tired of being weak. You hit her back and went to your room. She hollered and screamed and pounded on the door. You pressed the conch to your ear, listened to the ocean until her voice faded away.

When she fell asleep, you took her car. You didn't pack anything. You didn't need anything.

The gentle sounds of the ocean spoke to you the whole way back, leading you home. You drove all night.

The sky was empty. The ocean was black. She wasn't there. You felt insane.

You stepped into the waves, fully dressed, the shell dangling from your palm.

"Where are you?" The only answer was the crashing of waves, so loud it was deafening.

You were alone. It sounded like the entire universe was ripping apart. You had nowhere else to go.

You threw the shell as far as you could, regretted it

instantly. You lurched into the water, dove for it, missed, hit your head on something sharp. You came up for air and blood dripped down your cheek.

Your clothes were heavy in the water. You were heavy. You closed your eyes, got turned around. Waves jostled you. You didn't float like you used to, you had to flail your arms to keep your head above water. When you opened your eyes, the shore was out of sight.

Thousands of silent jellyfish bobbed around you, their luminescence your only light. The ocean reflected the sky, the sky reflected the ocean.

Something scrabbled at your feet, pulled. You kicked back. You only sucked in half a breath before it yanked you down.

Everything was dark and wet and heavy. You struggled, you resisted, you were lost in pure panic. Your arms and legs thrashed. You were pulled deeper. Hair or seaweed or *something* wrapped around your hand. Something huge and cold floated by, stroked your side. You couldn't move. Seconds without air ticked by, endless. Your hands opened, closed. You were so tired. Everything was coming to an end, this was it, you were dying, you couldn't hold your breath anymore and you were drowning and you couldn't hold it you couldn't help it, you opened your mouth and the water surged in.

And you found you could breathe perfectly.

You opened your eyes.

THE BACKWARDS PATH TO THE LIMBUS

IF HE KEPT slurping like that, Miranda would kill him. She'd have to. Between the dead fruit stench of the tea and his incessant old-man noises, if she sat here one more fucking minute she'd scream. She wouldn't be able to help it. Frustration bubbled in her throat, but instead she bit down until she tasted blood.

Just one night. She'd sit here patiently until the old widow up front got things started, and then she'd wait and wait and wait and she would get a taxi and listen to the radio while rain pounded against the windows and then she would lie on her dead son's bed and she would scream for as long as she fucking wanted.

Dr. Hopskin was right about a lot of things, but not this. She had never been a people person. Yeah, she had liked to read, but reading didn't mean she liked being surrounded by a dozen people she had nothing in common with, listening to the noises they made, and waiting, endlessly waiting while they small-talked and sipped tea and it was already quarter after six and they hadn't even started talking about the fucking book yet. The group leader, Carrie, had been standing there fucking around with her notebook since Miranda had walked in, underlining passages and adding post-its and highlighting sections with an agonizing precision. As if any of this could take her mind off Riley.

She would never come back. Fuck Dr. Hopskin and fuck all these people.

The woman sitting next to her grabbed her knee and Miranda jumped, sloshing her third cup of tea over the rim. She gritted her teeth, managed not to snap at the woman, and smiled instead.

"What did you think of the story?" The sad-eyed woman smiled, her lips drawn thin. Miranda shrugged.

"It was okay." No, it wasn't. Literary fiction or something. Reading should be for pleasure. Beach books. She would never have picked this up by choice. *The Backwards Path to the Limbus*. It was just endless meandering that put her to sleep. A protagonist —never named or gendered— walked a labyrinth. Overwrought description of the path, the sounds of the sky, the bones beneath their feet. She had forced herself to read it, to be prepared, but she fell asleep more often than not, with twisted dreams of pathways opening up to her and spiralling down, down, down.

"You'll appreciate it more the next time you read it," the woman assured her.

"I doubt I'll read it again."

The man next to her butted in, a smear of chocolate on his face. "Oh, you will. We've all read it lots of times. You'd be surprised at what you see on a second and third reading."

"Or a twenty-eighth." That was Carrie. Everyone laughed. Miranda tried a smile, but it felt wrong on her face. Jesus, who the hell read *any* book twenty-eight times? Not to mention one as boring as this. Maybe she just didn't have the same attention span anymore. But at least Carrie had tuned in to them, and maybe the meeting would start, so it could end.

Dr. Hopskin would just have to set her up with another activity. One without so much talking.

Something brushed against her leg, and she flinched. Mercifully, it wasn't Harold or any of the other weirdos here. A small calico cat wound through the crowd and darted beneath a chair.

"Is there supposed to be a cat here?" It seemed unsanitary somehow, but it was a bookstore, not a restaurant. Still . . .

"Oh yes," said Carrie. "Every bookstore has a cat. Or had a cat. Or will someday have a cat." The group laughed as if she'd told a joke, and the cat darted off somewhere behind the shelves. What a weird fucking thing to say; it could hardly be true. But the group looked at her like they wanted a response, so Miranda smiled and pictured stabbing a knife straight through the woman's chest.

Fuck this place.

Carrie smiled back and shuffled the books on her desk until she had *The Backwards Path to the Limbus* in front of her. Miranda noticed the ragged line of a scar snaking down her wrist as her sleeve shifted. Dr. Hopskin had mentioned that most of the members had been patients of his at one point. Did they all carry around the same sort of pain as hers? It was hard to believe, looking at them now, with their bland faces and casual conversation.

"Well, I guess we're ready to get started," Carrie said. Instead of feeling relieved that things were finally getting underway, Miranda felt the next endless expanse of time stretching out in front of her. Every time she'd tried to read the book, a headache had pierced through a deep part of her brain, triggering endless dreams of trudging an eternal path, the walls getting tighter and tighter as she spiralled ever inwards. She had muddled through, but she certainly didn't have anything to say about it, at least not anything they would want to hear.

"Miranda, would you like to start us off?"

"Uh . . . no, just do things however you usually do them." All eyes were on her, all these other social rejects stuffing down their pain to come to a bookstore and make small talk about boring books as though this was a reason to be alive, to keep on going.

Carrie smiled at her. Her smile was too wide in a way that made her look a little crazy. "We've all read this book before, it'd be nice to hear a new take on it." She waved the thin volume in front of her face, as if it would jog Miranda's memory. "You read the whole first section, yes?"

"Yeah, I read it." And she had felt every moment of it, too. The book had been divided into three sections, and the first concentrated on a man winding through a trail of tiny bones. Kinda morbid, maybe, but not even in an interesting way. It took her forever to read, as though she had to experience every single step he took, forcing herself to read each word, one at a time.

"I'm sorry. I didn't like it. Nothing happened." The group kept their eyes on her, chewing their lips as they waited for more. "Maybe I didn't really get it? I used to read a lot of thrillers and stuff, but this was kind of . . . *literary*?" She felt like she was rambling, but she had nothing to say that was of any substance. "It was written cool, I guess." She didn't really think that, but being stared at was driving her nuts. She had to keep talking so they could move on to the next person and stop fucking looking at her. "Like, the rhythm of it? If that makes sense. The words felt like they rhymed, even if they didn't." It had agitated her, actually, and the words had echoed through her dreams, and then *she* had been walking the path, the bones crunching beneath her feet. "It was weird to have the author focus on the mundane for so long. I spent the whole section just . . . waiting for something to happen. The author described every detail of the footsteps, but there was nothing to really anchor the story, to let me know where it was happening, or why."

"You'd be surprised how much you'll get out of it when you read it again. What did you make of it this time? What did it mean? We'll talk about some of our own theories later." Carrie leaned forward, as if Miranda's opinion of this stupid book were the most fascinating thing in the world.

"I don't really know . . . I actually looked it up online, and I couldn't find anything about it." That was weird too. She had checked Amazon for reviews, to give her a hint at what she was supposed to be getting out of it, but it hadn't been listed. "Not even anything about the author."

"Oh, that's a pen name. Not all authors want you knowing who they are." Everyone laughed again, and the sound was grating.

"What did you think of the bones?" Harold asked eagerly. "Did you work out what kind of bones they were?"

The bones had reminded her of Riley, of course, but everything did. They were too small, far too small, but they reminded her of him still. The bones that showed through his thin skin and the bones that by now filled his grave. To her absolute horror, her eyes filled with tears. She didn't want these people to see her cry, oh God, that would lead to sympathetic looks and soft voices and a whole event she just couldn't take right now. And would her doctor hear about it? Somehow, she believed he would. Miranda stood up. "Is there a bathroom here?"

"Yes, just down the back." Carrie gestured to the rows of bookshelves criss-crossing behind her, in a way that made Miranda feel slightly dizzy. Still, better to wander lost among books than be stuck with these people for another five minutes.

The bookstore went back farther than she'd expected. She just needed to breathe, to get back to herself. She stumbled deeper in, her pulse pounding hot in her head. What had she been thinking coming here, among these strangers, trying to heal herself?

As if they could ever understand.

The place was old; it had been here since she was a kid. She had visited once or twice with her parents, but they had hurried her out quickly and she'd never had the opportunity to properly explore.

She had never brought Riley here. He hadn't been much of a bookstore kid. He was busy, so busy, always

214

wanting to be outside. She had become that sort of person for him. And after the disease struck, well, books were the last thing she thought about.

The tightly-packed bookshelves insulated the sounds of the others talking, as if they were farther away than they really were. She was grateful for this moment of quiet.

She strummed a finger against the spine of a thick set of children's dictionaries.

Something was moving behind the shelves. Footsteps, Riley's footsteps, as he stumbled from his bed to the bathroom to vomit blood into the toilet. No—probably the cat. Her throat felt thick and pasty. Had they mentioned the cat's name? She couldn't remember. "Kitty?" She could still picture Riley, his beautiful eyes gone flat as he gazed up at her over the toilet seat, changed, as if he had vomited out some essential part of himself and she had no choice but to flush it away. It nagged at her. She needed to see the cat, to prove to herself she was crazy, to prove to herself Riley wasn't hiding just around the corner. Her head spun with the kind of paranoia usually reserved for the darkest moments of the early morning. She took a left turn around the shelves, away from the bathroom and towards the noise.

The cat sprinted away, so light on its feet it could have been floating. Then it peered back around the shelf right at her, and she stifled a scream.

Its eyes.

The cat had Riley's eyes.

Not the dead eyes that haunted her every night, not the eyes of the last few months when everything that had made him her son was drained out of him and he lay limp and unmoving in the hospital bed. No. These eyes were the bright blue eyes of his childhood, when he had been his real self. And they had seen her. Known her.

A wave of nausea swept through her. Dr. Hopskin wouldn't like this, she shouldn't do this, she was imagining things, but her brain was chattering quick and the impulse could not be controlled. Besides, she wasn't following the cat because it had Riley's eyes, of course not, it was to prove that the cat didn't look like him, that she was imagining it, to prove just how ridiculous she was being.

They aren't even shaped like cat's eyes.

She turned a corner and listened for the padding of paws, then turned again. A flicker of a white-tipped tail guided her further. Was it possible to get lost in a bookstore? To become lost between the shelves and never find your way out again? She didn't see the cat anymore. All the shelves looked the same. *They're probably wondering where I am by now.* The bookshelves stretched to the ceiling, and when she looked back, she wasn't sure which way she had come. Like the labyrinth, closing into tighter and tighter spirals, the walls were closing in, the tiny bones crunching beneath her feet, but now Riley's eyes peered out from the darkness and she was chasing him through the dimly-lit pathway and—

This was ridiculous. Time to go back.

Miranda retraced her steps as well as she could remember and stumbled almost immediately upon a dead end. Not exactly a dead end, though, because a narrow door yawned open onto a dark stairwell. A basement? Something dripped, and she heard a strange yowling that could have been a child's cry but must be the cat.

The light switch was near the door, and as Miranda fumbled for it, the dim light cast a shaky path down the stairs. As though in a dream, her body moving on its own, she found herself descending, each footstep slow and deliberate to avoid tumbling. She reached the dirt floor almost immediately; her neck cramped forward uncomfortably in order to clear the ceiling. The room was small and crammed full of crates spilling books. And in the farthest corner, Riley, his hands in his lap, sitting quietly on a box. Beautiful. Healthy. She couldn't breathe.

Immense relief, overpowering relief, weak jelly-legs that could barely stumble across the floor. She was at his side, *this wasn't real*, but it didn't matter, she had to hold him, pull him as close as she could, feel his warm cheek against her own. She was sleep-talking, words pouring out of her mouth, smearing tears onto his clothes, pushing his hair away from his eyes. He was still and silent, but his breath puffed onto her cheek.

His eyes were sharp blue, not the dull grey they had turned before he died.

He let her blubber over him for a moment longer, and then he was speaking, in a soft gravelly voice she had never heard before.

"I need to tell you something." But she couldn't stop touching him, his soft cheeks, the tiny hands that moved in hers, and the life that pulsed beneath his skin. He didn't move, didn't respond, and something about his frail coldness terrified her.

"Riley, what's the matter with you, please?" Her voice was sharper than she intended. "You're not acting right."

"Please, stop talking. I need to tell you something and I don't have long."

"What do you mean? Why don't you have long? Don't leave. Don't leave." It wasn't enough. She wanted to look at him forever, his cowlick sprig of hair, the sprinkle of freckles over his nose. She rained kisses and tears on his brow, but he didn't move.

"Please . . . " That voice was so awful and so unlike him that she stopped. He wriggled from her arms and squirmed away, but he let her take his small, cold hand in hers.

"I need to tell you . . . that time I was really, really little and we went camping. Me and you and dad. We had the tent and we were in that campground near the ocean, but we had to walk that path in the woods to get to the beach and I liked the woods so much more than the beach, so we went back there for lunch. There was a picnic table. I ate my sandwich really, really quick, and you guys kept eating, and you said I could go play but not go too far. I had my bucket and I peeled back the bark on some trees and looked at the bugs and put the bugs in the bucket and then I turned over a rock and there were salamanders. And most of them ran away, but I grabbed one and put him in my bucket but he didn't want to eat the bugs.

"I was gonna ask you if I could keep him. I loved him. He was shiny and his eyes were dark and he ran around in the bucket so funny. I'd name him Sal and put him in the old aquarium that my fishes died in and he could be my friend.

"I wanted to put him on my shoulder to show you him and me being friends, and I reached in and grabbed him and he flipped over in my hand and I tried to pet his belly but I pushed too hard and his guts came out, I pushed too hard and I killed him, he made a squishing sound and it all came out his mouth and he was dead and I couldn't tell you and dad why I was crying because I was a murderer and I didn't want anyone to know that I killed him, I killed my little friend."

A thin, bitter fluid filled Miranda's mouth. "Riley, that's not true."

"It kept coming to me forever. Until I died, every time I closed my eyes I saw his guts spurt out and his beady little eyes go dead." Riley closed his eyes. He looked like he was carved from marble. He didn't speak again.

Miranda opened her mouth. She didn't know what she was going to say, but she had to say something. Instead, she gagged. Bitter fluid flooded her mouth and took her breath away. She started coughing and Riley gazed impassively at her, barely blinking. She swallowed and thought the worst was over, but her words dribbled over a thick swelling in her throat.

The stink of panic rose from her armpits when she couldn't catch her breath, that familiar stink that had kept her awake so many nights. She couldn't breathe, and her son was just looking at her with those eyes that had haunted her for far too long. She tried to cough, and finally something loosened, and then something in her mouth was moving and it was slimy and bitter and she spat, and a salamander, squirming and dead-eyed, raced away. She screamed, but Riley didn't even flinch.

"Miranda? Where are you?" Reluctantly, she tore her eyes away from her son. That old creep Harold was snooping around looking for her. She didn't want to answer, not now, so she looked back toward her son, but he was gone.

The cat sat on the box instead. She blinked normal green eyes at Miranda.

"Miranda?" A female voice now. The cat blinked again, slowly, and hopped off the box and padded up the stairs.

Everything got blurry after that. There was screaming, and there was crying, and there were boxes torn apart in Miranda's hands. Eventually there were people all around her, and she was clawing away from them, screaming his name, pounding her hands against the walls.

Then Carrie was there, stroking her back, intoning something about the labyrinth, her voice low and calm, and the adrenaline spike faded, and Miranda slumped into her arms.

They led her back to the seating area. Someone placed a hot mug in her hands and helped her sit down. It was hard to breathe. All their eyes were on her, their dull brown eyes and dark green eyes and pale blue eyes, but none like Riley's. None even close.

"Can you tell us a little bit about what happened?" Carrie thumbed her book open, the one with all the post-its and the meeting notes. She had a pen in her hand, like there was going to be an accident report or something.

"No, it's not . . . my son was down there." Panic erupted in her chest again and she started to stand up. She had to find him. The group shifted and looked at each other. "You don't understand. He's dead. My son is dead." Carrie jotted something down in her book, then peered closer at Miranda.

"What color were his eyes?"

That bitter taste rose in her mouth again. "Blue. They were his eyes. They were blue."

"I knew it!" Harold said. "I had a feeling they would be, we haven't had blue in a while." Carrie was furiously flipping through the notebook, marking things with highlighter. Her brow was furrowed in concentration, but her mouth hinted at a smile. "You're right, it's been nearly six months."

"What are you talking about?" Murmured concentration went on around her. Carrie ignored her and flipped back to a new page.

"Did he say anything?"

Miranda stood up, but her knees wouldn't hold her. She slumped back into her chair. "What the fuck is going on here?" Tears streamed from her eyes, beyond her control. "I don't feel right . . . " Shelves blurred and twisted in her peripheries and she had to close her eyes to control the dizziness.

"It's fine. Please. What did he say?"

"He told me this story about a salamander. It wasn't true. Riley never lied, but this wasn't true." She opened her eyes to more of those simpering smiles, but felt too tired to be mad. "He never met his father. We never went camping. Why would he say those things?"

"Oh no, honey, it's not meant to be literal." Harold patted her knee.

"Camping and a salamander," Carrie was still writing. "Any other themes?"

"What do you mean, *themes*? He told me he killed a salamander and he couldn't stop thinking about it."

Carrie flipped through the book. "I think we've had salamanders before, haven't we?"

"What do you think it means?" Harold asked. He wasn't talking to Miranda. He was looking at Carrie. A dribble of drool shone on his lips.

"What does it mean?" asked Miranda. "What does any of this mean?" Something deep inside her wanted to scream, but everyone was so calm, and the tea was sweet and strange and instead she stifled a yawn. Idly, she wondered if she could retrace those steps through the shelves. She wondered about the book they had read, and if she mapped out that path and mapped out her own and sat one on the top of the other, how closely would they line up?

Everyone kept talking incessantly around her, and she caught fragments of the conversation; cross-referencing, and codes and riddles and how things came together, piece-by-piece-by-piece.

She remembered her son's face. The first one, the fresh one, the one full of promise. She remembered how it had fallen away, day by day, and morphed into his dying face, the one with hollow cheeks and holes for eyes. That dead face was the one she saw when she closed her eyes now, his eyes gone flat and dark. His new face, the one she saw today, was better, even if those blue eyes wouldn't quite look at her.

"Miranda?" Her eyes shot open. They were all looking at her again. The book had new flags and notes. She wanted to read it, to see what secrets it could possibly hold. "Can we expect you back next week?"

"Oh, yes. Absolutely. Yes."

SHE SLEEPS
WITH CROWS

GUILT CHEWED VICIOUS through her mangled heart. Outliving your children is bad enough; worse to outlive the entire world. Worse to be so alone.

Alice's raw tongue prodded the holes where her teeth had been. The taste of blood cut through the dusty air. Ash swirled with each footstep. She stumbled. She was not yet used to these feet.

In the bleak distance, a hunk of flesh.

She had fallen for this trick before. No doubt she would fall for it again. What else could she do? She couldn't die. She tried. She had tried to fall and her legs had been torn from her hips and the dark had swirled around her and she had woken, still alive, legs replaced with rusty rods and new skin.

She tried not to fall asleep anymore.

Today, her jaw ached and her gums bled, proving she was still alive. The streets refused to claim her.

Ahead, the blob of flesh faded, receded further away. It was impossible to judge distance. Everything familiar-unfamiliar. Sometimes she was in the desert. Sometimes she was on the street where she grew up. Sometimes she didn't know where she was. It didn't matter. She stumbled into a brick wall and a window shimmered and she winced away from its glare. She did not want to see what she had become. She did not want to see what survival had earned her.

She kept moving.

It was a hand, pink and plump, still spurting blood.

Her daughter's hand.

No.

Her daughter was dead.

No.

Not her daughter's. Her daughter's face was melted and twisted and ripped from her skull. Her daughter was gone.

She was afraid to touch it.

It was the only sign of life she had seen in weeks.

She followed the spurts and splatters, stabbed her tongue into the pockets of her teeth.

The trail led into an alley and stopped. Nothing. Empty. Dust.

No.

Not empty.

Another patchwork girl, shaking and crying and bulging with strange shapes.

Alice cleared her throat, croaked, "Hello?"

The girl turned. Her skin was thick and ropy and twisted in braids that pulled tight and painful, dancing up shoulders, peeling back the flesh from her face, revealing a jagged crow's beak. Dark, human eyes watered. Familiar. One bony hand fluttered at her side.

Alice swallowed.

The bird-woman's eyes softened. She came closer. Razor wire closed her beak tight.

"When does this end?" Alice wobbled, fell. The bird-woman crouched beside her, shook her head. Her body was cold.

They huddled together.

Fatigue pulled them down. The bird-woman's eyes blinked slowly, then opened in alarm. She warbled a fractured note and Alice took her hand, lifted her up.

Sleep meant restoration.

They walked.

They couldn't walk forever.

The bird-woman collapsed first. Alice collapsed behind her.

They prayed for death.

Alice dreamed of her daughter's face, and that it was she who ripped off the flesh and chewed and chewed and chewed.

And when she woke, the first thing she noticed was that the taste of blood was gone. She moved her tongue, felt the broken shards of shell that coated her throat in layers.

Renewed.

She was alone, clutching the fragile skull of a bird in her hand.

She screamed and tasted nothing.

She cradled the skull in her hands and prayed for it to grow.

She had grown back from less before.

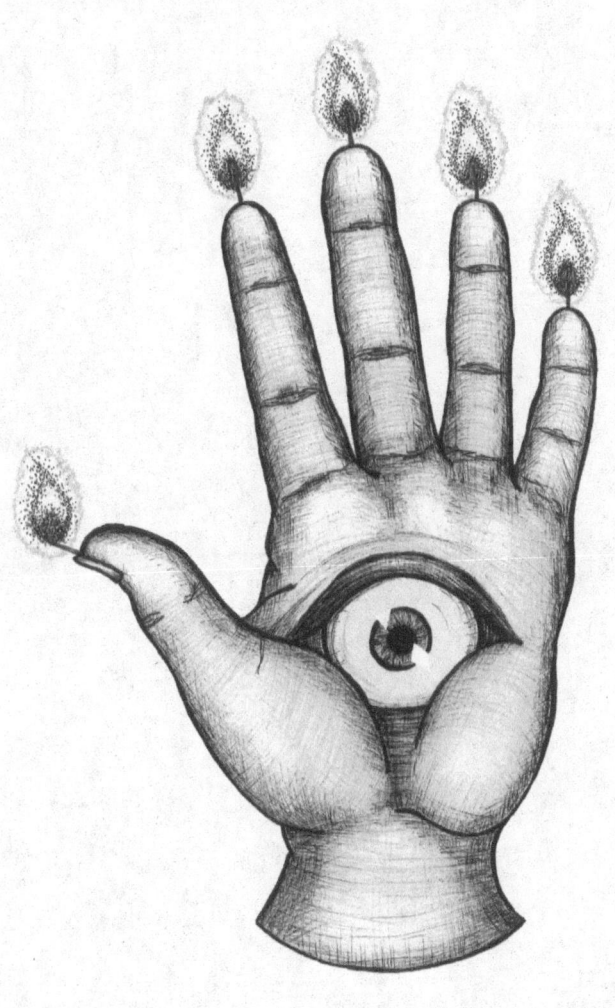

STORY NOTES

Love is Not a Handful of Seeds
I don't actually remember writing this story, but I did, and I think it is quite pretty and evocative and a great dreamy mood-setter for the collection. The cover was inspired by this story, but I also don't remember deciding to use this story for the cover, just suddenly having the rough sketch and color scheme and thinking yes, that's right.

Tiny Bones Beneath Their Feet
This story connects with the last story in the collection. They were both originally planned for a collection titled *The Cat Lives* that was going to be interconnected cosmic cat stories along these same lines, but my moods and interests move and shift and that never panned all the way out. I think these two are really cool on their own though, and love having them bookend the collection.

Something is Coming
A couple threads came together for the horror/surrealist aspects here. Thinking about the guy from the internet phenomenon Have You Dreamed This Man, and the creepy way his eyes and face look, and thinking also about how frightening it would be to notice the people on the television noticing you but pretending they didn't.

These Beautiful Bones
This is one of my favorite stories I've ever written, and

always the first one I think of when someone I know in real life tells me they're reading my work. It was built around the skeleton-fucking scene, really going for the extreme horror splatterpunk vibe.

The Botany of Desire
Trying to go a little bit more into character here, and how what they want can conflict, and trying to make the horror just a bit beautiful even as it's horrifying.

The Desert of Wounded Frequencies
I think this story was my first acceptance from PMMP/Ghoulish and the one that started my relationship with them. It was written for the anthology *Lost Signals*, which I really wanted to be part of but procrastinated writing something until pretty much the last minute, then just made it happen in two days. That's often Max's writing method as well, so it makes sense that it worked out.

Root Rot
I don't think I ever submitted this gross little story anywhere. I wrote it after a few different famous dudes were publicly blasted for shitty sexual behavior, and thinking about some of my own unfortunate past experiences, and built it around that.

Postpartum
This was written for the *Eternal Frankenstein* anthology. Really went into the story of Frankenstein and thought about what my take on it would be and what parts of it I wanted to work with and bring to life. The fire of creation, then the rejection of your creation, and the putting together pieces of something dead to make something new.

This Narrow Escape
When I first started taking writing seriously in my late 20s, I spent a couple of years writing very basic horror stories. I was starting to get the hang of some of the construction

parts of writing—beginning, middle, end, theme, but I was really having trouble finding a way to make it feel like mine, to make it matter and feel like mine. This was one of the first stories where I really leaned into the surrealist/dream imagery that is the hallmark of my work, and it was one of the first stories where I really felt I had hit upon something special.

The Language of the Mud
As a kid I was fascinated by Fortean phenomenon—things like raining frogs, cryptids, dopplegangers, and strange things that happen on the outskirts of science. I'd read a few where someone went missing in plain sight of their family, and built this story around that concept, and what it would feel like for the person left behind who had witnessed a sudden disappearance.

Lonely Hearts Club
This is another early story from when I first started finding the rhythm of who Betty Rocksteady was as a writer. Rhythmic language and surrealism were the focuses here.

Our Feral Skies
Another cat story, not connected to the other two. I think I started with the title for this one, and the idea of a strange weather event changing things irrevocably. The cat crawling into the throat imagery is a bit of a homage to the Stephen King story, but with a very different setting and result.

The Taste of Sand on Your Lips
Fifty-Five 55-Word Stories
This was written for a collection where the authors all wrote fifty-five 55-word stories. I really wanted mine to be connected and tell a larger story outside of the miniature stories, but also have each one readable on its own.

Dusk Urchin
I'm really happy with the vibe of this story. My main goal writing this was to make things feel very creepy and unnerving, but more because of what wasn't being said with a slowly building sense of dread, but you're not quite sure exactly why you're so frightened,

Larva, Pupa, Moth
This was written for a writing exercise that I don't quite remember what the prompt was, just that it involved three separate equal parts of a story. This was also around when I first started getting comfortable getting really, really gross in my writing.

Elephants That Aren't
The second of my Lost stories, from *Lost Films*. A couple years ago I started getting very heavily into old cartoons again. My dad had a show on the local cable channel when I was a kid where he taught cartooning, and I grew up watching his tapes of old black and white Fleischer cartoons. 1920s and 1930s cartoons are extremely weird and surreal, and just a bit frightening. This story was from the start of my deep dive back into cartooning, which has become a major influence on my art and writing since.

First, A Blinding Light
The third of my Lost stories, featured in *Lost Contact*. I'm very proud to be the only author who has a story in all three of the Lost anthologies. There's a walking path by my house that I go for a lot of walks on, thinking of spooky and mysterious things, and this story was thought up on those walks. It all takes place in the exact moment of an alien abduction, and leans heavy on the surrealism.

Lullabies from the Formicary
Written around a very early memory of picking blueberries and pissing on an ant hill, and going deep into the sense of sound and what all those ants sound like in your walls.

Crimson Tide
Another story from very early in my writing career, when I was just starting to touch on the things that make my writing unique and finding my voice. Some good imagery in this one, moody without being too heavy on the dreamlike aspects I often use.

The Backwards Path to the Limbus
This is the other cosmic cat story that connects with "Tiny Bones Beneath Their Feet". I wanted the bookstore conversation to be really obnoxious and unnerving in a subtle way. The awful story the false ghost tells about the salamander is based on one of my earliest, worst memories of squashing a salamander I wanted to keep as a pet. Whoops.

She Sleeps with Crows
This was written for a microfiction contest to promote the book *I Can Taste the Blood*, which it won. It was a book of five novellas, each with the title *I Can Taste the Blood,* and the microfiction stories were written to go with the same title. I wanted to fit the theme but also write something completely different than anyone else's entry would be, so I went in a really surreal, dreamlike direction.

ABOUT THE AUTHOR

Betty Rocksteady specializes in short fiction and weird illustrations. She is the author of the novellas *Like Jagged Teeth* and *The Writhing Skies*, and the graphic novel/novella hybrid *Soft Places*, all available from Ghoulish Books. She has also illustrated Cody Goodfellow's *The Flying None* and Kayli Scholz's novella *Saint Grit*. Find out more at www.bettyrocksteady.com

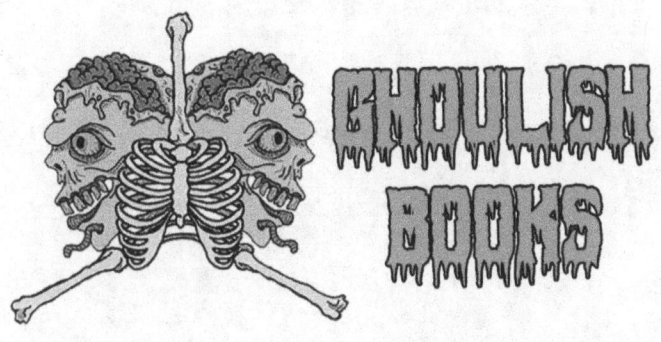

Patreon:
www.patreon.com/ghoulishbooks

Website:
www.Ghoulish.rip

Facebook:
www.facebook.com/GhoulishBooks

Twitter:
@GhoulishBooks

Instagram:
@GhoulishBookstore

Linktree:
linktr.ee/ghoulishbooks